About the

Helen Young is an author and digital editor. Her debut, *The May Queen*, was published in 2016. *Good Housekeeping* termed it 'an unsettling coming-of-age tale'. *Stylist* called her 'one to watch'. She is obsessed with questions of identity and geography – namely, the versions of ourselves we carry with us. *Breakfast in Bogotá* is her second novel.

Breakfast in Bogotá

Breakfast in Bogotá

Helen Young

unbound

This edition first published in 2019

Unbound
6th Floor Mutual House, 70 Conduit Street, London W1S 2GF
www.unbound.com

© Helen Young, 2019

This book is a work of fiction and, except in the case of historical fact, any
resemblance to actual persons, living or dead, is purely coincidental.

ISBN (eBook): 978-1-78965-050-1
ISBN (Paperback): 978-1-78965-049-5

Cover design by Mecob

Printed and bound in Great Britain by Clays Ltd, Elcograf S.p.A.

For Gerald

Super patrons

Anjola A
Geoff Adams
Gerald Adarve
Matthew Allsop
Laura Arends
Dawn Ashbourne-watts
Nasri Atallah
Stephanie Blackburn
Danny Blight
Thom Bonneville
Sabine Bou-Antoun
Dan Bracken
Liz Brealey
Nyree Bryan
Riina Cattermole
Maxine Mei-Fung Chung
Alan Clarke
Carol Clarke
Clare Clarke
Andreina Cordani
Hannah Cox

Jacqueline Crooks

Andrea Cunsolo

Dan Dalton

Emily Dear

Liz Dear

Charlotte Doherty

Paul Dornan

Stephanie Duncan

James Edwards

Heather Elliott

Chloe Esposito

Jonathan Eyers

Maura Feeny

Mia Fenwick

Karen Fickling

Michael Fields

Joanne Finney

Marthe Fjellestad

Matt Fox

Lisa Francesca Nand

Anne Gallagher

Rebecca Gillies

Carolyn Gillis

Andres Giraldo

Petra Glithero-Baldwin

Emma Goode

Anne Harris

Emily Harris

Veronica Hartley

Matt Hobbs

George Hull

Jorge Isaac Chiquillo Hurtado

Helen Jenkins

Robert Karl
Rahima Kasmi
Joseph Kershaw
Dan Kieran
Stefanie Kudla
Evalyn Lee
Mark Lewis
Robin Lewis
Laura Llewellyn
Ann and Colin Loxton
Iain Macdonald
Alison Marlow
Jim Martin
Carolina Massie
Elena Massie
Tom Massie
Rosalind Matchett
Jamie Maynard
Rob Mayr
Rose McGinty
Robert McKinlay
Rohan McLachlan
Michael Miller
John Mitchinson
Lindsay Nicholson
NnekaA
Denieca O'Neill
Emma Odwell
Arko Oige
Yudy Osorio
Valentina Palazzo
Dionysia Panteli
Antonia Parker-Jones

Steve Parks
Vicki Plomer
Justin Pollard
Laura Rees-Weeden
Mark Rees-Weeden
Ryan Ridge
Alejandra Rojas
Matt Rose
Sophia Rudkins
Lydia Ruffles
Ann Russell
Amanda Saint
Sandra Sanchez
Julia Scirrotto
Alexandra Shakespeare
Margaret Simpson
Richard Skinner
Roger Smith
Yara Somma
Ruby Speechley
Vincent Thomas Stephen
Richard Sullivan
Jessica Sutherland
Amir Tabatabai
Hannah Terry-mills
Amelia Tilney
Naomi Tomkinson
Helen Trevorrow
Benjamin Turner
Emma Vandore
Lisa Villiers
Rebecca Warrington
Kane Wheatley

Philip Willans
Laura Williams
Auguste Yair
Celia Yeoman
Jo Yeoman
Dave Young
Ian Young
Keith Young
Claudia Zubieta

1

Rocío was naked and Luke was not. For him, it felt the other way around. Why now, he thought, trying to stop his hands from shaking. He'd never had a problem undressing in front of a woman before.

'I need a beginning, that's all. A good place to start.'

'Papi, please, let me,' she said, rising from the crumpled bed and coming over.

She hadn't bothered to make it, he thought, looking beyond her to where it lay abandoned. Perhaps he had woken her? Stumbling up the wooden steps, he'd felt an intruder on the morning. But she had opened the door before he'd even reached it.

Rocío came towards him and he avoided her stare, instead noticing the bead necklace that she'd worn on each of his visits, an amber glow about her throat. He was drawn to it, and from there, down to the roundness of her breasts. Full and heavy above a fleshy waist. She wasn't young, but neither was he. At thirty-nine he knew what to expect from such arrangements and this wasn't his first visit to the modest-looking house in the district of Las Cruces, or to Rocío. He flinched as she reached out to unbutton his shirt and peel back the material. How close she came. He registered the static bounce between his newly revealed body and hers.

'Relax,' she whispered.

Her scent was sickly sweet and painfully human, athletic even. It made him want to hold his breath. To not let her in, not yet. And there, in the blur of her nearness, she smiled. He looked down at her face, a broad oval, and found the other, revealed faintly in the turn of Rocío's lips. The upward curl, a mocking grin, the idea of secrets shared, that made him want to die right then.

Rocío smiled again. She was the hot blood after a punch-up and the first lick of an ice cream. She reached down into his pocket to get at the part of him he couldn't avoid. It was what he'd paid for, wasn't it? What he'd asked of the old woman at the door, bringing out the photograph. He was tired of wondering how alike they really were. He wanted to see for himself, one beside the other.

Rocío snatched the image away. He stepped forward and made to take it from her, but stopped. It was remarkable. No one had come close before, but there Rocío was, before him now, parading with this other smile.

'I am like her, I think?' she said, holding the faded image up to her face.

'Are you?' Luke asked, feeling his voice catch.

She handed it back to him.

'I have her size.' Rocío seemed delighted.

She stepped back so he might see and went up onto her toes to meet his gaze. The eyes were wrong but the smile, and if he squinted, the body, could pass.

'I can't,' Luke said, un-wrinkling his view.

'Come, Papi.' Rocío took up his fingertips and led him forward.

'Stop,' Luke mumbled.

She turned, the smile gone, and, shrugging, went back over to the bed. Luke watched her bend, showing herself to him in ways the other never would have. He stood still, caught between remembering the face in the photograph and watching Rocío's body now, moving with purpose. He thought how easy it was to create some new version of the woman he had fled from, even here, thousands of miles distant. Rocío climbed up and writhed like something jungle-born, all the time looking back at him with the smile, making sure he knew that she had it. That thing he'd come for. He watched her, resembling something known yet strange as though that other woman were really here. His breath caught at the maddening idea that she was. That she had, in some supernatural way, pursued him across the Atlantic. Could it be so? A thick run of fluid flooded his veins, drowning out all sound, so that it was only his heartbeat and her name he heard. And somewhere in the shadow of his thoughts, he became aware of himself over by the bed and climbing. Covering, ready, rising. Luke closed his eyes and there she was.

'Catherine.'

'Señor?'

2

Luke fell out onto the street as though reborn. It was still early, but the promise of a hot day was right there, edging in off the Andes, laying claim to the Bogotá streets. He swallowed and looked back up at the room he had just departed. A sliver of light from the open window gave nothing away. Rocío would be standing at the basin across the room, cleaning the last of him from her thighs. No matter, he thought, raising a hand to mask a flash of sunlight reflected by a passing car. He hurried onwards, unable to find a regular pace in the aftermath of his expulsion.

At the corner of Tisquesusa Park he stopped a small boy selling coffee and found change for a shot. Black, hot and sobering. The boy was like the young, shoeless creatures that kept to the shadows in the boarding house, although he never looked too closely to see if any resembled Rocío. He returned the cup while the boy waited, squinting up at him, as though he might say or do something remarkable. Instead, Luke slipped him another centavo and walked on. It was a good hour on foot to the small apartment he kept in the district of La Merced. Despite the old pain in his leg, he enjoyed walking the city. One moment, the sun on your back seared with a tropical heat that left you sweating, then the next you were reminded of the altitude, all eight thousand six hundred feet of it. Bogotá never let you forget it was planted high on a plateau so that the cool mountain air turned all that heat to ice, often leaving you feverish and shivering. He didn't mind it. He liked going slow like the locals. They knew how to walk. He'd been perfecting his own slowness for eight months now. This city, so unlike the one he had come from, was full of wonder and he didn't intend to waste a moment of it.

Señora Rojas, his housekeeper, would have left him a plate of something for later, portioned out as extra from her own table. What the Rojas household ate, he did too, and today was predictably a chicken soup day. There was no need for him to hurry now. He would let opportunity lead, as it had earlier, when it took him to the only brothel he knew trading on a Sunday. On the whole, whores were as devout as housewives. His hands went to his pockets and he found the edge of the photograph. He breathed deep, leaving it there. His, guarded, safe.

When Luke reached Plaza de Bolívar, the alarmingly close ding-ding of an electric tram sharing his path snapped him back to the present. He jumped back up and onto the pavement. The trolley hurtled by. It was full, ferrying churchgoers who'd turned out in their Sunday best, now crumpled and ungodly inside. The driver looked harassed by the passengers against his back and Luke caught the stare of an old man pinned against a window. Why me, he seemed to ask, but the bus had rattled him away before Luke had an answer. It sparked on its rails as it turned the corner and was lost to him. The day had already found its feet and he had already lost his once, he thought, recalling Rocío's hot kisses, before sealing the door as best he could on this morning's encounter.

It was better to do that, he'd decided when he'd arrived in the country, to step forward, no matter how unknown the terrain, rather than dwell too deeply on where one had already been.

'Por favor, mister.' Dirt-stained fingers tugged at his jacket. Luke looked down to see its owner, a man dressed in a suit fashioned from rags, sitting in the dirt at his feet. At some moment in his life his leg had broken beneath the knee joint and it was fused now at an appalling angle. Luke sympathised fully, as though the break had been his. He felt the ghost of an ache in his own damaged leg, prompting him to empty his pockets into the man's palms before hurrying on. The square lay before him like a foundation slab turned to the sun. It was going to be a bright October day without a cloud in the sky. He stepped down off the kerb and picked his way over the tram tracks to where he'd spotted a squat cantina squeezed in between the grand buildings either side of it. He was ravenous and it would do. The cantina had a little plaque nailed to its door which read 'La Casa de la Risa', the house of laughter. It looked a joyless little place, he thought, although that was usually a good sign. The ugliest of them always produced the best food. Inside the cantina, it was dark and it took his eyes some moments to adjust. In a daze he motioned to the serving girl, a small creature with eyes black like draft ink, who found him a seat near the back. Luke blinked and checked his watch. It was eleven thirty. He'd have preferred a seat near the front but the cantina was full. He liked watching the street and the people on it. He'd been in the country the best part of a year but it still held that tourist's fascination for him. Luke removed his jacket and dropped it onto the chair back. The girl came over and in his cleanest Spanish he ordered the eggs he'd not realised he craved until then.

'Arepa y huevos.'

'Huevos pericos y tinto?' she asked, betraying a local accent that came out as though she were singing.

'Sí,' he said, sending the girl back to what looked like her father beside the grill. The older man took his order and looked up, nodding once in Luke's direction as though to thank him for his patronage. Luke returned it, although really he'd just come for the eggs. He removed the photograph from his trouser pocket. He shouldn't have taken it to the brothel, but the need had been too great. He placed it on the table, correcting the edges where Rocío had curled her dexterous fingers around it. We should stop this, he thought, looking at the face.

The waitress arrived with coffee. Luke sipped at the sweet black liquid and resumed his study of the picture – a sepia photograph of a pretty girl with a smile full of cunning. She was spread across the sands, somewhere that, given the ancient rock face behind her, could have been a brilliant cove on a Greek island. The truth was revealed in pencil on the back: *Catherine, Lulworth Cove, Dorset, 1932.* They'd been twenty-four; he, only just. That's why they'd gone; a birthday by the sea and everything ahead. He'd been qualified for three years and already practising as an architect. The last war had seen to that. He'd been just a boy, really, but bright enough to see that when many left and few returned, someone would benefit. Things had seemed golden then. In the photograph, Catherine wore a jumper and dungarees beneath. He remembered that trip to the Dorset coast as uneventful, other than how hard it was to unpin the clasps on the dungarees when they tripped back up the steps of her aunt's cottage. She'd giggled at his clumsiness. She wasn't nervous. She hadn't been in love though, not like him. Not then. Whatever happened to those trousers afterwards? Had she cast them off the cliff and into the sea? He smiled and took another sip. It would have been like her to do that.

The girl was before him again with eggs and the bread made with maize he'd taken to. He picked up the fork and ate like one starved. Not far from where he was sitting a loud discussion had broken out between three men. When he had finished eating, he pushed his plate away, ordered another tinto and listened in. Sometimes, it was the only way to learn the language, to develop an ear for how the people really spoke. He caught the eye of one of the group, a large man in a bright red poncho, far richer than anything else in the cantina's drab interior. Luke looked away. This man, if he was hearing it right, was arguing with the one beside him. From what he could tell, the argument was about the youngest of the group who it turned out was a family member – a son or nephew perhaps.

'Please. Not him…' the man spoke.

'It's too late, you agreed, you both did,' said the one in the poncho.

Something inside the boy's relative seemed to break, and, upsetting the table, he left. Luke watched to see what the boy would do. He looked as if he was about to follow, but the large man stopped him, handing him something from beneath his cloak. A folded piece of cloth, the same red as the poncho, Luke thought. When he looked up next the boy had gone and the large man too.

Lesson over, he called the waitress back and found coins for the meal. He was full, content even, and would save Señora Rojas' generous soup for the evening. He turned to reach for his jacket just as a deafening roar, like twisting metal, came from the front of the building. At first, Luke thought the cantina's shutter had fallen but it was something beyond that, on the square, which had caused everyone to rush outside. He followed the waitress out onto the street, where they stood together looking across at an electric tram partially shaken from its tracks, its front gnarled and ugly, beneath which the boy from the cantina lay, almost cut clean in half by the wheels. The waitress turned and screamed, muffling her face against his shirt front. He felt numb, an observer. Only minutes before he'd been sitting beside him in the cantina. He couldn't take his eyes from it. Not the stunned travellers dismounting from its steps, nor the body that lay like wet clay beneath it, but the roll of fabric – a flag – now unsheathed, wrapped tight like a vice around one hand, revealing a bloody hammer and sickle.

Luke detached himself from the girl. The owner of the cantina beckoned her back over. She went and Luke was alone again whilst those around him spoke fast in a local dialect he couldn't understand. In another minute the crowd had thickened and he could no longer see anything of the dead boy. The waitress was sobbing against the old man's chest and Luke thought about going over, to offer some words that might make sense of the destruction. Instead, he turned from them and slipped quietly away.

3

Inside of his office at La Merced, Luke searched the newspaper for any reference to the streetcar incident from the day before. He turned the page he was on and there it was, driven towards the back, near to the advertisements, the boy's life reduced to an eighth of a page. *Juan Manuel Muñoz Pérez, eighteen years old, yesterday endangered the lives of twenty-six people when he stepped in front of a streetcar. His distraught mother, Señora Pérez Beltran, said he had been struggling to find work...* Luke scanned the page and then read the article again, slower this time, in case he'd missed something. It couldn't be right. There wasn't any mention of the flag or of the two men he'd seen with the boy in La Casa de la Risa. They'd printed a photograph of the dead boy along with the article. A close-up from the day focussed in on his head, his right cheek grubby and worn where it had made contact with the pavement. He couldn't have been more than sixteen. The reader had been spared the rest of Juan Manuel. The way it was all phrased was wrong, though. The article spoke of criminal intent. Said the boy had acted alone. He was a vigilante thug, a criminal. And nothing but a worthless sacrifice in someone else's game, Luke thought, screwing up the entire page and tossing it across the room. Then there was the image of Catherine caught up in the whole damned thing. He'd left it in the cantina along with his jacket. He'd reached home and turned back, but it had been dark by the time he'd reached the square, and nothing but the abandoned streetcar remained. La Casa de la Risa was shut and the idea of her image lost there, at the centre of a city that swallowed everything, had been all he'd been able to think about since.

A knock at the door. 'Señor Vosey.'

It was Telma, his secretary. Luke closed the newspaper but didn't put it down. Telma knew how to knock, but not how to wait.

'Are the candidates here?'

'Señor, they've cancelled again.' She came into his office and adjusted the shutters. Luke blinked at the fresh light let loose inside the room. 'One couldn't afford his flight from Cali and the other, well, it looks like his papers were made up. People grow desperate.' She shook her head.

'And today's post?'

'I'll look again,' Telma began, edging closer.

Luke tried not to smile. She always smelled of hair lacquer. He was convinced it was an addiction of hers.

'There is my sister's boy; he could be here this afternoon, if it's only a junior you want.'

'The new draughtsman should have some experience, Telma, no matter how small, I'm sorry. And we'll need sound references this time, ones that can be checked.' It was the same script every time; she never listened. 'The board won't go in for anything less.'

'But you, señor? Since Señor Palacio upped and left that pile of half-finished drafts without a word, I thought…'

'You know I won't either.'

Telma straightened up. 'Another from the writer,' she said, placing a telegram on the desk in front of him. 'You can't avoid him forever.'

She turned and closed the door behind her. Luke looked down; to his left lay the discarded newspaper and to his right, the telegram from one of its staff writers. Camilo Osorio had sent six telegrams and, so far, Luke had ignored five. This latest was the shortest yet. *Have you considered?*

It didn't need to say more. Luke rose and went over to the window. It was impossible to see through its diamond-patterned glaze. What had he been thinking? He opened the pane. In the unfinished street below and as far as he could see, workmen, junior architects and engineers were busy crawling over his plans for the executive village – and Camilo Osorio wanted access to all of it. He wanted access to him, Luke Vosey. The architect behind the London Arts Institute (firebombed), Madrid's Centro Inglés (turned into a squat during the civil war, he'd read) and the garden suburbs of Heliotrope and Courtlands, three miles from London and Birmingham respectively. The past, Luke thought, taking in the scene in front of the house, was filled with nothing but forgotten vistas.

This latest commission had come from Anglo-Colombian Oil and he'd wasted no time getting it off the ground, pouring himself into every part of it. The plot had started life as a large farm run by Jesuit priests. Thanks to him it was very different to that now, although it had kept its name, La Merced, along with some of its land, which he'd turned into a pretty park. The houses he'd designed were in the Tudor Revival style; a nod to the medieval, with black and white plastering, bay windows, sloped roofs – that was what they knew him for, from before the war. They hadn't seen anything like it here. Most architects had trouble leaving England, the continent, family. He hadn't minded, he'd said. And after everything that had happened, they understood.

Luke watched a team of bricklayers surround and then climb a makeshift bamboo scaffold, passing batches of red tiles up for the sharply pitched roof. Above them, the tilers balanced on the new rafters, filled with the task of covering the timbers. From their bare, arched backs, the view inclined steeply towards Monserrate, more than a thousand feet above. He held up his thumb and closed one eye, obscuring the white church at its peak. Let Osorio come, Luke thought. I have nothing to hide.

4

'I'm not drinking, thank you.'

'A man like you should.' Señora Rojas came across the room of his apartment with the bottle of whisky he'd pushed to the back of the cupboard some months before. Luke smiled at his housekeeper and let her pour. It seemed unintelligent to argue with the person who washed and fed you.

'Will you join me?' he asked.

She shook her head at him as she always did when he encouraged her to vice. It was a game they played. 'Only at funerals,' she said, pushing the stopper back in. 'I must feed my husband.' She padded back to the kitchen.

He raised the glass to his lips, letting the alcohol lick his gums. He hadn't been back to the cantina for the photograph yet. He considered abandoning her there. He imagined it as something he was capable of doing but then lowered the glass.

It was raining. Luke listened to the tumult fire off the tiles and pepper the pavement below.

'Volver,' he sang, turning the volume up on the wireless beside him. The tango came at him like a flood. Luke closed his eyes. 'Volver…'

'What?' Señora Rojas came back into the room. She'd changed into her regular shoes and was wearing her coat.

'You'll drown if you leave now,' Luke said, turning the music down.

'And I'll sink if I don't.' She tightened the belt on her jacket. 'Señor Rojas likes to eat too, you know.' She looked down at the untouched glass in Luke's hand. 'And drink.'

'Your health,' he said, raising it.

When Señora Rojas had gone, Luke rose and went into the small kitchen-cum-maid's room. He poured the whisky down the sink and left the glass upright on the draining board. Perhaps he'd had another? Let her think so. He hadn't been drunk since those first few months in Bogotá. With the stress of the project, it was better to keep your head than lose it. There were other reasons too. Drink had stopped numbing the past as it used to. It had started to enhance it.

He crossed the hall and went into the bedroom. On top of the bed, a drawer from the dresser had been turned upside down and its contents scattered. He hadn't been able to find the other photograph of Catherine. The one from her brother Albie's party and their last night together before she'd left for France. In it, she was wearing the green dress that made him lose his mind, act crazy around her. He was there, leaning around her with the lighter, her face caught between the flame and the camera's flash so that she looked like a frightened rabbit. That's what you'd have thought if you didn't know her; didn't know that look in her eye that was anything but frightened.

From the bedroom window there was a good view of Seventh Avenue, running off into the distance towards the city centre. The apartment was close to the site as well, unlike those of the people he was building for. They lived up in

Barrancabermeja alongside the main oil refinery. All oil men up there, until they came down to Bogotá to play.

Luke went back over to the bed. He shovelled up the mess – lonely socks, pocket squares and an old cigar box that rattled tie pins, loose buttons and service medals, dropping it all back into the drawer. He picked up a pair of sunglasses and put them on, catching sight of himself in the window glass. Brown rims, barely worn and expensive, bought on the Strand after he'd signed the contract at Shell Mex House. They'd said he was going somewhere hot. They went back into the drawer with the last of the junk. Catherine wasn't there, which was undoubtedly a good thing. He had promised himself he would stop. Stop dragging her with him, not to the brothel, not to the cantina for breakfast, not anywhere else he chose to go. If he couldn't leave her behind here, thousands of miles from London, then where on earth could he? The moon? He looked out of the window. It was late and Camilo Osorio threatened the horizon, pencilled into his diary for one o'clock the next day. A mark in the afternoon that wasn't a blot, Luke told himself. He went over to the curtains and pulled them shut.

Early mornings were commonplace. Luke sat upright in the bed, his vision obscured by a palette of bright orange dots that he couldn't rub away. His leg felt dead, a slab of meat where he'd lain on it and stopped the blood. He pulled the covers back and tried to bring the damaged limb back to life. Resuscitation was agony. As always, it would be a waiting game. This time the death had been his own, met beneath falling masonry. So much dust. He coughed to try and clear his lungs of it but already the structure of the dream was becoming less formed, less concrete. This is real, he told himself, looking around the room. He leaned down for his wristwatch on the nightstand;

five o'clock. A reassuring milky light spilled in through the cracks in the curtains. Other real things occurred to him – the discarded drawer that lay on the floor beside the chest, the need to piss, hunger – so that he was able to forget what had not been real. He rose carefully and staggered to the bathroom to begin his day.

At La Merced, the rain from the night before had left puddles the size of small craters throughout the site. The men had worked out it was quicker to throw materials and tools to each other across them, rather than walk around. 'Don't!' he'd shouted but they were natural adopters of shortcuts and so he'd spent most of the morning trying to prevent tragedy. He had to admire their resilience. It was eleven o'clock by the time the sun had drunk most of the puddles dry. Luke sunk lower beneath the brim of his straw hat. He took off his jacket and threw it onto a pile of bamboo he knew was behind him. 'Tenga cuidado! Move it!' a man shouted from inside of the pile that had been on the ground but was now on this man's shoulders. He'd almost walked right through him.

'My fault,' Luke replied, picking his way over the potholes towards a quiet spot. Out here on site he was exposed, thrown in with the locals who didn't care who he was or who he had been. 'It's what you wanted, Luke,' he murmured. In front of him, a large red brick house was nearing completion. A new structure, unlived in, was a beautiful thing to behold, he thought. The bay window glaze was in, set tight into hand-carved lintels. Either side of the bays were two gabled wings – offices with bedrooms above. Mounted on top of each wing was a chimney stack and, clinging to each of these, a pair of workmen whose job it was to finish the pointing. Luke squinted up at them and walked over. The pair on the left kept twisting to catch sight of the other two across the drop. Someone is going to fall, he thought. Christ, it felt like a daily battle to keep them all alive. It had to be the foreman's doing, promising them a drink apiece if they finished first. That had happened before and, although he hadn't wanted to, he'd had to dismiss drunk men. He'd find the foreman before it came to that again. Further up the street he found only a cart horse being laden down with bricks. The horse was trying to buck itself free of the load. It didn't know that it couldn't get away from the cart like that and was churning up the dirt with its hooves. A roof tile smashed at his feet.

'Hey!' he called up.

The man who'd dropped it looked down at him with wild eyes. 'Sorry, sorry! You move!' he shouted.

'Move?'

'Move, mister, now!'

Luke heard the cry from the street then and saw the cart horse heading his way, spraying its heavy weight of bricks left and right. And there was the foreman, finally, standing in the middle of the road and right in the horse's path. Luke heard his own voice join the others, calling at him to get out of the way, and he did so, just in time, but the horse moved too. The cart tipped, and he didn't see the foreman after that.

The dust hadn't quite cleared when Luke found himself in the dirt, heaving the cart upwards alongside the other men while the foreman belched and groaned below. Luke hooked his weight against the cart's broken side. Everyone who had seen it was there too, lifting alongside him – some pushing, some pulling. 'Who is it?' someone asked. The foreman hadn't been popular. What was his name? Luke strained against the weight of remembering. Every time the cart looked as if it might right itself, it fell back and the crushed man cried out again. Isidro, his name was Isidro and his family came from Tolima. Luke wasn't going to let him die.

'Push, now!' Luke said.

The men worked together, but without the horse braced to it, there was nothing to help pivot the cart upwards.

'Lift again.' An unfamiliar voice came out of the dust, its owner holding a timber joist which he was already hooking under the cart beside the foreman.

'Now!' Luke shouted as they tried again.

The stranger put his weight against the joist, damp and red in the face. Luke listened as it cracked and then started to splinter – they'd all be thrown backwards into the dirt – but then the cart let out its breath and sprang upwards, rocking violently on its frame. Beneath, the crushed man was barely conscious. Luke helped to drag him free from the earth and lift him onto the back of the cart. Everyone crowded in. The men fought against each other to be in the group to lift the frame. Luke watched it being dragged away, taking the same path as the horse had earlier. They'd have to bring her under control. If they'd used vehicles, it would have been otherwise, but things were done differently here. He found another man and told him to run ahead to the doctor some six blocks away. The man wouldn't budge, not until Luke told him he would pay.

Luke tried to bring his breathing under control. Those who'd helped had tried to do right by the foreman, he understood that and was glad for it. 'Everyone here can collect an extra ten centavos this week,' he said to a sea of blank faces.

With nothing else to interest them, the men returned to their work. He should get back to his office too. The journalist would be here soon and he was filthy.

'Will he live?' It was the man who had given him his best chance.

'Let's hope so.' Luke turned. 'Good idea about that joist.'

'Simple physics.' The young man smiled and looked down at his feet so that Luke did too. Worn brown leather, the same as his satchel. He offered his hand. 'Camilo Osorio.'

'You are, aren't you?' Luke said, extending his. 'You're early.'

Camilo Osorio sat across from Luke wearing a look free from disaster. He didn't seem affected by the event with the cart. It isn't the story he's come for, Luke thought, wondering if he should offer him a drink. He wanted one and it would be the normal thing to do after a crisis, drink. He leaned back in his chair. It could not have been worse timing, Osorio arriving when a man's life hung in the balance.

'Don't worry, I won't write about it,' Camilo said.

'It might make for interesting reading.'

'You mean, the brave architect, his face in the dirt?' Camilo smiled and the door flung open. Telma appeared, carrying a tray laden with hot towels, coffee and papers. She put the tray down on the desk and handed over the cups with instructions to wash. Then she handed Luke his post for the afternoon. Memos from the board, questions from the executives and, on top of this, the updated employment file for the draughtsman role. Luke thanked her and pushed the pile to one side. Camilo's eyes followed.

'Tell me, how have you settled in here?'

'In Bogotá?'

Luke handed him a towel and took the other, blackening it instantly.

'Pack horses and competing labourers are different to what you're used to.'

'It's the same the world over.'

'Really? It was Madrid last, wasn't it?' Camilo put the towel to one side and produced a notebook from beneath the desk. He opened it and waited.

'I thought you'd have done your research, Señor Osorio?' Luke smiled and sipped at his coffee. He might be free in an hour.

'Camilo, please.' He paused. 'The Centro Inglés was one of the greatest examples of the new modernist style in Europe. It was a great loss.'

'It is still standing, you understand.'

'But sadly as a symbol of bourgeois oppression.'

'Right.'

Luke finished his coffee and noticed Camilo's cup was full.

The journalist picked it up. 'I followed the story of its capture.' He drank. 'It made me want to cry to think of the glass alone. Wasn't it the first time it had been engineered on such a scale?'

'The eyes of the city.' Luke smiled.

'Smashed through.'

'I prefer to think of it as it was.'

'And I've just reminded you otherwise.' Camilo leaned forward. 'I'm sorry.'

Outside, it had just started to rain again. He hoped the men would find the doctor. He wanted the foreman to live. His death would be so meaningless, but when had death ever been anything else? Luke watched the workmen climb down from their scaffolds and drag rough covers over the timbers at ground level.

'You know what's funny?' Luke said. 'I find the climate reminds me of home.'

Camilo followed the direction of his gaze. 'And the houses too, no doubt.'

5

When Camilo left his office, promising to return the next day, Luke had shaken his hand. Once to thank him for saving the foreman's life and again to get a feel for the man. Camilo had appeared at the right time. He wasn't altogether unlikable, as previous newsmen he'd run into were. It felt good to be reminded of his earlier projects. If he could keep things light, give the journalist what he wanted, glory in a little of what had been, they'd both come out of it unscathed. Yes, he could do all that, he thought.

'It's tonight you're at the Hotel Granada and there's still dirt under your nails,' said Telma.

'Tonight?' He hadn't heard her come in.

'The Chairman's Dinner?'

On top of everything he'd forgotten all about it.

'What did you think of him, Telma?'

'The boy?'

'Camilo, yes.'

'Cachaco.' She tidied the desk. 'You know, in the way he talks.'

'He sounds like you.'

'Of course not.' She lifted the tray. Cachaco was a word they used in Bogotá to describe a fancy, formal, old-fashioned way of speaking; of being.

'He's coming again tomorrow,' Luke said, rising. He considered the pile of post. He really should take a look before he left.

'Leave it,' said Telma. 'There isn't a draughtsman in there you'll like anyway.'

That evening, Luke left his apartment with ample time to reach the Granada. There was something he had to do before the dinner.

He made it to La Casa de la Risa as the old man was drawing down the shutter. As he ran across the square, ignoring the pain in his leg, he noticed that the smashed-up streetcar had gone. The cantina owner looked surprised to see him. He remembers me, Luke thought with some hope. But now that he was in front of him, the Spanish word for lost had completely slipped his mind. *Perder* meant to lose the game, didn't it? What about an object? What kind of loss was that?

'Fotografía?' he asked, pointing to the black interior of the bar.

The old man ignored him and went back to the shutter.

'Señor, por favor,' Luke said, putting a hand out to stop him. 'You know me.'

The man shook himself free.

'The photograph of the girl,' he tried in English. 'Please.'

'Girl?'

'I was here, just yesterday?' Luke pointed to where the streetcar had been.

'Somewhere else, perhaps,' the man said, looking across the square to this other place both of them knew did not exist.

'Look,' Luke said, but he didn't know how else to continue; what else he could say? It was obvious he wasn't communicating properly. 'Look here,' he said again, taking out his wallet.

'Oh, oh!' the man said, grinning. 'The dead boy.' His mouth held barely any teeth.

'That's right, I was here then. I comforted your daughter.'

'My daughter? Yes.' He laughed again. 'Let's see.' He reached inside the front pocket of his apron and brought out a small wedge of papers, receipts, bills mostly. From the pile he drew out a blank sheet and pinched it open. It was the photograph. 'Pretty girl, this,' he said, turning the image of Catherine in the air. His other hand came to rest palm-up before Luke.

Luke handed over a fistful of notes. Any notes, he hadn't seen and didn't care.

'Bye-bye, beautiful,' the man said, passing him the image.

It was her. The photograph was limp. Hot even, where it had sat close to the old man's body, and there was a deep crease across Catherine's face. He tried to ignore this and studied the contents of the scene instead, as though the position of the sitter might have changed. The cove and the rock were still there, and the tide flowing in just so, so that the next wave would catch at her ankles and she'd run into his open arms at any minute. But his eyes were drawn back to the crease. It made it impossible to tell who the sitter was now, unless you already knew, unless you had been there.

Luke looked up. The old man was just standing there, waiting for something else. Luke remembered the jacket he'd also left in the cantina. Yes, the man wanted a second note in exchange for that – but he'd only come for the photograph, hadn't he, and that was ruined. He looked at the man but didn't speak. Let him understand that I'm not going to pay him anything else, Luke thought. How long had she sat there, so close to his body? He could take a few more of those teeth, but the idea of it was more delicious than the act itself. Nothing violent could really be said to have happened. Not now. Not to anyone. Only to an image of what had been.

'Gracias, señor,' he said and walked away.

Luke limped the four blocks from Plaza de Bolívar to Santander Park and the Hotel Granada. Furious at himself for giving in to her again, he forced himself onwards with increasing speed. It was true that Catherine was his again but he did have to get back to the living. He should get back to them. He was sweating by the time he reached the corner of the park.

You couldn't miss the Granada. It took up a whole street junction, laid out in a frothy Victorian style he was done with. It was so unashamedly European and so different to everything around it. Walking, he'd passed many low terracotta-roofed dwellings that were much friendlier-looking, much warmer. He passed alongside the tree-lined park in front of the hotel, emptied and pleasant at this time of day. He didn't think anything of the group of young men chatting amongst themselves against its railings until a few of them ran to catch him up.

'Whatever it is, I don't want it,' he said, walking faster.

One of the men stepped in front of him.

'What?' he asked, turning to find the rest of the group behind him. 'Don't try me.'

'Lotería?'

'What?'

'Buy a ticket,' the man said, pulling out a roll of paper from somewhere inside of his jacket. 'Sir.'

'Yes, yes,' he said, fumbling about inside his trouser pocket for coins. He pulled out a centavo. 'Uno billete, then.'

'No change,' the man replied. 'That buys you a sheet.' He pocketed the coin and tore off a strip.

'Gracias,' Luke said, taking it. He didn't want the tickets but knew he had to have them. There had to be an exchange. This wasn't robbery. 'All right then, we done?'

The smallest of the group whistled through his teeth for them to move on. The roll was put away and Luke's path cleared. He walked on, clutching the strip of four he'd just bought. When he reached the safety of the Granada he looked back, but the group had abandoned the park. The doorman was grinning at him.

'Just take them,' Luke said, handing him the strip.

The main salon of the Hotel Granada was filled with executive types. He'd expected that and tried to calm his mood. The shift from the outside, the local city, to this one of privilege was disarming. At the height of his career, his had been the face everyone expected to see. One year, there had been a whole season of parties, of dinners, of girls that he'd thought he'd enjoy again here. But no, he wasn't enjoying it. He couldn't.

Deeper inside the space, he could hear the orchestra tuning up. He had been to the hotel before and knew some of the Anglo-Colombian Oil executives by face but not by name. They bored him. The men had one foot in the past, talking only of the first war. Most of them had been hiding out here then. Karl had told him that. A few of the men looked up from their drinks in recognition. 'Cowards,' he said, smiling back.

'Vosey!'

Karl Draper arrived at his side in a fug of cigar smoke.

'Mr Draper, I'm late, I'm afraid.'

'Nonsense, I know your game. Too busy with all those pretty girls over in Las Cruces, hey?'

'There was an accident.'

'I've got a good doctor.' Karl reached up and touched his sleeve. 'Discreet.'

'With the foreman, on site.'

'Don't talk to me about work, Vosey.' Karl threw him off and collared a passing waiter. 'Get this man a drink. Whisky, I'd say.'

'Yes sir.' The man bowed his head and made as if to disappear.

'Isn't there anything else?'

Karl raised his eyebrows. 'You won't get a beer, Vosey. Not unless you know a good working man's club.'

'Whisky's fine.'

'Remember, Vosey, the Americans are here and they want to meet the man responsible for this little building project of ours.'

'Then I look forward to it.'

The waiter returned and Luke took a glass. The foreman would live, he'd learned, but would be bedridden for weeks. Camilo Osorio, on the other hand, was returning tomorrow. He was looking forward to their next exchange. Luke lifted the drink to his lips. The liquid burned his throat but there was a kind of clarity after the searing. He'd always looked for that.

'Now,' said Karl. 'See that man there?'

Luke followed his gaze to a tall, immaculately dressed man, smoking alone beside the windows that overlooked the park.

'That's Gabriel Osorio, he works for the foreign ministry.'

'Osorio?'

'Yes.'

'And?' said Luke, letting the coincidence pass.

'Well, he's got his fingers in enough American pies to feed the country twice over. He's heading up the Pan-American delegation next year. What's more,' Karl whispered, 'he's shown a special interest in the project. Probably some work in it for you after all this. There's more of this shithole needs pulling down and he knows it. Come and see me tomorrow.'

'And what's in it for you, Karl?'

Karl's eyes narrowed. 'Bold, Luke. I like that. Osorio won't, though.'

At dinner, Luke was seated next to Karl's wife and a senior member of the board; a man who spoke too quietly to be heard. The chairman was two or three tables over with Gabriel Osorio, conspiring above the smoke from his cigar along with the other executives. Luke looked past them. He wanted another drink.

'You won't get him that way,' Mrs Draper said, clicking her fingers sharply above the music. A young waiter came over.

'Mine's a French 75,' she said. 'You know that one?'

'Yes, madam, and you?' he asked, facing Luke. The boy looked tired.

'Another whisky, please.'

The waiter left and Luke watched as the remaining guests went to their seats. A waltz was begun so they might have something to listen to while they ate, he thought, amused at the idea. Dinner was French; fresh lake-caught trout smothered in brown butter followed by calf's liver with parsley. Luke asked for water while the waiter kept up a vigil beside Mrs Draper's wine glass.

'You're a quiet man,' Mrs Draper said, leaning across Luke to his neighbour. 'I like quiet men.'

'Mrs Draper,' Luke said, smiling and removing her hand from his lap where it had fallen, 'how long did you say you've been in the country? I can't remember what you told me the last time we dined together.'

'You men never listen!' she giggled. 'Oh, I don't know what I told you. I come and go.'

'I think that's what you said then.' Luke smiled. You couldn't let your guard down around a woman like Mrs Draper, but she wasn't the worst of them.

'I come and go at his bidding,' she said, pointing at Karl across the room. 'And are you settled now, Mr Vosey?'

'Yes, I think so.'

'When we first met you had a wonderfully expectant look about you.' She leaned in closer. 'Like a young buck hunting for something, or someone.' She smiled.

'I don't think so.'

'Oh yes, it amused me greatly, but that's gone now. You're as tired as the rest of us. Too many late nights spent with my Karl, hey?'

'That must be it,' Luke said, trying to get the waiter's attention.

It was after the main course that both seats beside him became free and he felt momentarily unshackled from responsibility. Luke leaned back and closed his eyes. The orchestra played on. Around him the room felt generally satiated, chatting above the gentle rhythm. It suited the mood lent him by the alcohol and his thoughts turned to Rocío then. Did anyone take her out, he wondered. Perhaps when he got free of this, he would. She really deserved better than what she got.

'Has she bored you to death yet?'

Luke opened his eyes and sat up. It was the tall man from the foreign ministry.

'Señor Draper's wife, I mean,' he said, sitting down beside him.

'The answer might cost me my job,' Luke replied.

'Gabriel Osorio,' he said, holding out a packet of cigarettes.

'And you're the architect.' Luke nodded and took one. 'My friends call me El Lobo.'

'The wolf?' Luke asked, leaning in.

'Yes.' He smiled, lighting both cigarettes. 'And Vosey, that's French.'

'English.'

'It's a good name for an architect. Le Corbusier is French.'

'French-Swiss I believe.'

'Detail,' said Gabriel, waving cigarette smoke between them. 'Is Osorio a common name?'

'Common?'

'I know another Osorio, that's all,' Luke said. 'Camilo, a newspaperman.'

'My brother's boy,' he nodded, blowing fresh smoke. 'A mere pup.'

The orchestra stopped playing. Both men turned to watch. A clarinettist came on and blew a simple tune that was soon picked up by a man on maracas and percussion at his back. Unlike the food, the cocktails and the waltzing, it was familiar. Not to Luke, but to this place. Wasn't it called cumbia? It was the music he'd been listening to on the wireless. The music by Burmúdez or some other orchestra that was popular with the men on site. They whistled the tunes while they worked. He smiled, watching the few European couples who had been waltzing stop and try to change tack. None of them could.

'You see,' said Gabriel, rising and not taking his eyes from the clarinet player, 'we're pleased you're building the little English village.' He placed a hand on Luke's shoulder. 'Unlike this, it shows progress.'

6

The next morning, Luke was bleary-eyed. He could still taste the alchemy of Mrs Draper's lipstick mixed in with the cocktails. She'd insisted on kissing him goodnight, full on the lips, just as her husband rounded the corner of the lobby. There, Karl had met Luke's apologetic stare with an encouraging smile.

Luke dressed slowly in front of the open window of his bedroom, taking large gulps of mountain air. He'd expected to feel more breathless as soon as he'd arrived in the city. In the boardroom on the Strand, Karl had said the altitude could make even a brisk walk feel like a marathon. Was he a marathon runner? He wasn't, he'd assured Karl then, laughing at the idea. Only after a night of drinking did he feel the effects of the altitude on his breathing. It had been the same that time before, when Luke had just arrived and Karl had taken him straight from the airport to his club.

Today, Camilo Osorio was due back for his interview. Karl was coming too, to talk about some commission tied to the Pan-American Conference next year. There was also the project to sign off on before the weekend. It was progressing

31

but as a child might, in constant need of nurturing. He was optimistic about the draughtsman vacancy – there was bound to be someone in need of work; he just hadn't found him yet. He'd get that organised today as well. He needed them to start on the designs for the fireplaces and fittings. There were at least a hundred fireplaces to be drawn up and committed to wood by local craftsmen. He had no idea of timescales for that. It was worrying to think that the internal work might go on indefinitely. Camilo's interview and Karl's commission were ways forward, he thought, but the idea that part of the building work might be held up threatened to change that. Nobody knew where that fool Palacio had run off to. Luke swung the end of his tie into place and drew the silk towards his throat. He was reminded of Rocío's hands doing the same last night but in reverse, or was it this morning? He'd gone to her in the end. She was becoming a habit.

He left the apartment and headed down Seventh Avenue, which still laid claim to a few grand colonial houses. Once their sprawl of rooms and balconies had suited them, sitting very much outside of the city, but now, as they were slowly consumed by its girth, they looked out of place. He liked seeing what had been there before set against what was now. They reminded him of Spain, of the rural haciendas there. It gave him a strange feeling of home, even though he'd only spent weekends outside of Madrid when he'd worked there. Perhaps it was the friends he'd made and the skins of wine they'd drunk together? Nevertheless, it was a good memory to have held onto. Luke left them behind and passed through the national park. It was beautifully landscaped but in a juvenile state, having only been planted out some ten years previously. At its heart was a four-sided clock which told a quarter past nine from each face. Ahead of him, through the fronds of young palms, he could make out the building works of La

Merced leaning towards the side of the mountain. There was his contribution. In the early Andean light, he almost thought he could see its terracotta rooftiles glisten, like some sacred site within a city he was still eager to know. He'd always been aware of the gradient of the streets he worked on, although from this perspective he could see just how much they were building upwards, claiming the lower steps of the incline for the city. It meant everything had to be stabilised, calculated with mathematical precision, should any of the foundations choose to lean too far into the mountain, or worse still, away from it.

The familiar, comforting scrape of metal instruments against brickwork met him even before he had entered the site. When the workmen came into view, the scene exploded into one of industry. It looked as though there were twice as many men as the previous day, as though each man from the day before had hired another. They crawled like ants over the scaffold mounts, watching the supervisors who watched them, as though to beat the next man to an extra day's pay come Monday.

'Got to get things moving.' Karl Draper was at his side, his grin serving to frame a cigar stub clamped between his teeth.

'Things were moving, Karl, and safely.'

Karl frowned. 'Christ, Luke, don't talk to me about safety. When have rules ever helped anyone? This is work, that's what it is. And done in half the time.'

'And time wouldn't have anything to do with the Pan-American project next year?'

'Bingo.'

'OK, Karl, I understand there's a bigger prize in the offing…'

'Good, good.'

'But this has to be respected. This village, La Merced, has to be completed as planned; as we imagined it.'

'God, Vosey, you really are a pro, aren't you?' Karl slapped him on the back. 'Ha! I actually hired someone worth hiring.'

'So, you'll let me run it with no interference?'

'Yes, yes. I see you took my advice and brought in extra security.' Karl gestured towards a man standing watch over a large stack of roof tiles.

'They're checking everyone who comes in and out.'

'Good. We can't be too careful. People will take anything, even the seat from the john.' He laughed. 'That happened to me on another project. Damned humiliating, squatting like an animal to shit.'

'I suppose it can't hurt, if we can afford it. More men means we'll finish faster,' Luke said, contemplating the walls of a red brick garage that was taking shape before them. 'I wonder if any of them can draw?'

'Draw? Hang on, hiring men *and* women, hey?'

Luke turned. A group of men had forced their way through the security block and, led by a single woman, were heading straight for them. These weren't people who worked for him, he was sure of that. They had that look about them that said things were better taken by force than worked for.

'Are you Señor Vosey?' the woman asked.

'I am.'

'Isidro Gallego is my husband.'

The injured foreman. Luke looked at the men at her back. 'And these are?'

'His brothers.'

'All of them?'

'They're his brothers in the cause,' she said.

'I'll be in your office,' Karl whispered.

Luke watched him leave. Around them, the workers closest by had stopped what they were doing to stare.

'Señora, will you come with me?'

She shook her head, planting her feet in the dirt.

'Bring one of your companions if you like.'

She turned her back on Luke and spoke low in soft, coaxing tones as though these brothers, whoever they were, needed soothing towards diplomacy. When she turned back, one of them was at her side.

'The rest of you can wait here,' Luke said, nodding at the security guards who'd been overpowered at the gate. The pair had run over not long after the group. They had their clubs ready. They wanted blood and he understood it. The need to show you could be forceful too. Luke didn't want fighting, not here. Not when there was an arsenal of bricks and chisels to hand. He led the foreman's wife and the brother after Karl. It would serve Karl right if he walked right into his office with these two. Wouldn't do, though. Karl was his boss and that had earned him the right to some cowardice. Instead, Luke took them to the foreman's old office on the floor below his and invited them to sit. The man refused. He was the kind of man who didn't look comfortable being invited to do anything. Isidro's wife sat down in the chair Luke offered and fanned out her skirts. Luke leaned on the corner of the desk, which seemed a good middle ground between the two strangers. He didn't want to get too comfortable, if things were to go that way with the brother.

'How's your husband?' he asked her.

'He's unable to work, señor.'

'I understand that.'

She made a show of removing a handkerchief from her pocket and dabbed at her eyes. 'The doctors say he will not walk for some time.'

'And the company will pay his salary and medical bill for the next two weeks. His family were told this. You were told this.'

She looked back at the brother.

'Did you know he was in a union?' the man asked.

'What kind?'

'The kind that looks after its own.' The brother lit a cigarette. 'We don't care what his family were told. The union sent us. We're to take his place.'

'You mean the six of you?'

'We insist.'

'You don't have the right to do that.'

'You people think that,' the brother spat. He seemed to grow taller, but really he had just moved fast so that he was standing over him. Luke could smell the unwashed perfume of him, a stale sweetness lost inside the burn of fresh tobacco.

'We just want what's right,' the woman said, rising to guide the brother back to her side. 'The work is there, we can see it with our own eyes.'

'I'm not used to being threatened,' Luke said. It was a lie, of course, but it was what you said in such circumstances.

'It isn't a threat,' said the brother. 'If it can't be arranged today, it can be tomorrow, or the next day. We'll keep coming. We've been encouraged not to stop.'

Luke thought about asking who had sent them, or what idea perhaps. It was like one of those protests the liberals encouraged the people to take part in. The ones that saw them erect obscene banners in Plaza de Bolívar and pelt raw eggs at politicians when they didn't agree with policy. He'd read about them in *El Tiempo* but never imagined they'd find him here. He'd always been fair, he thought.

'Today we are six brothers, perhaps tomorrow we'll bring his cousins. He has a lot of cousins.'

'All right,' Luke said. 'What if I take two men and no more?'

'They all want to work,' the woman said. 'Take three.'

'I can't.' He thought of the army of men Karl had already employed without his knowledge. Could they afford more?

'It just went up to four,' she said.

Luke smiled. 'I'll take three, and if you go on insisting, I'll ask for references too.' He rose. 'Decide amongst yourselves who it is to be.'

'We'll have to speak to the others,' she said, rising too. She had stopped crying or forgotten, in the exchange, that she had begun.

'This is his,' said the man, taking up a jacket and hat that could have belonged to the foreman from a hook on the wall.

'Take it,' Luke said, leading them to the door and then back onto the street.

He waited while they discussed the outcome with the others. None of them looked alike and he wondered afterwards if the foreman was actually married. He'd never mentioned a wife but what did it matter now. Part of who he was respected what they were doing. He watched as the men split into those who would stay and those who would leave. The woman had taken ownership of the foreman's jacket and hat and he realised then that she'd arrived with neither of her own.

After they'd gone, Luke went in search of Karl, finding him in front of the window of his office. Karl's thick limbs stopped most of the morning light from entering the room. He'll never go without, Luke thought. He went over to his desk and retrieved a new bottle of whisky he'd bought on the journey into work that morning, promising himself it was more to have should Karl drop by than to drink himself. He found two glasses. Telma hadn't been through with the morning post yet. She had been right about yesterday's, there wasn't a good draughtsman anywhere in the pile. He'd checked. What had begun as a promising day was starting to slip. At least there was the journalist to look forward to.

'I must say, Vosey,' Karl eyed the whisky. 'You handled that well. I'd have run.'

Luke smiled. He poured and handed over one of the glasses. 'Is that why you hired me?'

'I didn't hire you.'

'Who did, then?'

'The board.' He raised his glass and Luke followed. 'Knowledgeable men with an eye for talent. You're famous.'

'Salud,' Luke said, taking a deep draught.

'Only question is why you came?'

'Is that why you're here today? To get to know me better?'

'Of course not! Christ, Luke, you could have come to fuck all the whores in Bogotá for all I care.' He grinned. 'Perhaps you have? Cigar?'

Luke shook his head and sat down at his desk. Karl sat across from him.

'As I said, the Pan-American Conference is coming next year. Lot of money to be made then. That gives us a little under four months.' Karl lit his cigar. 'All eyes on us. A man with your talent could benefit, if you take my meaning.'

'Four months for what exactly?'

'To get going. There's a lot of cash pouring in. Trying to modernise the place. More than a lick of paint, you know.' He slid his empty glass across to Luke. 'If what I hear is right, wouldn't surprise me if a few more of these building projects went up before the rest of the Americas, including our friends in the States, descend. All this nonsense with the socialists, crying out for the land to go back to the people. When was it ever theirs? Fat chance, not when Osorio and his pals own most of it. Nothing but commie whingeing, I say.'

'Perhaps it's their desire for a fair chance, or the suffering that follows when it's denied,' Luke said. He thought again of the woman and men who had begged to be employed. He thought of the boy and the streetcar.

'Suffering? Don't get involved with any of that, Luke.

38

They're in for a bit of a clean-up as well, Gaitán and his righteous lot. Can't have the reds making trouble when the conference comes.'

'And you think this Gaitán will?'

'He'll try. Half the country listens to him.'

'And the other half?'

'Sense.'

Karl stopped and looked at his empty glass. Luke poured.

'You won't join me, Vosey?'

'Not this time.' Why did men like Karl work in binaries?

'The place needs bringing up to speed, inside and out. There was talk of some big architect, someone you've heard about of course, coming here to redesign the city. I forget the name. Doesn't matter. You're here now. Osorio wants you for the job.'

'Camilo?'

'Who? Come on. Gabriel Osorio, you met last night.'

'Of course, El Lobo.'

'Better lay off the drink, Vosey,' Karl joked.

'And why does Gabriel Osorio want me?'

'Truth of it is, I've been lying to you.' Karl rose and went over to the window again. 'I said I didn't know about you when we met, but I did – I mean, I do. I know what you've lost.'

'What I've lost?'

'Is there an echo in here? Yes, what you lost. It can't have been easy.'

Luke poured himself another drink. 'It wasn't.' He thought of Catherine. As much as he tried, hers was always the first face he saw when he looked back.

'And in the way you did? I wouldn't wish that on anyone. No, you've got principles, Luke.'

Luke watched him, waiting to see how far Karl might go.

'I know something about it myself.' Karl rose and went over to the window. 'I had a horrible little brush with the law back in '42.'

'You're talking about my profession?'

'What else?'

'I came off lightly,' Luke said.

'But your career, it was in shreds after the trial, wasn't it? So public as well. There was no need for that. Doesn't give a man a chance to make himself up again afterwards. You know, once the game's done.'

'War isn't a game.'

'You'd think it was, talking to some of that lot last night. Did you hear them? So many victories. You'd think they'd all made General.'

Luke looked up at Karl and squinted. Framed by the sunlit window, he was nothing more than a charcoal outline of the man who had promised him a fresh start. Karl, in his management role, hadn't asked questions in London. Why was he asking now? They were far from the Strand, though, and Karl operated differently here, it seemed. He appeared different too – his suits were brighter and his hair shinier. In fact, everything about him had been dialled up a notch. Luke looked at his empty glass; his second. Karl picked it up and filled it again.

'All I'm saying, Vosey, is that this is a chance for you to step back onto the world stage.' He handed the glass to Luke. 'Osorio sees potential. Christ, so do I.'

Luke nodded.

'I'm arranging a little get-together, next week. We'll talk more then.'

7

Camilo didn't show that day. It didn't bode well for the newspaperman, Luke thought, considering how easy it had been to ignore him the first time, and he really didn't want to ignore him. Something about El Lobo left Luke keen for the arrival of the nephew. He wanted to know more about the man who called himself The Wolf. The man who, according to Karl, wanted to hire him. He needed to understand it, this new Pan-American project that was supposed to be greater than La Merced. Without the certainty of some future success, the past still had a way of bleeding into the present. Despite his best efforts, there would always be someone like Karl, with knowledge of the past, to remind him.

He couldn't just wait. Sleep was a nightmare. It was always the same scene drawn up and repeated; whole cities crushed and people too. And, some mornings when it was time to rise, he woke screaming to be free of them. It had become normal, almost, and not just for him. Señora Rojas had arrived early one morning and heard him. Afterwards, she'd said nothing, keeping her head down and her eyes on her work as though there were worse things he could have brought into her life. It was another week before Camilo appeared again.

'The newspaper boy's here,' Telma said, standing in the entrance to his office.

'Thank you, show him up.'

She didn't move.

'Has something else happened?'

'It's tonight, you know, the lecturer I told you about,' she whispered, 'and now the boy is here I'll need to stay late. Not that I'm one for politics. Work has no party and all that. I just wanted to hear Gaitán speak...'

'Enough, please.' Luke held up his hand. 'Tell Señor Osorio to come up and you can go to your meeting, or whatever it is.'

'I knew you would understand,' Telma said, smiling and stepping aside to reveal Camilo Osorio behind her.

Luke gestured to the seat across from him. Camilo took it and produced pen and notebook from his bag.

'You know you're late,' Luke said. 'By a week.'

'Late? I was here the next day. Didn't she say?' Camilo jabbed his pen back towards the closed door.

'Of course.' Luke smiled. Telma hadn't said a thing. There were things he wanted to know though, about Gabriel Osorio. He'd be polite and sacrifice a few details from his past if needed. 'Shall we pick up where we left off?'

Camilo opened the notebook and frowned.

'Forgive me,' he said, flicking through the leaves. 'Much news since then.'

'Perhaps I can ask you a question? About your uncle,' Luke said. 'There might be some coffee, if you want it too?'

'No coffee, thank you.' Camilo placed the notebook down on the desk. 'You must mean Gabriel Osorio?'

'We met last week.'

'He's my father's brother, but I don't know what I can tell

you.' Camilo sat up and reached into his pockets. 'Do you mind if I smoke?'

'Please.' Luke rose and opened the window.

Camilo lit the cigarette and inhaled deeply. 'Would you be shocked if I said he despises me?'

'Why would he do that?' Luke asked, leaning against the frame. 'I imagine it would be useful to have a nephew in the press.'

'I wrote something about him once which he didn't like. Now I'm an outcast of sorts.'

'And if I asked what it was you wrote?'

'I'd tell you, it's no secret. Something that implicated him in a deal he didn't want made public. Unseated a couple of his friends from office when it did,' he laughed. 'But the details would be boring, Señor Vosey, to you and to me! Now, where shall we start?'

'Well, I could start by saying that I'm an outcast too.' With Camilo it was easy, like talking to an old friend. 'You can write that down.'

Camilo smiled and stubbed out the cigarette he'd just lit. 'And why are you an outcast?' he asked, picking up the pen instead.

'I'm here, aren't I? Far from home.'

'Where is that?'

'England. A place called Liddington, actually. It's a small village somewhere called Wiltshire where nothing much has changed in over three hundred years.'

'Unlike here,' Camilo replied, nodding towards the scene outside.

'Yes, unlike here. Everyone seems caught up with it.'

'Yes, they are,' Camilo said. 'But it should be the right change. Not only this.' He gestured to the window.

'Something greater, real social movement – to see the people rise and not the skyline.'

'That's very well put. Not something your uncle would go in for, I bet?'

'Not in the slightest. Anyway, they're not my words, rather those of the people I write about. There isn't an original thought in my head.' He smiled. 'Are you hungry? I mean, if you're not too busy?'

'As you've seen, my secretary's in charge and she's gone for the day.' Luke rose. He took the key to his office from the drawer. 'Let's go.'

'I thought I was asking the questions.' Camilo pushed his bowl aside and sat back. The cantina was hot and busy. Luke lowered his spoon. Camilo had taken him somewhere new, although it was an old place, by the looks of the patched-together interior. They'd left the building works on foot and headed down Seventh Avenue and into the city, past the solid stone prison scheduled to become the national museum, the bullring that dominated one corner of Independence Park, and the Hotel Granada, walking straight through to the bustling old town district of La Candelaria. Luke would return tomorrow night, he thought, to meet with the elder Osorio and Karl at the Teatro Colón, but Camilo didn't need to know about that. Today, he was pleased to have a chance at a head start.

'It's good to talk to someone not connected with the building project,' Luke said. 'I haven't always gone in for the suburbs. I mean, I started there but I moved on. But you know that – if it doesn't sound too vain to admit it.'

'So, you've come full circle?' Camilo grinned and called the waitress over. 'Another coffee?'

Luke nodded.

'Say, have you been to the bullring?'

'Not here, I went in Spain,' Luke said, thinking back. He had been terrified at the time, not by the animals that sometimes broke free into the stalls, but by the wild crowd that frothed at the mouth in their blood-red rage. It made beasts of all of them.

'I always hated it,' Camilo said. 'My uncle used to make me go, although few children were ever invited.'

'I hated it too,' Luke said. 'But why do you ask?'

'It's my litmus test,' Camilo said, regarding him. 'You can tell a lot about a man by how far he is willing to benefit from suffering.'

'Then I hope I passed the test,' Luke said.

'You did,' Camilo said, smiling. 'Tell me something else about you, the man. For the article.'

'I live for my work.' Luke looked at the notebook on the table in front, its text pinched and small.

'The war,' Camilo said, pen in hand. 'You weren't building then. What did you do?'

The coffee arrived and Luke picked up his cup. He would have to say something about that. 'I was at the Ministry of Economic Warfare. I never left London. I wanted to.'

'What stopped you?'

'An order.'

'From a commanding officer?'

'Actually, a woman.'

Camilo smiled. 'And is this woman still giving orders?'

'No, she's dead.'

'I'm sorry, please forgive my intrusion.'

Luke swallowed. 'Back at my office, you said the people should rise up. How do you think they'll do that?'

'You're interested to know?'

'Yes, I find I am.'

Camilo put his pen down. 'Nothing like your European war, if that's what you're thinking.' He took a cigarette from the pack in his bag and lit it. 'There are other ways.'

'Such as?'

'Gaitán.'

'The liberal leader?'

'Yes.' Camilo leaned in. 'He's a man of change – he brings a fresh wind with him,' he smiled. 'Where he blows, people follow.'

'A man of the people.'

'The pueblo's jefe único, you know that phrase? He used to be the mayor too, so he knows how this city really runs. If he's elected to the presidency, it'll see an end to the old code and way of rule. An affliction the Republic thinks it's been suffering from for years.'

'Does it? The people are pinched, that's clear. The workers on site are paid well enough but they insist on jobs for their relatives too.' Luke sighed. 'Sometimes people turn up and I have no idea who they are.'

'Yes, they all want to work on the American project. They're idiots! Forgive me; it's just that it won't change anything. Your European war cast a long shadow. People like my uncle hardly noticed a change but the poor are still reeling from the rise in prices and it's getting worse. They're getting worse. Failed harvests, grain in short supply, the rich getting richer. They think Gaitán will save them.'

'How?'

'Like a hero in a fairy tale, of course. He wants to take from the rich and give to the poor.'

'El Robin Hood?'

'Yes, that's good, but with teeth. The man orates like a lion. He doesn't ask for change, he demands it. You should hear him speak.'

'I'd like to. Have you?'

'Many times, parades too.' Camilo leaned in. 'In '45, thousands of people followed him through the streets by torchlight. That was something. The city covered with flags. They say the man's a genius. That night, Bogotá came to a standstill because he asked it to. That night, everything changed. It pushed me into journalism. His followers have organised a lecture tonight but there's another two days from now.' Camilo tapped the table. 'If you want to see the true mood of the people, come then.'

Luke paid for lunch and walked with Camilo as far as the newspaper offices on the corner of Jiménez. He watched the reporter disappear into the dark interior and crossed the street, before looking back and up for the headlines on the public board. The twelve o'clock news told nothing exciting: a fugitive on a crime spree finally brought to justice followed by tomorrow's weather; rain, again. Over lunch, news about Gabriel Osorio had been less forthcoming. Camilo had, in truth, revealed little. For his part, Luke had kept quiet about their meeting.

When Luke arrived back at his apartment, Señora Rojas had already set the table for one. The smell of cooked meat, not unlike that which he'd had for lunch, drifted out from the kitchen to meet him. That smell mingled with thoughts of Camilo in his head, and before long he was back in the cantina and thinking about the interview and what he'd let slip about the war office. What had he revealed? That he hadn't fought in Europe as this world expected he had. He'd mentioned her too. Catherine. Luke went into the bedroom and sat down. He loosened the tie around his neck and dropped his head, letting it find the palms of his hands. He hadn't revealed her name, though, had he? That he held safe within himself. Someone he loved had died, though, Camilo understood that much. Would he print it? *The bachelor architect building to conquer his grief,* or *The Englishman designing English homes for a wife he'll never have?* How tragic, Luke thought, sitting upright.

'The bedlinen is drying, señor. It's hanging in the maid's room.'

'Thank you, Señora Rojas,' Luke called back. He rose and went to the kitchen. 'What you've prepared smells very nice.'

'Ajiaco,' she said – so it would be the same as his lunch.

'I'll wash first,' Luke called.

'I'll be back in the morning,' she said, coming into the sitting room for her coat.

Luke waited until she had left before returning to the bedroom. He fell backwards onto the bed. He thought about what he had abandoned, letting everything he'd kept hidden earlier flood in. He closed his eyes. Catherine on that rock with the waves foaming around her, licking at her ankles and spraying her cardigan with water that at that moment seemed to have become airborne just so it could touch her. That look on her face when it caught her unawares and he, a spectator, drinking the whole thing up as though it were a special show just for him. Luke opened his eyes and, breathless, reached down, loosening his trousers to touch the part of him that had once belonged to her. He closed his eyes. This time, she didn't get up from her rock and come to him, waiting behind the camera. She stayed there, willing the next wave to strike, knowing it would. She wore the strangest smile, he thought, seeing her now in his mind's eye. He watched, and from somewhere imagined she watched him back. She didn't turn to see, wasn't aware, even, of what lay in store as each wave hit, growing in strength and threatening to throw her off. He felt the full force of each one against her back, losing himself inside the space between them on that deserted beach. He wanted her to remain there, perched – willing her to devour him with that strange, strange smile as she was being devoured by those waves. Then the old feeling returned, guilt stumbling along to wreck his pleasure. As the water rose around her, he realised, even now, he couldn't watch her drown. He had to warn her. Luke cried out and realised he'd done so for real, guttural and with intent. He blinked, returning to the room. There was a hollow feeling that something had been lost, or something discarded and left behind, like an empty shell, kicked about the sands. Luke opened his eyes. Señora Rojas stood in the door frame holding a pile of clean sheets.

'Dios bendito!' she said, staring at him. 'Extras, I forgot to give you.'

'Señora, I...' Luke buttoned up his trousers and sat up, compelled to move, to be anywhere that would distance himself from the bed and what secrets it had revealed to his housekeeper.

'I have three grown sons, Señor Vosey.' She walked forward and handed him the sheets. 'Please close the door if you wish to be alone.'

'Yes.'

'Goodnight.'

Luke followed her from the bedroom and watched her leave. When he heard her steps in the hall fade to nothing, he went over and drew the chain across the door.

8

———

Luke rose around five the next morning, refreshed and at first thinking only of the two Osorios. Until recently, he hadn't known any Osorios. Now, he could claim knowledge of a pair. Then there was Señora Rojas – poor Señora Rojas – how much had she seen? Christ, add it to her list of peculiarities, he thought, stumbling to the kitchen for coffee.

His housekeeper was already there. Luke went back to his room for his robe. He joined her again and worked up the courage to search her face for any semblance of disgust – something that might show they existed now on very different sides of decency. Señora Rojas looked the same as she always did, head down, busy over a jug of coffee boiling away on the stove.

'Good morning, señor.'

'Mrs Rojas, I…' Luke began.

'Señora, please, I'm not an Englishwoman,' she snapped.

So, I am not forgiven, he thought.

'You didn't touch the ajiaco,' she said, handing him a cup of coffee and smiling. 'Never mind, you can have it tonight.'

'Tonight I've a business appointment,' Luke said, sipping the sweet, dark liquid.

'Yes, this came for you.' She passed Luke a folded card.

He left the room and opened it over by the sitting room window where there was more light.

I'm counting on you tonight. Dreary opera! Karl.

'Who delivered this?'

'A boy,' she said, poking her head into the room. 'There is something else, señor.'

'Yes, Señora Rojas?'

She was buttoning up her coat. 'Will you come to mass with me? It might do you good.' She looked nervous. 'It might help, with your loneliness.'

If that's what it would take to absolve his soul. 'Of course, Señora Rojas.'

After breakfast, he dressed, and they left the apartment together. He followed his housekeeper down the street. He'd never been outside with her before. Out here, she looked different. Not closed in by his Englishness. She knew where she was going, for one, but it was more than that. Out here, he was strange, and she was not – as though any question he asked of her out here would have a different answer to what she'd give inside of the apartment. Had he thought of her as his? No, not exactly – it was more that she hadn't existed whole for him until now.

They crossed Seventh and then Fourteenth Avenue where the spiral of a modern church loomed up before them. Together, they slipped inside the silent building. Mass had already begun and so they found a pew towards the rear. At his side, Señora Rojas bowed her head to hear the creed. Luke had never been a religious man. There wasn't space for God in architecture, but he did have a way of filling buildings after they were built, as this fat priest was doing now. Señora Rojas tugged on his sleeve.

'Look,' she said. 'How he singles out those in need.'

The priest had a man about his own age on his feet. He had his head in his hands and the woman seated at his side was crying, sobbing in fact. From joy or holy fear, Luke couldn't say. It was like theatre. He thought of the opera tonight and wondered what role he'd be expected to play then.

After the service, they walked back to the apartment in silence. It was a happy sort of silence. He was glad to have come. He vowed to treat her better, thinking he meant Señora Rojas, but then extending this to every person he'd tried to wall in in some way. But he couldn't get the image of the woman in tears out of his head. It had jarred with his expectation of what the mass should have been. He had seen her again after the service, on the other side of the street, half-running to where she needed to be. There were moments in this city like that, where tragedy was easy to find, but easier to forget when it belonged to someone else.

A little before seven that evening, Luke left the apartment and went on foot to the theatre. He arrived to find the orchestra smoking and laughing on the front steps. The theatre was neoclassical in an Italian way – a lot like the elder Osorio, he thought. This was just the sort of place he imagined finding him. It was a style completely out of keeping with its surroundings. There were many good examples of the older, Spanish-style dwellings here – big inner-city estates two, three storeys high and built around central courtyards you wouldn't guess existed behind unassuming doors at street level. Then there was the theatre and its kind. Even the Andes, he thought, appearing at the end of every street junction like the ghost of a god he could not shake, were keeping watch over this imposter. Luke navigated his way past the group of musicians and entered the theatre. The ticket hall was dimly lit, but from here he could make out a small atrium and the beginnings of a grand staircase that must, he thought, lead to the upper tiers. There was a young woman manning the desk behind an iron grille.

'What's tonight's performance?' he asked.

'*Otelo*,' she said, unable to stifle the yawn she'd begun before speaking.

'The moor.'

'No, Verdi. You have tickets?'

'Yes,' he smiled.

'Come back at eight. It starts then.'

He'd agreed to meet Karl and Osorio at seven thirty. He thanked her and checked his watch. It was just past seven. He stepped back out onto the cool street, colder now the sun had completely set. The musicians had departed so he took a seat where they had. A man passing turned his head to stare right at him, unembarrassed. Luke would never get used to the false celebrity that came with being European here. Maybe hanging around theatres before showtime was something only the workers did, and to smoke. He hadn't arrived in a fancy car, or with a woman in furs. He didn't have any cigarettes. He opened the front of his suit jacket and leaned back on his forearms, content to wait it out.

Karl arrived first, a little after eight. 'Vosey! Up here,' he shouted, standing high on the theatre steps behind him. 'What are you doing down there? There's a bar, you know.'

Luke rose, taking care to stretch out his bad leg. He dusted himself down.

'Where's Osorio?'

Karl shrugged. 'I keep no diary for the man. Let's go in – it starts soon.'

Luke followed Karl back into the box office and through the doors of the atrium. The attendant was there, free from her metal box. Karl handed her the tickets and went ahead.

'Otelo, the moor,' she said, smiling at Luke.

'Shakespeare,' Luke said, pretending to yawn.

'Vosey! Vosey, this way.'

Luke took the stairs two at a time to catch him up. At the top, before he was swallowed by the crowd, he turned to catch sight of the girl again but something the architect had employed in the curve of the step concealed everything below. Upstairs, he thought of Europe and the opera houses he'd visited there; Naples's San Carlo and the Staatsoper in Vienna before it was firebombed by the allies. Karl was at the bar, puffing away on a cigar. He'd already found himself a drink.

'That's for you,' he said, indicating another beside him. 'Always with the ladies, hey?' He grinned. 'Hey?'

It was embarrassing, Karl acting like a drunken uncle whenever they were together. Luke picked up his glass.

'Good health.'

'Health? Damned opera always gives me indigestion.'

Karl sank three more whiskies in the time it took Luke to drink one. He needed a clear head. The saloon, he noticed, was stuffed with society women, soft and undefined, along with overfed dignitaries, but not one of them was Gabriel Osorio, who, he thought, would have stood out, lithe and alert, from the pack. It was the same dull crowd as the Chairman's Dinner and Luke wondered if Osorio, who had slipped into his life then, would try to do the same tonight. A bell rang, signalling the performance was about to begin, but nobody moved. It was at the second ding that the room slowly emptied towards the upper tiers. Luke had taken control of their tickets and led an unsteady Karl through the crowd and up a second, smaller flight of stairs to a narrower corridor. Theirs was a palco, a box. He opened the slim door and invited Karl to enter, stepping through after him.

'Take the front,' said Karl, gesturing at the seats there. There was another empty row behind these.

'Is anyone else joining us?' Luke asked. 'Besides Osorio?'

'I shouldn't think so.' Karl shuffled in next to Luke and dropped down into one of the free chairs. 'Can't do business in the stalls, Vosey.'

Luke took the one beside him. He leaned over the balcony and looked down into the auditorium at the people fussing below and then over at the orchestra beyond. The palcos on this level extended the full width of the theatre and those within sight looked full to capacity. Theirs was the only one with seats to spare.

'You found your draughtsman yet?' Karl asked, leaning over the velvet cushion that divided them.

'Almost.'

'Almost? So, not yet.' He shuffled closer. 'For Christ's sake, Vosey, how do you suppose we're going to convince Osorio the other project should come our way if we can't get this done?'

'We're on schedule, thanks to the extra hands.'

'That may be,' Karl said, raising his voice above the orchestra. 'But you should know that Osorio sets his own schedules.'

'Forgive me, but Osorio wasn't in the plan until last week.'

'Osorio's always been in the plan,' Karl spat, half mindful of the volume.

When had that been, Luke thought? The lights dimmed. They'd have to have it out afterwards. He wasn't going to be kept in the dark. He turned to the front. The stage was lit and the curtains parted, revealing a Venetian street scene, although it was very hard to think of Venice then.

At the close of act two, at the point when Iago and Othello sang vengeance upon Desdemona, Luke became aware of a third person within the box, one he hadn't heard arrive. Karl, who breathed heavily, had succumbed to sleep early on. Luke tensed, conscious of a shift in the air behind him, as though it had been forced to find new channels around the space. He looked down at his feet and, in the gloom, caught the tip of a shined black shoe, like a little dart, placed close to the back of his own chair. He straightened and looked forward with renewed focus, as though his ability to concentrate might return him to his previous state of anonymity. Iago and Othello were on their knees when they stopped singing and the curtain went down.

'Are you enjoying the show, Señor Vosey?'

Luke turned as the house lights rose to find Gabriel Osorio seated behind him.

The theatre emptied in search of refreshments. Gabriel Osorio had risen too and gone to find them a waitress. Luke leaned across to Karl and woke him.

'Still not here, hey?' Karl said, looking lazily about the space.

'I've ordered champagne,' Osorio replied, slipping back into his seat.

'Oh, I see.' Karl pulled himself straight. 'Hello, Osorio.'

'Unless you'd prefer something else?'

'No, no.' Karl reached inside his pocket and brought out his cigar case. He placed one between his teeth. 'Either of you two?'

Osorio waved his hand to the negative.

Luke shook his head. 'Perhaps we should talk now?' he suggested. He didn't want to wait until afterwards. He didn't want to see Desdemona killed without knowing.

'We are talking,' Osorio said, smiling at him.

The champagne arrived and the waitress poured. Osorio handed a glass to Luke. 'Tell me, how is the building project in La Merced progressing?'

Karl tried to catch his eye.

'It appears I've lost the only draughtsman in Colombia.'

'Really?'

'There aren't any others, I've looked. Not here in Bogotá or anywhere else, it seems.' Luke raised his glass to the men and drank. There was an acridity to the champagne that extended beyond the glass.

'Then we'll fly one in,' Osorio replied, as though it were fact. 'And this other business? No doubt Karl has informed you?'

Luke caught Karl's eye.

'I see he has,' Osorio continued. 'Good. I need an architect I can put to work on this city. One who inspires greatness.'

'Before this Pan-American business?' Luke asked.

Osorio reached across and refilled Luke's glass. 'That's it! But we're not miracle makers, Señor Vosey. The delegation – the USA and our neighbours – arrives this January. That's only four months away.'

'But the contracts are ready?' Karl said, reaching over for the bottle.

'They are,' Osorio continued. 'We want to build a city of the future. The project in La Merced got you here but you must see, even that is tied up in difficulty.'

'How so?' Luke swallowed.

'Well, you've workers who just disappear. You admitted that yourself. Perhaps who just arrive without warning, too?'

Luke swallowed. 'Something like that.'

'This new project will allow you free rein; a steady workforce. We want an end to the tenements close to here and the cathedral. In fact, this city is riddled with them. They're nothing but pockets of the past.'

The people in the auditorium were returning to their seats. The mood felt heavy and oppressive somehow. Osorio was offering a commission, so why wasn't he more excited? Offering – perhaps that was it? It felt more like a command.

'A clean slate?' Luke asked. 'You want to start again, is that it?'

'Yes, like your Victorian slums – wiped off the map so a better city could rise in their place.'

'And those who live there? What about the people?'

'The people?' Osorio asked. 'We're doing it for the people.'

Luke looked over the balcony at the orchestra who had returned and were limbering up. In the half-light, the tips of their bows and elbows flitted unconnectedly, like tiresome insects above the pit.

'Then there's the question of your name,' Karl said, drawing out the words. 'Your time in London wasn't so fine, if I have it right.'

Luke laughed. 'Are you going to wipe out the past?'

'You can do that yourself,' Osorio said. 'Let the dead have their history. Why not live again here? Be the architect you were before.' He leaned forward. 'There's always more than one side to every story, Señor Vosey. Which one would you prefer to see in print?'

Luke set his champagne down. 'I thought you didn't talk to your nephew.'

'Careful, Vosey.'

'It's all right, Karl. Señor Vosey needs time to think it through.' He filled Luke's glass. 'I will admit one thing, even though it pains me to do it, because it seems you need reassurance, shall we say? It's true, the tie between my nephew and myself has been severed. To my regret, he no longer looks upon me as his uncle. But you have a young man's spirit, like he does. Don't waste it – put it to good use. It would be my greatest joy if you would join us on this project.'

The lights were fading and the theatre was silent. Osorio and Karl were waiting, not for the performance, but for him. Luke picked up his glass and sipped. He had to say yes. He wanted to say it. Let them make a success of him when he had failed to do it himself. Principles were exhausting to maintain, God only knows he'd tried. Let me only be a success now, he thought. Let me agree to this.

'Yes,' Luke heard himself say. 'All right, but I'll finish La Merced myself. I'll find my own draughtsman.'

The three men went on to a small private bar after the opera. A nameless place, dark and ugly and as far removed from the Teatro Colón as it was possible to get. He'd gone to take a piss and read above the basin: 'If you don't fear God, fear syphilis' on a public health poster half disintegrated by stringent ammonia. After the drinking was done, Luke left them on the edge of Las Cruces, drowning in the chicha they had ended the night on. For a man who only drank champagne, Osorio's enthusiasm for this fermented corn drink was unheard of, but he'd drunk it too; bowl after bowl for courage. As they'd left, Osorio and Karl had embraced him in turn before retreating into the back of a chauffeured car. Its sudden appearance seemed mythic, set against everything that had come before. Gabriel Osorio was capable of conjuring up anything, Luke thought as he swayed on the roadside, insisting he would be fine. He promised Karl he wouldn't get murdered and could find his own way home. He had something else in mind and he wasn't afraid, neither of God nor the alternative. When he was free of them, he turned and walked the single block it took to reach the familiar boarding house. The female inhabitants were awake when he knocked and asked if he could step inside. Luke had some trouble persuading the woman on the door it was Rocío he'd come to see, and no, he wouldn't like to visit one of the newer girls. The old woman left him in the hallway beneath the glare of a single lamp and went ahead of him up the stairs. He stayed behind and it occurred to him he might be refused. He heard her creaking about above his head along the distance it took to reach Rocío's room at the end of the hall. He'd made the same journey enough times now to know. The first time he'd waited in this hall he'd had the photograph of Catherine. He'd asked if there was a woman like her and bingo, he'd found one. But it was all wrong. To think, he'd gone looking for Catherine to try and satisfy that old need and found her likeness here. What would she have said? He heard laughter from upstairs. Catherine. She was laughing at him, even here. He put his hands to his ears. I should leave, he thought. It isn't fair. She'll think she means more to me than she does.

'Go up. She's waiting.' The old woman had reappeared. 'You OK, mister?'

'I'm fine,' he said, pushing himself away from the wall and staggering towards her.

9

Rocío's eyes were brown. Miel actually, like honey. He'd spent the night at the boarding house. Some attachment was forming, he could tell. It would be easy to blame the chicha but it was his fault. He should stick to the normal times if he wanted to keep his distance. He had made it back across town to his apartment without being murdered, though. He must remember to tell Karl that. Tonight meant the other Osorio; Camilo. Tonight meant the lecture and hearing Gaitán speak. He wasn't sure how he felt about that now, though.

Luke stood over the small enamel sink in his apartment and drew the razor up his jaw. He winced and pulled back, lifting his chin to the mirror in time to see a thick drop of blood form and then fall into the basin below. Last night, once Rocío had understood he hadn't come with the photograph, she'd seemed relieved. Encouraging him forward, she had guided his path across the floor of her bedroom, and he remembered moving cautiously then, uncertain of all that lay there, chemises and other soft things; the two women blurring to one. Luke dabbed at his chin with a towel. Last night. When he'd had the courage to look, he was relieved to see it was only Rocío, kneeling in the moonlight, he saw.

Luke finished the rest of his face and washed away the blood from the sink. He placed a corner of tissue over the broken skin and went into the bedroom to dress. Señora Rojas hadn't been this morning and it was good he was alone. He needed time to think. To go over again what had happened in the theatre. A new commission. It was wonderful to have something to line up after La Merced and then down the line, perhaps a whole new career in the Americas? Why not? There had to be a contract, though. Something concrete to say Karl would finish with him. Karl, who worked for Anglo-Colombian Oil but was mixed up in this new deal too. Parts of what had been sold to him didn't make sense but there'd be plenty of time for detail, he was sure of that. Luke took a fresh shirt from the closet and pulled it on. It was the promise of a clean start that had blindsided him. The idea that what he'd started in Europe before the war could be finished here. Europe – which had been purged by fire and falling hell, as he had. Better not to think of that. Something modern would do it. He longed for it. Structures dotting the horizon as far as the Andes – sweeping vistas of concrete and glass, uniform and functional, with bright living spaces for all, communal zones and gardens. Yes, something that was harder to burn through. Luke pulled on his jacket and found his keys, drawing up plans in his mind's eye that could easily translate to ink. The draughtsman, though. The one he didn't have. First, La Merced had to be put to bed, if it was to be finished by Christmas. To do that he needed to find the best match from out of the pile mounting on his desk. Luke finished dressing. On his way out of the apartment, he drew the crumpled photograph of Catherine out from his pocket and left it on the table. He'd leave her behind too.

'There's someone in your office.' Telma came around her desk towards him as soon as he arrived. 'I'm sorry, señor, he insisted.'

'Who did?'

Telma gestured towards the glass window of his door. 'Ask him! He's come from Señor Osorio.'

Luke turned the handle and went in.

'Mr Vosey,' the man said. 'I'm your new draughtsman.'

'Telma,' Luke said. 'Bring coffee, please.'

She left, closing the door behind her. Luke went around his desk and sat down. The man was slight in the extreme. No wonder he'd slipped past Telma.

'What experience do you have?' Luke asked.

'Señor Osorio already interviewed me.'

'Well, you'll be working for me.' He thought he'd been clear with Osorio in the theatre: he would find his own man.

'Perhaps you can tell me what hasn't been done.' The man leaned forward. 'I hear things are behind.'

'Where were you last?'

'New York, Gooch & Gooch.'

'Impressive.'

'Yes.'

'You're not American, though? Didn't fight for them in the war?'

'Correct on both accounts.'

The door swung open and Telma entered. She placed cups on the desk and gathered up the spread of unopened job applications. 'We won't need these.' She sighed, taking up the pile and letting her gaze rest too long on the stranger.

'Leave them, Telma.'

Luke waited for her to leave.

'And your name?'

'Alfonso Blanco.'

'Señor Blanco,' Luke said, raising his cup. 'Seeing as you're already here, we'll have a trial period. One week.'

'But Señor Osorio said...'

'A trial period, and then we'll see.'

Luke drank his coffee. Alfonso Blanco picked up his own cup. Something flashed in his eyes, Luke saw, and in that moment, he thought the draughtsman meant to smash it. Instead, he took a measured sip.

'Burnt, I think,' he said, placing it down. 'I'll start now, if you don't mind.'

On the tram ride south to meet Camilo, Luke was still reeling from his encounter with the draughtsman. Alfonso Blanco wasn't a likeable man, but, after a couple of false starts, he had completed a half-finished workable sketch of one of the fireplaces and a series of outlines for the exterior reliefs. Nothing original, but he was good at picking up where the previous draughtsman had left off. He'd stopped wondering altogether what had happened to Palacio. He had someone now, even if it was Blanco. Luke had him set up in the room below his, cramped in alongside the new foreman, mainly to keep him out of Telma's way.

Luke had agreed to meet Camilo at six sharp at an area known as Tres Esquinas – one of the main stops south on the tramline. He was looking forward to it and wondered if he saw something of himself, as he had been long ago, in the principled young man. Long, long ago something of himself had torn his father's heart in two. He'd refused the family farm. He'd had Camilo's energy then to fight the old man, and fight they did, with his mother looking on. It took the strength of his younger brother, William, once he'd reached them from the lower field, to tear them apart. Luke had lost a tooth. He'd kept it for years afterwards out of respect for that first trial of his principles.

Luke left the site early, when the day was still bright, and boarded the first car he saw at Centenary Park. The tram slid smoothly through the city, old and new building styles blurring into one as though throwing up all future possibilities of what they might be. As he got further from La Merced, he felt strengthened by all that he passed, buoyed by the knowledge that soon he'd have a hand in shaping it. At an intersection, another tram, quite different to his own, passed his. Inside, tired men clung tight to its sides as though they might be bucked off at the next turn. He watched three local women who'd stopped outside a shop, their heads thrown back, sharing some punchline. The possibilities seemed open and endless. As the vehicle turned onto Plaza de Bolívar, a wide Ford Sedan shot out of a side street, sending the tram driver straight for his rosary. Luke gripped the rail above his head. It would be good to remain guarded in some respects, though. He didn't have to tell Camilo about his uncle's plans.

The journalist was waiting for him on the pavement. He looked tired.

'What's keeping you up?' Luke asked, smiling.

'You.'

'Surely not?'

Camilo shrugged. 'Come on, let's go.' He crossed the road and Luke followed. 'I'm sorry, the venue's changed,' he said, stopping in front of a different tram stop. 'Power cut in this part of town. Somebody didn't pay the bill; at least not to the right people.'

They didn't have to wait long for a tram to take them back into town, pushing on behind a group of men. Luke found money for the two of them, feeling his pockets for more coins in case they might return.

They stayed on until Seventh. About halfway down the main thoroughfare, Camilo jumped off and Luke followed. The journalist led him down one side street after another, slowing his pace until the two men were level.

'How are things progressing?' Camilo asked.

'Good, good. I've just hired a new man.'

'For the draughtsman role?'

'Word travels fast on the news desk.'

'Actually, your secretary,' Camilo said.

'My education is progressing, you'll be pleased to hear. I went to mass yesterday.'

'I didn't know you were devout.'

'You're surprised?'

'You want me to write about it in the article, to endear you to the populace?'

'Not exactly. You see, the priest was a little crazy, intense, I mean. I can't stop thinking about it.'

'A religious fanatic?'

'Reduced one man and his wife to tears.'

Camilo nodded. 'Listen,' he touched Luke's arm and the two men stopped. 'The church is powerful here. If you went back there tomorrow or any day after that, I bet you any money you wouldn't find that man, or his wife, again.'

'What are you saying?'

Camilo shrugged. 'I'm not saying anything.'

Luke thought about it. 'If I didn't find them, it could be that they just changed churches.'

'Could be.'

They walked on in silence. The street ahead filled. They had to slow their pace as the crowd thickened. They were students mostly. Young men together, women by themselves or the two mixed up into groups.

'I'm sorry to hear you've already hired someone for the

draughtsman role. I thought I'd found someone for you,' Camilo sighed. 'With real talent.'

'You Osorios are so helpful.'

'We try,' Camilo said. 'Although I don't know what you mean.' He stopped. 'I'm sorry – she's here.'

'She?'

'Yes,' he said, grinning. 'And I said I'd introduce you. Can you just play along? I've already said you're coming.'

'All right, if you like.'

They'd stopped before a large building, standing aside to let the crowd filter in around them. Luke looked up. The word *Faenza* was carved into the lintel above its vast doorway that was more like the opening of a circus tent, he thought. The building took up most of the street. You couldn't miss it. It was a very public venue for a political meeting organised by a party that wasn't in power.

'It's a cinema,' Camilo said, watching him. 'And her name's Felisa Mejía.' He entered the building and Luke followed.

Inside, it didn't take long for him to lose sight of Camilo. The journalist left him in the lobby and went in search of his friends; friends he said he wanted to introduce to the British architect. Luke stood to one side, feeling wholly different. From the street every type of person poured in: street cleaners, shop clerks and those who kept the administrative arm of the city running.

'Will he be here? Dr Gaitán?' Luke asked a passer-by. The man frowned at him and walked on.

'He thinks you're policía.'

Luke turned to the woman at his side. Her eyes were darker than honey, black almost, like molasses. She looked at him and blinked.

'Do you think I am?'

'Yes,' she said, quite seriously. 'You don't belong here.'

'How so?'

'You're too exotic.' Her smile was different to Catherine's, more alarming in fact. 'Here comes Milo.' Luke turned to see Camilo walking towards them.

'Luke, I'm sorry,' Camilo said. He was breathless. 'I see you've found Felisa. Señorita Mejía, I mean.'

Felisa bit her bottom lip. 'Ah, the architect.'

'Shall we go in?' Camilo asked, putting his arm around her.

Luke followed behind. The pair looked about the same age – and about half of mine, he thought. While Camilo affected a type of poverty in the way he dressed, Felisa looked like she was trying to raise herself above this. Inside the hall, most of the seats had already been taken. Camilo found three towards the back. Felisa tried to take the furthest one, placing Camilo in the middle, but he refused, insisting she sit beside Luke, and he on the side closest to the wall. Neither of them spoke.

'Camilo says you're looking for work?'

'Does he?' Felisa turned to face Luke. In the darkness, her eyes shone brighter. He was aware he was staring.

'That you're a draughtsman,' he said, coughing.

'I'm not,' she said, laughing self-consciously so that he was embarrassed. He looked over her head at Camilo who caught his eye and shrugged.

Luke turned to the front. For Camilo's sake, he had tried. The crowd was silent now. From offstage a man appeared, sending the room wild – it was the kind of rapture heard after a performance, not before it. Luke wasn't used to it – the way the people beat the floorboards to pieces with their shoes and all for this sinewy man with a bald top.

'This is Gaitán?' he asked her.

'No,' Felisa whispered, coming close. 'It's one of the contributors to Gaitán's newspaper, *Jornada*. His name is Over Gómez.'

She pronounced the 'v' softly, as though coaxing it towards a 'b'. Luke did the same in his head, trying to get it just as she had. He wasn't that exotic. Over Gómez approached the lectern.

'Gaitán thanks his loyal friends for attending tonight's meeting. We apologise for the earlier confusion over the venue; as you know, these things are never simple.'

'Will Gaitán return my ten centavos for the tram?' a man shouted.

Gómez was silent for a moment.

'What is your name, my friend? No, you don't have to say. Tell me, is this the first time something in your life has changed course?'

'It's not.'

'And usually, is it not your employer, your boss, who decides that course for you?'

'And my wife!'

The room erupted.

'Yes, yes,' Over Gómez said, joining them. 'So, tonight there was a change in your course, but it was you who decided. Not another man. After that first disappointment you could have gone home, but no, you came here. You chose to continue.' Over Gómez addressed the room. 'You're all responsible for your individual paths. We're equal in that.'

The audience loved that and beat the floor again. Seeing that they loved it, this Over Gómez took a little bow.

'That man's path is ten centavos down, though,' Felisa whispered.

'You must keep the spirit of what we are trying to achieve alive. In fact, you must raise it above spirit. You must make it concrete, make it flesh. If the politicians take from you, take from the politicians. They're just men.'

'We'll be arrested!' someone shouted.

'I'm talking about organised marches, protests and pickets, not vandalism. No man, woman, or child should act alone. You know the government is weak. You know they're fighting to keep you low by starving you of hope. They seek only to fill their own bellies and leave yours empty. It's what their fathers did and grandfathers before that, all the way back to the shores of Spain.'

'Gaitán didn't win last time, he split the party,' said another.

'Because people were afraid. He's a man who cannot be bought. He fights for absolute change, not partial. He demands absolute loyalty, not half-vowed allegiance. Look what happened to Karrera who was once his friend. He who called himself liberal. He refused to give up his parliamentary position when Gaitán was shunned by the rest of them. He refused to stand with him when the time came to show his loyalty. No! That's why Gaitán asked that the people punish Karrera. That's why it had to be done.'

Luke knew this. He was talking about the politician who'd been pelted with eggs so publicly. It frightened all of them, these politicians, that Gaitán could ask such a thing and the people would deliver.

'To some, that commitment is a terrifying concept, wouldn't you agree?' Gómez continued. 'If you trust yourself to Gaitán, he will stand by you. The purpose of tonight is to leave here with this message. There are pamphlets and flyers on two tables positioned at the back of this hall. Take this literature with you and return to your homes. Give them to your neighbours. Push them through letterboxes. Through the will of the people we will change things, but only through the will of *all* the people.'

After the session, they filed out with the crowd. Camilo led them on foot to a coffee shop two blocks over that he said was the regular post-lecture meet-up. Inside, it was packed and the three of them sat hunched awkwardly around a too-small table.

70

The mood inside the café was high, like they'd all attended a wedding and loved both the bride and groom.

'You see,' Felisa said, staring at Luke across the table, 'these lectures are nothing new. Gaitán only shows for the big ones that pull in the huge crowds now.'

'Not always, Felisa,' Camilo said.

'Milo, it's what he wants,' she said, gesturing at Luke. 'He only came to see Gaitán.'

'Not only,' he said. 'Tell me more about *Jornada*.'

'It has an incredible circulation,' she said.

'I'd like to read it.'

Felisa caught Camilo's eye. He couldn't decide if it was a look that said: when is your friend leaving? He didn't want to. And he'd handed Blanco the draughtsman job. When there was—

'Milo here will lend you a copy.'

'Idiota, Felisa! He has money. He can buy his own.'

'But I wouldn't know where to find it,' Luke said. Camilo was not a tactful man.

She began again but softer this time. 'Tonight you heard the same words that all Gaitán's council repeat so that the pueblo won't forget, but if you hear Gaitán himself speak, well, that's different.' She refastened a piece of hair which had come loose: 'Liberty, freedom, workers' rights. You'll find it all in *Jornada* if you're serious.'

'She's in love with him,' Camilo said.

'So the talks themselves are meaningless without him?' Luke asked, ignoring him and leaning in closer.

Felisa moved closer too. 'No. People need reminding that things can change. Without that, there's just tomorrow, and the day after that, and so on, with nothing to make your life any different from the rest.'

The waitress came between them with hot coffee. For a moment he thought he was back inside La Casa de la Risa.

'There are good and bad ways to bring change,' Luke said. 'Do you know La Casa de la Risa? It's a cantina…'

'The socialists meet there,' Camilo said. 'It's known for that.'

'And here?' Luke asked.

'Liberalism reigns!' Camilo rose. 'Excuse me, please.'

Luke watched him cross the café and disappear behind a narrow curtain. Felisa fell silent. It surprised Luke how shy she could become so quickly.

'Actually,' Felisa said, her tone measured, 'I can draw.'

10

It had been two weeks since that meeting in the café. Luke hadn't seen anything of Camilo since then, but he knew now that the journalist kept his own schedule. He had a habit of reappearing only when there was a reason to do so and the next time, Luke suspected, would signal the publication of the article. Camilo had sent notes, tidying up the details, but that was all. In his replies, Luke hadn't told him about Felisa coming to work for him. They'd worked it all out while they were alone together in the café. Felisa had said she wanted to break the good news to Camilo herself. In fact, Luke hadn't told anyone. Alfonso Blanco had turned up for work one morning to find the young draughtswoman sitting in the tiny office he already shared with the foreman. Luke had wanted it that way, so that word would get back to the elder Osorio, hot-tongued and angry. In future, Gabriel Osorio should leave the detail to him.

In the days that followed, Luke set about putting Felisa to work on the more intricate designs that Blanco laboured over, such as the carvings for the plasterwork set above the door frames. These were needed quickly, so that they could be worked up into moulds and the casts set in place for painting. She sat in his office and listened to what was needed, performing quick sketches, which she would complete in more detail later. In the afternoons, these would find their way back up to him for sign-off. In the pile of forgettable outlines that Blanco delivered, there was skill in Felisa's hand. She had natural talent, going beyond the brief to deliver imaginative coats of arms interlaced with alien flora he could only assume she had seen in magazines. Blanco, who saw himself as every bit her superior, was a thorn in Luke's side and hers too, he imagined, sometimes listening out for proof of his whining drifting up from the floorboards below.

There was a knock at his office door. When he didn't answer immediately, it crept slowly open. Felisa stood in the frame.

'Excuse me, Señor Vosey, she's gone out,' she said, signalling Telma's empty desk in the hall.

'Would you like to come in?'

Felisa slipped into the room and closed the door behind her.

'He's left for the day too. Señor Blanco, that is,' she said.

Luke offered her a chair, but instead, she went over to the window. She wore her hair long, he noticed. It fell in dark waves, trailing to her waist. As black as her eyes, he thought.

'Are you happy with my work?' she asked, turning.

'Has Señor Blanco said otherwise?'

'All the time,' she said, sighing. 'I haven't studied like him. That's what he says and it's true.'

'Being taught something doesn't mean you'll ever understand it.'

'I agree.' Felisa walked over to the chair opposite his and sat down. 'I wasn't sure, you see. Because I haven't been paid and the others have.'

'I see,' Luke said, feeling the temperature in the room go up a notch. 'I'll speak to Telma about that.'

'She doesn't like me.'

'It's her nephew. She wanted him here first, and then Blanco came. But it's no excuse.'

Felisa bit her top lip. 'Jobs aren't easy to come by. If the junior role was her nephew's, he should have had it.'

'I decide who works here, not my secretary.'

She looked up and their eyes met.

'I know jobs are scarce,' he said.

'Do you?' She raised a hand to her mouth. 'I shouldn't have said that.'

'It's all right, perhaps I don't. Camilo talks of real struggles, violence outside of the city. It makes sense that with everyone pouring in, there'd be less work to go around.'

She nodded and he could see her relaxing slightly, wondering just how much she should. He wished she would. Luke watched her eyes fall first on her hands and then move up to the desk between them. It was a solid reminder of his role there, as her employer. Felisa spoke first.

'Where I'm from, south of here, there isn't much chance to leave – to escape from that life.'

'Is it so very bad?'

'Now it is. Have you ever seen real poverty? It does terrible things to people, that and fear.'

'I've seen what rationing does, but not real poverty first-hand. Fear, I know something about. It goes hand in hand with ignorance.'

Luke thought back, remembering the latter days of his posting during the war. He'd been sent to some backward, out-of-the-way place then. Shame was another emotion, he recalled, but no need to speak of that now.

'But you escaped the south?' he asked.

'I was given a chance to study when I was very young. In part, Camilo was to blame for that.'

'Blame?'

'Perhaps it isn't the right word.'

'The two of you are close, then?'

Close. That wasn't the right word either.

Felisa shrugged. 'I'm not sure why he helped me later on, but he did. I only know that as soon as I could read in English, I got hold of every book I could. I wanted to know everything.' She smiled. 'I was a better student than him, even if I wasn't sent to any college. He was, and he let the chance he'd been given fly away.'

'He tells me he's fighting the life that's been chosen for him.'

'That's good. Dear Camilo,' she said, smiling. 'I suppose he is.'

Luke rose and went over to his jacket. He drew out his wallet and removed a handful of notes; enough, he hoped, for the weeks she was due with a little extra besides. Telma he would deal with later.

'Here,' he said, holding it out to her.

'I don't know,' she said. 'It should be official.'

'It's yours.'

Luke stood there, feeling ridiculous holding the money out in front of him, with something of the same awkwardness he supposed she felt in not taking it.

'Perhaps if you wrote it down,' she suggested, 'as proof.'

He looked around the desk for paper, pulling open the drawers in search of something to write on. He found his diary and tore a sheet from the front. On the back of the clean page he wrote: *Felisa Mejía, paid two weeks' wages by Luke Vosey*, followed by the date. He signed it.

'There,' he said, handing it over.

Felisa took the sheet and studied it.

'Will it pass?' he asked.

She nodded and he handed her the money.

'You'll be paid along with everyone else next time.'

'Thank you.' She turned to leave. 'Actually, there is something else.'

Luke waited.

'A rally. Not like the one before, a little more secretive.'

'I'll come,' he said.

'But you don't know what I'm going to say!'

'A guess,' Luke said. 'An assumption you hadn't given up on my political education.'

'Now you're teasing me.'

'When is it?' he asked. They could go together.

'Later this week. I'll explain tomorrow.'

After she'd left, Luke recalled that he'd been the same at her age, brave and afraid together. If he was younger it would be easier to start again. The past seemed so far away now, and he a different person in it. Catherine had been brave, in her way. Look where it had got her. Stuck behind enemy lines and he powerless to do anything about it.

Out in the hall, the phone on Telma's desk rang. He crossed the room but by the time he'd answered it, he only got the operator. He heard voices on the street outside. He thought everyone had left. Luke went back into his office and over to the window. Opposite the building he saw Camilo. He looked up once in his direction, but Luke knew he couldn't see him through the glaze. There was a second figure. Felisa, her coat pulled around her shoulders. She was running across the new street to join him.

The next afternoon, Camilo returned to collect her again. Luke was out on site, inspecting the last of the buildings to go up, a turreted red brick mansion that owed nothing to its surroundings.

'She's doing well, yes?' Camilo said, coming up alongside Luke.

'Yes,' he replied. 'I think we'll be finished on time. You were right about her.'

'I'm the only one that sees it.'

'Then she's lucky,' Luke said, 'to have a friend like you.'

'Excelente trabajo, Luke, look at it, the little English village.' Camilo surveyed the buildings. 'And all finished by January?'

'Or earlier. She really is quite wonderful, you know – her drawings, I mean.'

Camilo waited for a man to pass. 'I came to talk about the article but, if I can speak plainly—' he kicked up the dirt at his feet '—I wish she and I were much closer.'

'I'm sure, if she knew…'

'Yes, if she knew. She knows. And after everything I've done for her.'

He looked at Luke and grinned.

'You can't know her the way I do, Luke.' He leaned in close. 'When I found her, she owned only the clothes she stood up in.'

'You're right, I don't know her the way you do.'

Camilo sighed. 'It's hopeless.'

The sun was low in the sky and both men turned to look as it momentarily split the road they were standing on in two.

'Nothing is without hope,' Luke said.

'That's true. Felisa and I belong together.' He grinned. 'But I'm sorry. I wanted to ask if you're coming to this little gathering tomorrow? Felisa said she'd invited you.'

'You know about that?' Luke said. 'I thought you might be working.'

Camilo seemed to consider this. 'I'll be there, Luke. Anyway, for me, it is work. I was rather hoping you'd keep her company in case I need to run off. These things can get a little lively. I know she trusts you, like a father.'

'Did she say that?'

Camilo waved the question away. 'She says many things. Anyway, I came here to ask for something else. For the article.'

'What else could you possibly need?'

'A photograph. Do you have one?'

11

The secret rally Felisa spoke about was to take place at Tres Esquinas as well. Felisa and Luke got through the day not talking about it and at five o'clock left the office together. Telma eyed them with suspicion, as though she expected to be invited too. Out on the street and in the afternoon crush, they were bundled onto a tram together and made to endure a forced intimacy. Felisa, he noticed, closed her eyes when they were pressed closer and he tried to make space for her, feeling in some way responsible for his nearness.

'This is us,' Felisa said.

They disembarked and he recognised the place from before. Felisa went ahead. She walked fast and he followed close behind.

'Where's Camilo?' he asked, feeling the question come reluctantly.

'He'll meet us there.'

Felisa left the main thoroughfare and turned into a side street. About halfway down she stopped in front of a low doorway whose door was broken off its hinges. It was nothing

like the Faenza cinema hall, the scene of their first meeting, and
that saddened him in a way he didn't understand.

'We're here,' she said, going through.

Luke followed and found himself in a small courtyard,
enclosed on all sides. It was standing room only and the space
was already filling, as was the upper terrace which ran its full
length. He expected the same people as the meeting in town,
but this crowd was harder. He stood out a mile.

'Who are these people?'

'These are the real pueblo,' she whispered. 'They aren't afraid
to act because most of them have nothing to lose.'

A man pushed past him. The armband he wore caught
Luke's attention. Red and unmistakable. The same as the flag
the boy from La Casa de la Risa had tried to pin onto the
front of the streetcar last month. Communists or labour party
members, Luke thought. Some of them anyway. He looked
back towards the exit but it was hard to locate now that more
people had piled through. Luke turned forward and crossed his
arms. Felisa smiled up at him. Did she really see him as a father
figure?

'Luke!'

Camilo appeared beside them.

'How did you get through all that?' he asked.

'Press papers.' Camilo grinned.

'Really?'

'No, not really,' Camilo said. 'This is more Felisa's doing, I
told you.'

Camilo smiled at her but she didn't go to him.

'Who are these people, really?' Luke asked.

'The Workers' Communist Party,' Camilo said, placing a
finger to his lips. 'We've come to see if they'll support Gaitán.'

The crowd grew still. Up on the balcony a man appeared,
surrounded by others, carrying pistols and machetes. He

scanned the crowd below, letting his gaze rest on Luke. 'Our membership grows,' he shouted. 'Our cause is your cause. You come here because those elected men have not served you.'

'Thieves,' a man beside Luke spat. Any mention of politicians would do that, Luke thought. He shifted on the spot. He was drawing quite a lot of attention to himself, he couldn't help it.

'You demand a better way,' the man on the balcony said. 'But I can't give you anything you don't already possess.'

He threw open his arms. A couple of machetes were unsheathed in the crowd and used to stab at the sky.

'You like this?' Luke leaned down and asked Felisa.

'Just listen,' she said.

It had been a mistake to come. Behind them, a fight had broken out.

'They drink too much,' Camilo said, looking back.

Luke doubted he could know that. He was taller and still couldn't see a thing.

The speaker continued. 'Soon, there'll come a chance to put words…'

The crowd surged forward and Luke grabbed Felisa so that she wouldn't fall.

'…to put words,' he said again, but he wasn't looking at them, he was looking over their heads at the exit, '…into action!'

The speaker stepped backwards, signalling to the others. Luke watched the group form around the man. Together they backed away from the balcony edge and were gone. Nobody seemed to have expected them to do that.

'What's going on?' Felisa asked, as they were pushed forward from behind.

Camilo was knocked to the ground. Luke was pushed too and winded, propped up by the man at his side. Other people had fallen and were screaming to be helped up. It was impossible to get at them, though. They were too packed in. The men with machetes still had them raised, not because they wanted to, but because they couldn't drop their arms without cutting their neighbours.

'Take my hand,' Luke said, fighting his lack of breath to pull Camilo to his feet.

'Policía, policía!' was being shouted now.

'It's a raid,' Camilo said, grinning. 'But we need to leave.'

Around them was panic, as people looked for places to run to, finding one exit only to discover it blocked and pushing through the crowd to reach another. He couldn't be arrested. Not here, not before this new thing had a chance to begin. Luke struggled to keep his footing. Felisa was knocked in the head by someone's elbow and he pulled her towards him, looking for a place, anywhere, that might offer a way out of this one. For once, he was glad to be taller than the rest of them. Over the heads of the crowd, he spotted an open door, on the far side of the courtyard. It was how the speaker had disappeared so quickly.

'Camilo?' he said, turning and finding him gone.

'What do we do?' Felisa asked. She looked terrified.

The people were fighting back. As the police moved in from behind, beating and cutting the crowd down, the men who'd brought weapons retaliated. He saw a large man launch himself from the balcony onto the head of a young officer. The men fell to the floor together but only one got up.

'Take my hand,' Luke shouted.

He pulled Felisa low through the knot of people. His stomach was bruised but he tried to focus. He tried to breathe. He had to find the door he'd seen. He thought he had, but instead ended up backing them into a corner. He'd taken them the wrong side of the pillars at the far end. They'd have to go around.

'Stay close to the wall,' he told her.

Two police officers almost fell on top of Luke, going after one of the men he'd seen on the balcony. They'd come for men like this one. Felisa screamed as the wanted man grabbed her arm and shoved her forward. Luke took her other arm and fought to keep her beside him. She cried out and he worried that he was hurting her too. Luke pushed the man off with his free hand. He heard a crack and saw that one of the officers had split the man's skull with a baton. There was blood everywhere. The officer swung again, cutting the air between them in two. Luke backed off and pulled Felisa away. They kept low and to the sides. Then he saw it, a small chink of light. He broke out into the open and lunged towards the exit, dragging Felisa after him. They fell through, gasping for air, as though they'd been holding their breaths the whole time. They'd emerged onto a deserted backstreet behind the building. They were both breathing heavily. After them, more people flooded out, scattering in all directions. He still had hold of Felisa's hand. He smiled down at her with relief. The smile was also an invitation to let go, if she wanted to. Instead she came closer, so he kissed her.

12

Luke hadn't slept. After walking Felisa back to her lodgings, close to Tres Esquinas, he'd gone home on foot. Felisa's building looked worse than the meeting place. She didn't seem to mind and said it wasn't so terrible on the inside, although she hadn't invited him to see. It had taken him hours to get back to his apartment because of the number of police and people on the streets but he didn't care, slotting his key into the lock sometime around two. He lay on the bed all night in a state passing between brilliance and nausea. That night, things had shifted between them in the most unexpected way. He couldn't sleep. He felt sick. Had he taken advantage? It would look like that, wouldn't it? That's what Felisa might have thought at the time or soon afterwards. Even if that wasn't the way it had gone, Camilo wouldn't like it. When Luke eventually rose, exhausted, he poured himself a coffee, had a second cup, and then a third before leaving the apartment. He'd washed, dressed and scented himself in something he'd forgotten he had.

He arrived at the site, took the stairs to his office two together, avoiding the urge to knock on the closed door of the draughtsmen's room. Not yet, he thought, greeting Telma at the entrance to his own.

'You're early,' she said.

'Am I the only one?'

'So far.'

He went into his office, removed his jacket and threw open the windows. Now he was back on site, he felt full of hope, and coffee – feverish, almost. The street below had been scrubbed clean and now glistened under a rising sun. He stared at the almost-finished vista, feeling brave and triumphant in a way he hadn't in the apartment. As an architect, he was on his way to being celebrated again. There was nothing to be afraid of. A man passed below the window and looked up, squinting and wondering perhaps who this grinning figure was. I shouldn't stand here, Luke thought. She might think I'm watching for her. He went over to his desk and sat down.

He waited until nine, ten, and then eleven came and went. The waiting was exhausting in itself, making it impossible to work. There was a lot of paperwork to sign off to start the process of closing the site down. That kept him tied to his desk. It was approaching twelve when he'd finished with it. He slipped his arms inside of his jacket. The room had grown cold. Everything ached.

'Isn't it cold, Telma?' he asked, propping himself up on her desk.

'Cold?' Telma rose and put the back of her hand to his head. 'You've a fever.'

'I didn't sleep well.'

Telma nodded. 'Yes, because of the fever.'

Luke left her there and, gripping the banister for support, made his way down to the draughtsmen's office. 'I'm going to check on the work,' he called back up.

Blanco and Felisa's door was open.

'You look terrible,' Blanco said. 'Just awful.'

The draughtsman was alone. Felisa's desk was empty.

'Is Señorita Mejía at lunch?'

Blanco shook his head. 'Oh no, she never came in.'

'What? She isn't here?'

Having imagined her there all morning, Luke was confused that she wasn't. 'What?' he asked again, falling limply into the chair that Blanco, having risen, had put out for him. 'Why didn't you say anything?'

Blanco shrugged. 'I saw it as no great loss.'

'No,' Luke said. So, she simply hadn't shown. She hadn't wanted to face him. He coughed and drew his hand across his forehead. He felt hot, as Telma said he was, but he was still cold, shivering in fact. 'No loss, no,' he repeated, realising that Blanco had left him talking to himself.

Blanco returned some minutes later with Telma.

She put her hand to his forehead again. 'Burning up!'

'I'm fine,' Luke said, trying to rise and finding he couldn't.

'Go upstairs and call him a car,' she told Blanco.

Telma left the room too. She returned with a glass of water. Luke forced himself to drink.

'I had an awful amount of coffee this morning,' he said.

She took back the glass. He'd only managed a sip. Telma looked concerned. He was fine – if he could just lie down, just for a moment, he'd be better.

'One of the workmen has flagged a car down. They're waiting outside,' Blanco said, reappearing, although he refused to come any closer than the door.

'Let's get you up and home,' Telma said, trying to lift him by herself.

'I can walk,' Luke said.

He insisted on going alone in the car, promising to have his housekeeper phone Telma when he arrived home. It was the only way she'd let him leave.

When the car pulled up outside his building, the driver helped him out. Luke forgot to thank him, stumbling past the doorman without a word. He had to lie down and it could only happen once. He might not be able to get back up again. When he reached his door, he could hear laughter coming from inside of the apartment. He took the key from his pocket and turned the catch. Inside, there wasn't any sign of his housekeeper. Instead he found Karl in the chair closest the window, nursing a tumbler of whisky. The near-empty bottle was on the table beside him.

'Jesus, Vosey, what happened to you?'

'Why are you here, Karl?' He went over to the sofa and collapsed onto it.

'Just passing, wasn't I, about to leave this.' Karl waved a note in the air before pocketing it. 'Hey, Mrs Rojas?'

She came into the room.

'Looks like Luke here is unwell.'

She put her hand to his head as Telma had.

'Burning up, I know,' he said, pulling his knees up to his chest.

Her hand went to her own head. 'And me at my mother's in Soacha this week; I'll cancel.'

'It's all right, Mrs Rojas, I'll look in on him,' Karl said.

Luke turned his face from them to retch.

'Perhaps for now, though, I should leave you to it.' Karl got up.

'That might be best.' Señora Rojas had taken a blanket and was tucking it in around him.

'Before I do,' Karl said, getting down on his knees so they were face to face, 'I need to tell you the reason I came. Remember the executives?'

Luke nodded, using the blanket as a mask. Karl's breath was rancid.

'They're coming to see the project. It's out of my hands. I said it was short notice but they want to see the city homes you've created for them. Coming in with their uptight wives and screaming brats. All flying down from Barrancabermeja.'

He struggled with the vowels.

'Unfinished,' Luke whispered.

'What?'

'It's not finished!' he said.

'All right, Luke, I can hear you.'

'Perhaps you should come back another time.' Señora Rojas held out Karl's hat.

'Right you are,' he said, rising. 'It's very short notice, Vosey. Sunday in fact. This Sunday. Do you think you can get well for then, Luke? Because that's when they're coming and there's no stopping them.'

13

———

Señora Rojas stayed as late as she could, helping him to his bed before she had to leave. She left him a jug of water and a bucket, because he'd already been sick twice, and brought a weight of blankets down on his body. His poor, aching body – he couldn't breathe and kicked them off as soon as she'd left. He slept for what felt like forever, but because of what Karl had said, he couldn't rest. The executives were coming. He kept waking, thinking he could hear them, their screaming families too, gathered at his bedroom door.

Luke woke up for real on what felt like the next day. He rolled onto his side and attempted to push the remaining sheets away but ended up twisting deeper into them and, from there, found himself on the floor. He vomited again, getting some of it in the bucket and the rest on the floor and himself. Exhausted but relieved to have purged something, he stayed there for the rest of the day, drifting in and out of sleep, staring at the forgotten space beneath the bed. When he woke again it was still light. It felt like the same day but could have been another. The vomit on his clothing had dried. Both his legs ached. He used the last of his strength to pull himself back onto the mattress where he stayed the rest of that day, drifting in and out of consciousness. He wasn't sure how long he'd been there, but when he opened his eyes next, the moon outside the window was high and his bedsheets and pyjamas were clean.

'Luke.'

It was Camilo. The journalist smiled and rose from the chair beside him. He must have carried it in from the other room.

'Nice to have you back.'

'What time is it?' Luke asked, trying to sit upright.

'What day, more like – it's Tuesday, Luke.'

'Tuesday?'

Camilo came over and helped with the pillows. 'You had a nasty fever by the looks of it. You should have seen the mess when we found you yesterday. Half of your workers went down with it too. No one's dead but they closed the site at the weekend.'

'They closed it?'

'Yes.'

So the executives hadn't come. He was absolved.

'How did you get in?'

'We persuaded the doorman it was a matter of life or death.'

'We?'

'Yes, Felisa's here. She raised the alarm yesterday when you didn't show for work. Be grateful, Telma tried to join us. I told her you were still infectious.'

'Is he awake?' Felisa entered the room. She was wearing Señora Rojas' cooking apron, the cord looped twice around her waist. 'Please drink this,' she said, handing him a steaming cup.

'Felisa,' he said. 'You came.'

'That's right, Luke, it's Felisa.' Camilo turned to her. 'He's delirious!'

'Stop it,' she said, but Luke had seen her blush.

He looked down at the contents of the cup. It contained what looked like cooked seeds swimming in a murky gravy.

'Drink,' she said, standing over him.

Luke raised the cup to his lips, poured the contents into his mouth and swallowed. It was awful.

'It's native medicine,' she said. 'It's the only reason you're not dead.'

'Are you sure?' he coughed. He could feel it, sliding like mud to his gut.

'Felisa is a witch,' Camilo said, ducking as she swiped out at him.

She took the empty cup and left the room. The bulk of the liquid had reached his stomach; he could feel it bubbling away inside him. He was starting to sweat again. It must have been an effect of the potion. He untangled his feet from the sheets. He might need to run to the bathroom. He might need to do that soon. He sat up, his stomach cramping.

'Excuse me,' Luke said, jumping up. 'You can both leave now, I'll be fine.' His legs were weak and Camilo lunged forward to support him. Luke pushed him away and staggered towards the bathroom. Once the door was locked he sat down and his bowels relaxed. Whatever Felisa had given him was quick to work. Once the third wave had passed, he collapsed onto the cool tiled floor and closed his eyes.

'Luke, are you all right?' It was Felisa. She was standing on the other side of the locked door.

Luke pulled himself upright. He still felt weak but better in some sense. She knocked again.

'Come on Luke, don't die in there.' Camilo had joined her outside.

Luke made himself rise. He checked the room was clean before opening the door.

'How do you feel?' she asked him.

'What was in that?'

'Dandelion, a little guarana for your stomach and other things for taste.'

'Taste?'

She smiled.

'Thank you,' he said, managing a weak smile of his own and pushing past them. He stumbled into the lounge. Felisa and Camilo followed. Luke collapsed into the armchair beside the window.

Felisa went back to the bedroom and returned with a blanket. 'I'm fine,' he said as she tried to cover him.

She ignored him and came close, placing it across his lap.

'I have to go back to work,' Camilo said.

Luke pointed to the cupboard behind the journalist. He did feel better. Alert even. Another side effect of the potion, perhaps. 'Up there,' he told Camilo. 'Take that envelope.'

'What's inside?'

'A photograph, for your article. You wanted one, didn't you?' He'd found it the other day by chance. The envelope had become lodged behind the top drawer of the chest in the bedroom. He hadn't seen it until he'd tried to get the drawer back in and couldn't.

Camilo took the image out. 'You're so young,' he said, showing Felisa. 'And this one?' There was a second photo stuck to the first. He pulled the two apart and turned it to face Luke. It was the missing image of Catherine from Albie's party.

'I'll take that,' Luke said.

Camilo handed it over. 'See you soon, then, and thanks for this.'

Luke waited for him to leave before looking at the image. She was as he'd remembered, Catherine, in all her dangerous beauty. In it, he had his arm around her. They had been deeply in love at the time, he'd thought. He brought it closer to his face. There was something there he hadn't seen before; a hand creeping in at the side of the frame. It was resting on Catherine's arm. Luke turned the photograph in the light, trying to make sense of its presence there. Something about the angle meant it couldn't have been his. The rest of its owner was out of shot. He looked again. He wasn't hallucinating. It was there. He couldn't remember anyone from that night but his thoughts were still muddied by fever. He could ask Felisa, ask if she saw three people too. She was busy across the room sorting something out on the floor. No, it wouldn't do to ask her that. He looked again. In the picture, Catherine wasn't leaning into him at all, but towards this other hand; towards this other person. He'd never have seen it even then but Felisa's potion had sharpened his senses. Luke tried to remember, but the party had been before the war and there had been so many… Felisa returned. She was clutching a pile of newspapers.

'*Jornada*,' she said, holding them out for him to see. 'They're old editions. I went and got them. I thought you might have time now, while you recover.'

'Thank you,' he said. He placed the photograph face down on the table beside him. She dropped the pile on top.

'About the other night, Felisa.'

'With the sickness, I was so worried you might die.'

'But about before…'

'And Camilo was worried.'

'You didn't come to work the next day.'

'I suppose I was sick too,' she said, sitting down beside him.

'But not like I was?'

'No. In a different way.'

He wondered what she meant. She was always with Camilo. Perhaps she was sick for him. 'He's in love with you, I think.'

'Camilo?' she said, looking horrified. 'Please don't say that.'

'I'm sorry,' he coughed. 'I must still be unwell.' She went

silent. 'Perhaps you should go.' It was wonderful, her being there, but he'd ruined it now. Catherine and that stupid photograph had set him thinking of the other man in Felisa's life.

Her eyes narrowed. 'Your housekeeper isn't due until Thursday, Mr Draper said.'

'Was Karl here?'

'Yes, he came yesterday and left this.' She handed him an envelope from the top of the pile of post on the dresser.

'I think I've upset him by being ill. He'll worry we're behind.' He'd open it after she'd left. Why wouldn't she leave?

'We're not behind,' she said. 'You shouldn't worry about that.'

'Well, all right, but Karl's not good at hiding his emotions.' Another bout of nausea briefly stopping him from speaking. 'I don't want it to get back to Osorio.' He tried to rise. 'He shouldn't think that I'm stalling.'

'Camilo won't care.'

'Not Camilo, and he will if he's told.'

'I don't understand?' No, she didn't. Gabriel Osorio needed to know he was on board. 'You stay where you are. If you have a message, I'll take it to Mr Draper or Telma.' She went back over to her bag and pulled out a piece of paper and pen. 'Look, write it here.'

It was the same sheet he had given her, torn from his diary.

'There's clean paper in a notebook over there,' he said, gesturing to the bureau.

'Of course,' she said, folding the sheet and putting it back inside her bag. Felisa brought over the notebook and placed it open on his lap. She handed him a pen but it was awkward to grip.

She pulled a chair over and sat down. 'Shall I write it for you?'

'Leave it,' Luke said.

He just needed to sleep. Felisa took the notebook and pen back. From the open window, a cool breeze caught the back of his neck. Luke closed his eyes. Better to be well and face Karl and the executives in person. He was still so tired. He opened his eyes to find Felisa had risen. He heard her moving things in the kitchen, trying to be quiet. She really should leave, he thought, closing them again. But he was glad when she didn't.

He woke sometime in the early hours and knew immediately that he was alone. The window behind him had been closed and the blanket pulled tighter. He freed himself of the covering and rose, feeling weak but mended somehow. He'd slept dreamlessly, like one returning to life after an absence. He went into the kitchen and poured himself a glass of water. The small room was spotless. Back in the lounge, he went over to the table where Felisa had left the copies of *Jornada*. Beside them, there was a single sheet of paper that had been torn from the notebook. He picked it up. It was a freeform sketch of a sleeping man drawn from life. He looked worse in the image than he realised, but it was a good likeness. She had signed it: Felisa Mejía.

14

Inside of the envelope was an invitation from Osorio to join him for dinner when he was better. Alongside this was a letter from Karl. He wrote that the executives and Osorio thought the fever might finish him off. That it was a good bit of luck for everyone that La Merced was almost complete, and as for the Pan-American project? Well, perhaps it was best that he hadn't started it, if his intention had been to die.

A week later, Luke had regained enough of his strength to join Karl for the trip to Osorio's hacienda outside of the city. Beside him in the back seat, his boss talked the entire journey. Luke tried to drown him out. Outside of the car window, there was another exodus along the highway – workers returning to their homes on the outskirts, mules weighed down with onion and potato crops, construction workers, dusty and tanned as old hides and other types of labourers with tools and battered machetes slung across their shoulders. Listening to Karl, he'd have given anything to join them. The car slowed at a junction alongside the caravan. He smiled at a man close by, knowing any reply would have been toothless and rare. He gave the rest of the journey over to thoughts of Felisa.

When they'd crossed paths in the office, she hadn't mentioned the visit to his apartment or the role she had played in his recovery. She kept her head down. Since nursing him back to health in whatever godawful state he had appeared to her in, she'd become withdrawn, so that the moment came and passed in which he might bring up the drawing. The kiss seemed even further lost to time. He'd wanted to remind her. To talk to her about *Jornada* too, which he'd read cover-to-cover. His recovery could be attributed as much to what he found there as to Felisa's medicine. Even on the page Gaitán spoke with an urgent need for justice with a capital J: legal Justice; social Justice; Justice in the workplace; Justice in the home; Justice in the field. One road and all upon it, he said. This man worked the people up into such frenzy that they probably dreamed about him, tossed and turned for him; saw him lucidly, keeping watch as they slept, Luke thought. He'd seen a picture. There was always a picture of Gaitán in *Jornada* – dark headed and titan-like in the fullness of his features – he was a broad-browed, wide-eyed demi-god and the people worshipped him. They opened their doors to him. They loved him.

'When we're inside, just agree to whatever Osorio says,' Karl said, interrupting his thoughts.

'Agree?'

'You know, say yes.' Karl sat forward. 'We're here, Luke.'

They'd stopped in front of a wooden gate as wide as it was tall. The driver wound his window down and one of the two guards stationed there came forward. He was armed with a gun, and as an alternative to that, a silver-bladed machete. The guard shone a flashlight into the back of the car, blinding them and then the driver.

'Are we going to be kept here long?' Karl asked, shouting through his window. 'Let us through, good man.'

The man sucked on his teeth and spat on the ground. 'Abra esa mierda!' he said, shouting across at his friend on the gate.

'That's better,' said Karl. 'I haven't had a drink since we left.'

The gates were opened, and they drove through. It was a short distance to the house itself. The car rolled to a stop in front of the main building and Luke got out. So, this was Osorio's hacienda. It was vast and whitewashed. Each set of windows was flanked by a pair of heavy wood shutters. Above these, a sloped roof of terracotta disappeared beneath a horizon of trees. He thought of all the generations of Osorios who had prospered under that roof, as far back as those who had claimed the land and planted out the estate.

'A sweet pile of bricks, wouldn't you say so, Vosey?'

'Yes, Karl.'

The night was crisp and filled with the sound of a thousand crickets and above this, an indigo sky purpled the horizon. Here, it might be possible to forget the city with its cramped streets and wild order. Osorio came out of the house to greet them. Luke smiled up at him. If he were to prosper, he needed to learn to like the man, at least.

'Just telling Luke, here, that if this project comes off he might be looking at his own little hacienda, no?' Karl went up the steps and shook Osorio's hand.

'Perhaps,' Osorio said.

'Nothing as big as yours, of course,' Karl said.

'Welcome, Mr Vosey.' Osorio greeted Luke, taking his hand. 'You know, when Karl was last here, he brought his wife.'

'We're acquainted,' Luke said.

'A well-dressed woman,' he said, smiling. 'Lets her spend all his money on fur, here in Bogotá of all places! Isn't that right, Karl?'

'I suppose it is.'

'That's how he's different to us,' Osorio said, leaning in close. 'No control.'

'What's that?' Karl asked.

A dog ran out from behind the house and then a man soon after. 'Neron!' the man shouted.

'Jesus!' said Karl as Neron took off, leaping up and onto the porch. The man caught the lead before Neron could reach Karl. They watched the man fight with the dog until it tired and allowed itself to be reeled back in.

'Dangerous fish, that,' said Karl, breathing quickly.

Luke tried to bring his own breathing back under control. Control, that's what he needed. That's what Osorio expected.

'Shall we go in?' Osorio asked.

Luke smiled and followed his host into the house. Osorio led them past a number of closed doors, through a paved hall studded with hurricane lamps and out into a courtyard garden. It was lush and in full bloom. The scent of citron and sandalwood hung heavy in the air. At the centre of the courtyard was a working fountain. He saw now that the house was arranged around a quadrangle with an internal balcony running the full sweep of the upper floor. All of this lay open to a sky now black and twinkling above.

'What will you take?' Osorio asked, going over to a small trolley that had been wheeled outside for their use.

'Anything,' Karl replied, sitting down on a low bench close by.

'Cold champagne, then.'

The man who'd brought the trolley went back into the house for the bottle. Luke went over to the fountain for a closer look. It was Moorish in style with four glazed frogs, seated one on each corner, spurting water into a giant lily pad at its centre.

'All the way from Andalucía,' Osorio called over to him.

Luke nodded and rejoined the two men. He sat down beside

Karl. The champagne arrived and Osorio got busy twisting the cork out with a cloth.

'I like to do this myself,' he said. 'It tastes all the sweeter for it.'

The cork was freed and disappeared into the shrub on the far side of the courtyard.

'Salud,' Luke said, taking the offered glass and raising it to the others.

'So,' Osorio said, placing the remainder of the bottle into an ice bucket. 'You're well again?' He sat down and crossed one leg over the other, revealing the immaculate silk of his socks.

'The fever was out of my control, you understand,' Luke said. He could mention Camilo's involvement in his recovery but wouldn't.

'Had us worried it might slow things down, though,' Karl said.

'Which it hasn't,' said Luke.

Osorio nodded. 'You were lucky.'

Luke wasn't sure what lucky meant in this context.

'Let's continue our conversation from the opera. The one we started before you were sick?' Osorio nodded. 'Now we're in agreement, plans need drawing up of the new city centre.'

'You can get your draughtsman onto it,' Karl said.

He hadn't thought to involve Felisa but perhaps he should. A maid came out of the house and over to their host.

'There'll be time to discuss details after dinner,' Osorio said, rising. 'Shall we?'

At table, Luke found himself seated across from Karl with Osorio at the head. They were an intimate little group.

'Just us three?' he asked.

'My wife is in town tonight,' Osorio replied. 'We have a modest villa there.'

'Not as modest as mine,' Karl said.

Luke ate sparingly, picking at his trout. The fish arrived whole. It had been submerged in a garlic and cream sauce that was too rich for his stomach. The fever had not left him. It had waited until he needed to feel strong, to remind him he wasn't. Across the table, Karl didn't seem to be having any trouble with his fish. From somewhere on the estate, a dog howled. If he could just get through dinner... Luke heard the sound of a motorcar approaching the house. A moment later the room was illuminated and the three of them were half-blinded by the glare from its headlights. Soon after, a man could be heard in the hall.

'Please, don't get up,' he said, entering the room.

Osorio rose to greet this new arrival and the two men came to rest at Luke's side.

'You're the architect? Señor Vosey, yes?'

Luke looked up at a fleshy face that seemed completely without structure.

'Sit down, Tomas, join us,' said Osorio.

The newcomer took the seat beside Karl and grinned over at Luke. He smiled back. Beside this man, Karl was the picture of health. The maid brought a fresh plate. The cook herself followed personally with the fish and a series of other small dishes which hadn't been served before. Karl filled his neighbour's wine glass to the rim. If he had to watch this man eat, Luke thought, he might be sick after all.

'This is Don Tomas Caicedo,' Osorio said, addressing Luke. 'Don Tomas is the Mayor of Bogotá.'

'It's a pleasure to meet you,' Luke said, although the moment for formal greeting had passed. The mayor wasn't paying attention anyway. He was busy picking his fish clean.

'Gabriel, you know this is my favourite.' He stabbed his fork at Osorio and then at Luke. 'Good, isn't it, Señor Vosey?'

'Call him Luke,' said Karl.

Luke smiled again. The three men had clearly dined together before.

'Mr Vosey, forgive us,' Osorio said, placing his cutlery down. 'The Pan-American Conference is on your mind. You're ever the restless architect, or genius, or both perhaps.' He laughed.

Luke swallowed. 'If we're to get it underway and begin building by the new year, we should start now. I want to start now.'

'That won't do.' Osorio signalled for more wine. 'The president won't like it. Ospina trained as an engineer, you know, he likes order – planning. If we can get drafts together for the conference then that's enough. What happens after is a different matter – it's what we can tell the delegates that counts. Important people, like General Marshall – the Secretary of State, he's heading the American Delegation – and the foreign press, naturally. No, it's what comes next – investments and capital pouring in from overseas. This is just the beginning, for us and for you.'

Luke smiled. 'Progress on a world stage?'

'Yes.' Osorio took a pen from his pocket and laid his napkin flat on the table. 'The actual conference is held at the Capitolio Nacional on Plaza de Bolívar, here.'

He marked it on the fabric.

'The areas selected for improvement are here, here and here.'

He drew lines representing some of the streets Luke recognised as those surrounding the main square and government building. He then drew three crosses.

'The Church of Santa Clara, the House of Juan Flórez Ocariz and the College of San Bartolomé, all close to the main square, and in the way of progress.'

'I've been there,' Luke said, placing his finger over the church. 'It's from the 1500s.'

'Then you'll have seen the havoc the roosting pigeons wreak on the cars?' This was the mayor.

'Can't scrub that shit off,' Karl chimed in.

'The people don't care about the buildings,' Osorio said, sighing. 'Luke, they want homes. How can I put this? You've heard the protests, yes? Let's say that the pueblo has spoken, and we have listened.'

The mayor laughed, almost choking on a fresh forkful. Luke understood. He'd heard words like those in *Jornada*.

'Poor Gaitán,' Luke said, without thinking. 'I guess, once you've made heroes of yourselves, no one will think of him, or his party.'

'Poor Gaitán?' Osorio sent his fist into the table so that the glassware shuddered. 'Let me tell you about poor Gaitán – he's a man who will not bend. He's a man who wants to take democracy apart, brick by brick, and he demands that the people do it for him. Who is he to demand anything? Of the people or of the president? What is his parentage?' They were all of them silent, the only sound the chink of the mayor's fork against his plate.

'Yes, you're right, of course,' Luke said, smiling faintly. 'I guess I'm still learning.'

Osorio nodded. 'You're a stranger here, Señor Vosey, our ways are hard to understand – perhaps it's better not to try.' He raised the wine bottle and filled Luke's glass. 'We've kept the priests happy and, naturally, God has given his consent. Karl will handle things on the ground – lower level administration and such. Tomas here will take charge of the paperwork; get the right people to stamp and sign. We need drawings first, though, something official we can document. You can do that, can't you?'

Luke was silent. The three men looked at him. He'd already

said yes at the opera but it seemed he needed to do it again here, in front of the mayor.

'Vosey,' Karl said. 'You going to say yes?'

He looked at the men. Here was his chance. 'I'd want control over the design,' he said. 'I won't put my name on just anything.'

'Of course.' Osorio leaned forward.

'And we'll build in housing?'

'Naturally,' Osorio said.

'We haven't got all night, Luke, and if you…'

Osorio held up his hand to silence Karl.

Say yes, Luke. Say it, he thought, making quick calculations of how it could be. He'd get Felisa to work on it. It would make her career as well as his. Why not alongside his? He'd explain to her about the buildings for the poor – she'd like that. She wanted change, didn't she? Did it matter who was offering it?

'I'll get Felisa to draw something up,' he said.

'Felisa?'

'My draughtswoman,' Luke replied.

'A woman? No good. Get Blanco on it. He's discreet.'

'No good,' Luke said, meeting his stare.

Osorio shrugged. 'As you wish.'

Luke pushed back his chair and rose, steadying himself against the table edge. It took the last of his strength to stand up to Osorio – to a man who wasn't used to being questioned.

'You don't look at all well, Mr Vosey,' Osorio said.

'Is there a bathroom?'

Karl rose. 'I'll show him.'

15

Luke left after dinner was over. He said goodbye to Karl, the mayor and Osorio and took the car back into the city alone. Before the car left the hacienda behind, he peered back at the house, seeking out the three men one last time. He imagined them changed somehow, into something nightmarish and true. Anything is possible here, he thought, loosening his collar. He found them inside of the dining room. They were just sitting there, smoking cigars. Then he was too far down the drive to see anything at all, save the flare of a few fireflies that could have been the tips of their cigars.

The driver pulled up outside his apartment block. Luke was glad to see the doorman. It was as though he'd been away longer than an evening and this was a homecoming of sorts. The man smiled oddly, but Luke felt this reproach was a sign he understood; that change was coming for him too. It was only when he reached the floor of his apartment and saw the figure leaning against his door that he realised he should have known better.

'Hello, Rocío,' he said.

'Luke.'

Her mouth was painted an achingly deep shade of red. When she smiled it was with Catherine's smile. Rocío, Catherine, what did it matter? He was finally moving on.

'The boarding house is locked now,' Rocío said. 'I waited too long.'

'You can't stay here, I'm sorry.' He slipped the key into the lock.

She stepped forward. 'You've been unwell, Papi. I was worried.'

He looked at her and sighed. 'You're really locked out?'

She smiled eagerly.

'OK, but it can't be like before, Rocío.'

She nodded and smiled again. It will never be like before, he thought.

When he woke up the next morning, he was alone, though the far-off sound of running water told him this wasn't true. There was someone in the kitchen, and his first thoughts turned to Señora Rojas. Since learning of his illness, she'd taken to arriving early on Saturdays before heading to market. He rolled over and saw Rocío's dress draped over the table lamp. There were two versions of what the morning could be: the first – in which Señora Rojas was readying his breakfast – and the second, in which Rocío had turned up at his door last night and was now naked, boiling water for coffee. He sat up fast and felt complicit; he was naked too.

'Good morning, Luke.'

Rocío stood in the door frame. She was wearing his robe and, over this, Señora Rojas' apron. She handed him a cup of hot coffee.

'I don't think you should be wearing that.'

She grinned.

'I don't have to.'

Rocío undid the apron string and removed it. She made her way on to the robe.

'Leave that,' he said, sitting up.

She retied the belt and positioned herself on the corner of bed.

'It's nice here.'

'How did you know where I'd be?'

'A friend,' she said, looking at him and then away again. 'I hope it was a nice surprise?'

'Very,' he said. 'But I don't think it's a good idea – the doorman for one.'

'I'm sorry,' she said. 'If they knew, back at the boarding house, I'd lose my place there.'

'You want to leave it?'

She shot him a look of disbelief.

'That was a stupid thing to say. I'm sorry,' he said. 'Shall we dress and go out?' Luke reached down to the floor for his trousers.

'Together?'

'Unless you're embarrassed to be seen with me?'

She giggled, genuine and true. He thought of Felisa then.

'I'll walk you back.'

'Oh, OK.'

They dressed quickly and while Rocío was in the bathroom, Luke washed up the cups and made one final check of the bedroom to make sure nothing was out of place. 'I only look after you,' Señora Rojas had said on taking the job. He met Rocío in the corridor coming out of the bathroom. They smiled awkwardly at each other. Her mouth was clean of lipstick and up close, looked vulnerable and small. I should kiss her now, he thought, but couldn't bring himself to do it. The moment quickly passed. They headed out of the apartment.

There was a different doorman in the lobby but he wore the same grin, Luke thought, holding the door for her himself.

He walked Rocío as far back as La Candelaria. A street before the boarding house, they stopped to share coffee and fresh bread, purchased from a café they'd passed. Rocío had taken ownership of a bench and moved to make space for him when she saw him approaching, laden down with supplies. Luke sat down beside her and they ate in silence. The coffee was tepid and the bread dry and hard to swallow. She nibbled hers and he felt instantly wanting, thinking she deserved more than the meagre meal he'd provided. She expects more for herself too, he thought. At least the fever had passed. Perhaps Rocío had something to do with it. No, he thought, dismissing the idea. It was Felisa who had saved him, and that potion of hers. After they'd finished eating, there was nothing for it but to go their separate ways. Rocío looked up at him with those big eyes and tried the smile again but it had lost most of its allure. When Felisa smiled it was as herself. Luke kissed Rocío once and promised to call at the boarding house in a week's time.

Alone again, he wandered without thinking. Luke took streets that wound upwards through La Candelaria, finding himself pulled closer to the mountain. After the evening spent with Rocío, the morning surprised him, as though it were a new idea that day should follow night. Over his shoulder and further down the basin, the city was still lost in shadows. Before him the mountain seemed to glow. He wanted the warmth of it. Luke turned his back on the city and climbed. People passed him, heading down into Bogotá's wide belly. Today, he didn't have the stomach for it. The new commission was there, at the front of his mind, but Rocío's unexpected visit had left a mark on the day. She shouldn't come again, he thought, he should find a way to tell her that. Her longing, though, to be loved, was sincere. He walked faster. Guilt was an emotion he could do without. Not on top of what he already had. The past was harder to shake than he'd thought and now this familiar woman had some stake in it. Why had he shown her the photograph? It gave her some hold over him; a false intimacy, he thought.

He reached the small white church of Las Aguas, perfectly framed by the mountains of Monserrate and Guadelupe, rearing up steeply behind. It was a pretty spot. The San Francisco river started here, flowing directly down from Monserrate to slip beneath its foundations and out the other side. When it reached the city it would change colour, depending on what washed through it, he'd learned that. Soon, Luke ran out of street and was faced with the mountain proper. Monserrate became his left and right and eventually his up. It dominated the skyline. He craned backwards and looked up. There was the little white church at its peak, sweet and promising as a curl of icing. The rest of the time, Monserrate imposed its will on the city and all its inhabitants but right now, right now, Luke thought, it wants to conquer me. I'll put paid to that, he thought. He crossed the road to the ticket office, bought a ticket at the booth and boarded the train. The car fit a good twenty people, in five stacked, standing carriages, although there were only a handful at this time – tourists and a few nuns. It began its ascent. From the open windows he watched the city slip out of reach and lose definition below. Up here, it was easy to see how Bogotá tightrope-walked a straight line from north to south. At its centre stood Chapinero, the commercial district, with the main avenues of Seventh and Jiménez running like arteries through it. As the car climbed higher, entire blocks were reduced to the grid-like simplicity of a circuit board. In Candelaria, the buildings were packed in, in a tighter formation. He looked for La Merced but it was as if it didn't exist at all from up here.

The car stopped, locking onto the platform at the summit. He exited the carriage along with the small mixed group. The tourists scattered, turning their Kodak 35s left and right. The nuns had departed silently for the church. He decided to follow them; to keep climbing. The air was thin and made any ascent slow and laboured. As his body struggled, he thought of himself as a building of sorts, made up of material framed only to last in the right conditions. His heart, lungs, muscles all depended on air, as the structures he founded did on the people who inhabited them, bringing to life that which was really an empty shell. People, the body, life itself, this had been Catherine's field, not his – the nurse and the architect.

He stopped. There he was again, thinking of her. He truly didn't want to. It was because he'd allowed Rocío back into his life. Maybe it was OK to have those thoughts up here, though, on the mountain? Up here, he might finally be free of her, of all the shame associated with her, shame that surrounded him like nervous energy. He walked on, picking up his pace, despite what it cost his lungs. His leg had started to ache again. Catherine. He could cast her off the summit if he wanted to. He recalled long nights spent with their own limbs fused temporarily together, at the height of making up over some argument over whether his creations lived or not. She believed not, and he always argued against her. She always bloody won. She had a way of doing that. Luke reached the cobbled veranda in front of the church. From here, he could see the monastery of Guadalupe on the sister mountain. He went across to the ledge in front of the church and peered down. God, he hated her. It was a long way back to Bogotá. A low wall was the only thing separating him from a fast descent through the overgrowth and then a hard arrival onto the streets below.

16

Their last few weeks at La Merced finally arrived. Telma took the end personally, flitting around the building with Felisa close behind, making an inventory in her sketchbook of anything the secretary asked of her. Luke's room was to become the concierge's office and the one below a mailroom. The bulk of the furniture from the buildings had already departed along with the larger machinery, all shipped back up the Magdalena River to the refinery. Soon, there'd be no trace of them at all. La Merced was deserted. The red brickwork shone and behind each façade nothing but empty, expectant space. The last of the workmen had been paid off a week ago so that besides himself and the temporary foreman, Telma and Felisa were the only ones left. The foreman was busy overseeing the transportation of the last of the machinery onto the back of trucks at the far end of the works and Telma he could hear below, loudly opening and closing filing cabinets and drawers. That just left Felisa, who, as well as helping Telma, he'd employed in sketching the buildings as a series. He looked out of the window for her now. He'd wanted the sketches for himself and paid her out of his own pocket, providing a box of watercolours for her use.

'I don't think we can keep this.'

Luke jumped. It was Telma, standing in the doorway with a large potted fern.

'Why don't you take it?' he said.

'I'd never make it on the tram,' she said, sighing and looking down at it. 'No, take it for your apartment.' She went over to his desk and placed it down.

'Is Felisa still here?' he asked.

'That girl!' Telma rubbed her hands together. 'I asked her to pack up the cabinets but she's off with her sketchbook.'

Luke smiled. 'I can help if you like?'

'You?' Her hand went to her mouth. 'Excuse me, señor.'

'I'm going to need a secretary, Telma. I have a new commission. Not yet, but when I do, well, the job's yours if you want it?'

Telma let out a little cry. 'Yes, Señor Vosey. I would like that very much.'

Luke left her picking over the files and went outside. He walked upwards on 34th Street and took the forked road left onto Fifth. It ran parallel to the piece of land they'd turned into a park. Banked up against it was a single row of houses, the grandest they'd built.

Felisa was sitting on a low brick wall with the park behind her. She was sketching a large corner house. Her head down, she was completely absorbed by the structure, guiding every aspect of its form down through her arm and onto the page. He turned and tried to retrace his steps unseen.

'Luke!' she called.

He waved and went over.

'Look,' she said.

He sat down beside her. Felisa flicked through the pages of

the sketchbook. It was full of buildings, but full of life too, as though La Merced hadn't really existed until then.

'And this is three days' work?' he asked.

'Yes. I'm too slow?'

'It's more than that,' he said, looking at her.

She was an artist. Perhaps not the best person for the draughtsman job, but one who fully felt the work she engaged in. It was like when he watched her talk about Gaitán. The way her eyes lit up with feeling; with life. He'd thought to ask her about the commission for the city, but she wouldn't be right for it, he realised now, seeing how unrestrained and fluid her style was. Osorio wouldn't like that. She should be in art school or somewhere less forced. Maybe he could help her with that.

'Camilo is coming today,' she said, returning to her study of the building. 'He has something for you.'

'Oh?'

She smiled. 'His article about you, Luke. For the paper. He's very excited about it.'

'Have you read it?' Luke reddened.

'No, of course not,' she said. 'He shared the news with me Saturday night.'

Saturday night – she had been with Camilo then. And he had been with Rocío.

'Perhaps I have something to share with you,' he said. 'You can tell Camilo if you like.'

It was her turn to blush.

'There's a new project I'm commissioned for and I need sketches done, of the city.'

'Of Bogotá?'

'It's tied to the Pan-American Conference next year.'

'I'm not sure I have the skills,' she said, resuming her work. 'You should ask Señor Blanco.'

'Yes, well, he's an idiot.'

Felisa laughed.

'It's very important, Felisa. Listen, can you leave the site tomorrow? I've an appointment at the mayor's office to look over the plans and the draughtsman should be there.'

'Caicedo's office?' she asked. 'Yes, I can do that.'

When they arrived back at his office, Camilo was waiting for them.

'It's here,' Camilo said. 'Hot off the press!'

They crowded around the table where Camilo laid the fresh paper flat. What Camilo had pitched as a column was actually its centre spread and the lead feature for the day. He angled it to face Luke.

'What do you think? Don't look so embarrassed, Luke!' He turned to Felisa. 'Doesn't he look embarrassed?'

'It's just more than I imagined.' Luke swallowed hard. Camilo's enthusiasm was infectious. Photographs of his earlier projects glared up at him in stark black and white. The evidence of a life once lived.

'This place looks like here,' Telma said, placing a manicured finger on the image of *Heliotrope, 1930*.

They all gazed down at the aerial view of his earliest project. The Arts and Crafts houses with their pinstripe cladding were more uniform than those of La Merced. He was twenty-two when he'd been given that commission and not long out of design school. He'd worked under a man named Hassberg. Hassberg liked order and Luke worked hard to make sure he had it. It was his first taste of what money could and couldn't buy. In contrast, here, everything had to be bolder, everything grander. The oil company had deep pockets, whereas they'd barely pushed a profit on Heliotrope after the last lot was sold. Luke looked at the image of his earlier project. It was so conservative, so safe.

'And this is in Madrid?' Felisa asked, singling out another structure. *Centro Inglés, 1934.* 'It's beautiful.'

'That is quite different,' he said, swallowing. At the time, it had meant everything, catapulting him into another league. He was written about after that. His name jostled alongside Eames, Lloyd Wright and Mies on the pages of the leading architecture and design magazines. Catherine had raved about it. 'I've never loved you more than I do now,' she'd said, devouring him with kisses, 'never, ever, more than now.'

'There's nothing like it here, not yet,' Luke said, looking at Felisa.

'Imagine.' She leaned in for a closer look. Her hair brushed against his hand in what was a perfect moment.

Luke skimmed the text. His heart raced the whole time and he wondered if they could hear it, if they knew it meant something else to him than it did to them. Not since before the war had anything good been written about him. He was afraid to find anything that might cast him in a negative light, convinced that there must be something small that would find him out here. Then he imagined he'd found it. There was a short paragraph that spoke of his time in the war: *During the European conflict, Señor Vosey's expertise was required by the British government at the Ministry of Economic Warfare. He ceased work as an architect during this tumultuous time. Putting his creativity aside, he downed tools to take up his country's cause. His sacrifice, during this period of conflict, has been our gain.*

Camilo, he realised, was watching him.

'Who told you this?'

'You did, Luke. Don't you remember?'

Telma rose. 'I think fresh coffee and almojábana are in order. Señorita Mejía, will you help me?'

The two women pulled on their coats and left. Luke and Camilo listened to them arguing on the stairs over which bakery sold the best cheese rolls.

'Did I get it right?' Camilo asked after silence had been restored.

'Close enough.'

Camilo nodded. 'There wasn't much I could edit out.' He produced a cigarette and lit it. 'It's a good piece though, isn't it?'

'Yes, Camilo, thank you.' Luke closed the newspaper and folded it.

'It was a good distraction, Luke. You are a good distraction.'

'Me? From what?'

'The country tearing itself apart.' Camilo dropped down into Telma's chair. He looked tired. 'Last week, I was sent down to Fusa – Fusagasugá, to give it its proper name. Two hours by road from Bogotá. One half of the town against the other, but all of them joined in hatred against a local landowner; a man named Robledo. The people grew tired of the way he threw his money around, using the local police to control them, to threaten them. Killing off anyone rising to Gaitán's tune, you see? It's the same everywhere but here. The people in this city don't know how good they have it. The real poverty, the real crime, doesn't reach them here.'

'So the people of Fusa fought back?'

'Not quite. This Robledo was dragged from his house in the middle of the night and, in front of his family, stripped naked and tied to a mule. The poor creature was kicked and lashed by the townspeople. Worse things were done to Robledo.'

'What kind of things?'

'Unchristian things, and with his wife and child looking on.

Eventually, I guess the mule had enough. He took off with Robledo still attached, right through the town and out the other side to cries of "Go back to the arse of hell!" The funny thing is that when the town woke the next day, the mule was back, but without its cargo.'

'But what happened to him? To Robledo?'

'He was found eventually, cut up, wandering naked across the savannah, sent raving mad by sun exposure and by what the people had done to him.' Camilo inhaled deeply. 'But he was lucky.' He stubbed out his cigarette in the ashtray on Luke's desk. 'Not so the main ringleaders; they should have killed him. They'll pay for that mistake.'

17

Luke arranged to meet Felisa at ten the following day outside the Palacio Liévano on the main square. He arrived early, wandering into the centre of the square, past the fountains and statue of Simón Bolívar. He was restless, excited even. Across the street was La Casa de la Risa. The cantina's shutter was up. He tried to pick out movement inside the dark interior but couldn't. He hadn't returned since Camilo had said it was a socialist meeting place and wouldn't, now this thing with Osorio was coming into being. El Lobo was the kind of person with eyes in every cantina.

A couple of days after the dinner at Osorio's, he'd asked Telma to arrange a meeting with the mayor but had been set up with the deputy instead, a man named Jorge Martin.

'You're early, Luke.'

He turned to find Felisa standing before him.

'We both are,' he said, smiling.

Felisa pulled her jacket straight. It looked like it had started life too big for her but had been made to fit.

'I borrowed this,' she said.

'I shouldn't have asked you to come,' he said, thinking he'd put her to too much trouble.

Felisa looked hurt.

'The bother, I mean. You shouldn't have.' He swallowed. 'You look nice.'

'Shall we go in?' she asked.

They made their way back across the square towards the palacio in silence. The deputy mayor's office was on the first floor. In the cramped waiting room, the two of them took up position on a low sofa. Sitting there put him on edge, this feeling of early submission. The receptionist, a woman with a head of golden hair, wouldn't take her eyes off Felisa. From her expression, it was obvious that she saw herself as superior.

'Will he be long?' Luke asked.

'I shouldn't think so,' the receptionist replied.

Felisa smiled at him. She was nervous as well, he could tell.

The deputy's door burst open.

'Señor, Mr Luke Vosey,' the man said, his small hand outstretched.

Luke rose and Felisa did too.

'And your secretary?'

'Señorita Mejía is our draughtswoman.'

'Mejía, of course, and I'm Jorge Martin. There, we are all present. Shall we begin?'

He led them back to his office where they sat down before a large desk. It was one of the only pieces of furniture in the room.

'The mayor has informed me that you need access to the files – to the initial report drawn up by the board?'

'Yes.' Luke cleared his throat. 'I'm to leave with the proposals for the new centre.'

'Precisely,' Martin said, looking at Felisa. 'Our idea for a new Bogotá starts today. Exciting, no?'

Felisa didn't answer.

'We're all excited,' Martin said for her. He leaned back in his chair and studied them both. The silence was long and awkward until the receptionist came in with a thick file. She handed it to Martin. 'Thank you, Ingrid.'

Luke watched her leave.

'She's German,' Martin said. 'Or at least, her father was.' He shrugged and opened the file. 'Here it all is.' He turned over the first sheet.

'Scheduled for clearance...' he read, 'The House of Juan Flórez Ocariz, the College of San Bartolomé, the church of Santa Clara, my goodness, the Palacio Liévano – the very bricks beneath our feet!'

'I'm aware of this,' Luke said.

'And the people who live alongside?' Felisa asked. 'Surely not their homes too?'

Martin looked at her. 'Señorita Mejía has decided to join us.'

Perhaps, Luke thought, I should have told her something. She had only come because he had asked.

'Mejía is a very old name,' said Martin. 'Did you know that some of the first to step foot here carried it all the way from Spain?'

'I don't see what...'

'And do you think they lived side by side with the natives when they did? Lived in their huts, ate their food?'

She opened her mouth to speak but Martin was faster.

'They improved the land and the people, using whatever means at their disposal. Whatever means. There,' he said, sliding the report across to Luke, 'everything you need to make your plans.'

'Shall I send a message to the mayor when it's done?'

'Through Ingrid is fine,' Martin said, rising. 'A pleasure to meet you, Señorita Mejía.'

They found their way back out through the maze of rooms, taking the stairs in silence. When they were out on the square again, Luke stopped her.

'You can't speak like that, Felisa. If you question the deputy, it's like you're questioning the mayor, and through the mayor, like you're questioning...'

'Who? Who, Luke?'

'Me. Like you're questioning me, Felisa.'

'You didn't say they meant to destroy the city. That you meant to.' Her eyes filled with tears. 'Men like that... those people he spoke about... those people are me.'

'No one wants to destroy anything,' he said. That bit was partly true. 'A lot of good can come...'

'Luke,' she said, 'don't you see? They're filling their own pockets. There's no way they're going to help anyone but themselves.'

'You have no idea what's possible, Felisa. Can't you trust me? I thought you wanted something better,' he said.

'What do you know!' She turned and walked away from him. People were staring. A few boys sniggered. Luke went after her. He was thinking of the people, and, yes, of his career and hers. She had no idea how important this was. No, he wasn't sure she quite understood at all. Felisa was practically running now and had almost reached the corner of the square.

'If you don't want the job,' he shouted, almost catching her up outside the cathedral. 'I'll find someone else.'

Felisa stopped. When he reached her, he was out of breath, but she looked worse.

'Wanting is not the same as needing,' she said, looking up at him.

There were real tears in her eyes now and his heart sank. He'd have said anything to stop her walking away, but he hadn't acted kindly and she hated him for it.

'There isn't anyone else,' he said. 'I didn't think. Felisa,' Luke took her hand. 'If it's not us, then they'll get someone else. Would you rather that?'

'I don't know. Luke, please.'

'I can't do it without you.'

Her face softened. 'Luke, you have to let go of my hand.'

He did. Things would be all right. He'd show her that.

'Gaitán is staging a huge public meeting in two weeks' time,' she said, wiping her face.

'Yes, I've read about it, it'll take place here, won't it?'

'That's right. Camilo is working, you see. He's covering it. Will you come with me instead? I'd like you to hear him. Then, you might understand.'

18

On the day of the public address, Luke agreed to meet Felisa on the corner of Plaza de Bolívar a little before five in the afternoon. He left his apartment at four and walked down Seventh Avenue. When he reached the commercial centre, the crowd that had been mounting along the route filled the road as well as the pavement. It looked as if most of the city had turned out for this one. Gaitán's loyal followers – calling themselves the Gaitanistas – were dressed in black as though heading to a funeral and not an address. Gaitán had asked them to do that. He'd written it down in *Jornada* the week before. Luke had read that issue and was also wearing black. He wasn't going to indulge Gaitán but at the last minute he'd changed his mind to please Felisa. She was already there when he arrived.

'Isn't it wonderful?' she said, reaching up to kiss him on the cheek.

'It is, yes.'

'Come.' She laced her fingers through his and led him across the square.

What struck him was the silence. The only noise the shuffling of feet; the unchecked coughing of children and the elderly. It was the second request he'd read about; the silence. And these people are never quiet, Luke thought. The city usually droned like an enraged hive and here they all were, subdued. This Gaitán, it seemed, could make them do anything. Felisa led him through the crowd towards the centre, past the cathedral, draped in workmen's sheets. The two of them squeezed in alongside men and women carrying homemade banners of black fabric mounted onto bamboo poles. An old man at his side prodded Luke in the ribs and gestured for him to take his banner and hold it higher than the rest. Luke let go of Felisa's hand and did as he was asked. She smiled in approval when he sent it skyward. They pressed on slowly into the square with the old man at their side. Hundreds of Gaitán's supporters had accompanied Luke down Seventh Avenue, marching out of step like the civilian army they were. Now, the number had exploded. He looked out across the heads of thousands of others, waiting for Gaitán to appear. At their backs was a makeshift scaffold. Some men had chosen to climb this and sat now on the different levels the platform afforded. The whole structure appeared flimsy, as if it might collapse on top of them.

'It'll start soon,' Felisa said.

He lowered the sign and handed it back to the man. As soon as he was free, Felisa sought out his hand again. Hadn't she said Camilo was here, somewhere? Luke looked around him as though the journalist might appear. All eyes were turned towards the municipal building. Luke recognised it from the mayor's plans. It was one of the structures to be cleared under Osorio's commission. The blueprints for its destruction were safely back in his apartment.

'All of this will be lost,' she said, moving closer.

'I know.'

He could feel the warmth of her, her arm pressed against

his. He thought about saying he'd go back across town to tear Osorio's plans in two, if only she'd go with him.

Felisa let go of his hand. 'The Pan-American Conference will be there,' she said, pointing behind them. 'At the Capitolio, where the Senate and House meet.'

'And Gaitán?'

She shook her head. 'Not him. He hasn't been invited. Can you imagine? All of the world flying in and the door slammed in his face.'

'So that's why we're here today? He's hosting his own conference.'

'Perhaps,' Felisa said, grinning.

'There!' someone shouted.

Luke turned to see a man step out onto the balcony before them. It was Gaitán. It had to be. He wasn't a delicate looking man, not like Osorio or any of the other dignitaries Luke had met. He recognised the full head of dark hair and large, powerful features he'd seen depicted in the press. He has the face of a native, Luke thought. He understood then why Osorio and his lot hated him. His appearance would have been enough. Gaitán lifted his hands.

'Señor Presidente Ospina Pérez, under the weight of a profound emotion I address Your Excellency, interpreting the wishes and will of this multitude that hides its burning heart, lacerated by so much injustice, under a clamorous silence, to ask that there be peace and mercy for the nation.'

At Luke's side, Felisa drew breath and reached up for his ear.

'Peace and mercy,' she whispered.

He felt it like a chill wind blowing. 'Peace and mercy.' It was like a plea, the last desperate bid of someone confined to the scaffold. Gaitán was speaking about them. Even those around them who had coughed and whispered their way into the square were silent now. All across the city, he thought, others will be feeling like this. President Ospina in some fine room inside the presidential palace will be feeling it too. Gaitán's words repeated to him down the line, 'peace and mercy', from aide to politician, 'peace and mercy', until finally someone brave enough will have whispered in his ear, 'peace and mercy,' knowing the message was meant for him alone. Gaitán, their chief mourner, addressed the people again. They were hanging on his every word, urging him to tell them to strike; now was the moment, they would do it, if he only asked.

'Go home,' he said at last.

Go home? Had he really said that? Go home? He wants us to leave, they now repeated. The address hadn't lasted more than ten minutes. Felisa tugged at Luke's sleeve.

'It's done,' she said. 'Let's go.'

The crowd began to disperse as Gaitán had asked. Some people were angry. They had come thinking something was about to begin, that they had been invited to start it.

'Stop that!' Luke shouted at a group of boys who were trying to shake one of the scaffold poles loose behind them. There were still people climbing down from it.

'Don't, Luke. Come away.' Felisa pulled at his arm.

'Ospina is a dog,' someone close to them said.

'My brother was beaten last week, outside his own house and only an hour from here,' said another, and then a third: 'He won't help. Ospina doesn't care, none of them do.'

'If Gaitán told me to spit on any one of them politicians, I would.'

'I would do worse.'

Gaitán has brought his cause to the president's door, Luke thought. Ospina had only to open the windows of his office to hear the decree; to hear the public cry. He had made the people bold.

'Do you think Ospina will step down?' Luke asked as they made their way back onto Seventh.

'He might.'

'Or worse,' Luke said. 'He might be pushed.'

'Why would that be worse?' Felisa asked.

'If it brought more instability, it might be.'

'We're knocking at his door now, he can't ignore us, Luke.'

They walked on in silence. It was as though, in some way, they were still under Gaitán's spell. For Luke's part, it was shyness too. He didn't want to be the first to own it, when Felisa knew so much more than he did. Perhaps she is waiting for me, he thought, wondering how or in what way he might get her to speak again. In the end he found himself asking after Camilo. He was their only common ground.

'He will have been there,' she said. 'Covering it.'

He thought of the moment in the square when she had taken his hand.

'And what do you think he'll write?'

'Gaitán spoke well, he'll say something about that. The main thing is the challenge to Ospina.'

'From the people.'

'What do you mean?' Felisa stopped.

'They offered up their silence so Gaitán could speak for them.'

'You saw that?'

Luke swallowed. 'I read the copies of *Jornada* you gave me.'

Felisa nodded.

'And I've been listening to Gaitán's question time on the wireless.'

'I don't have that luxury,' she said.

'Then come over and listen to mine, whenever you like.'

Felisa blushed and they were returned to silence. She looked cold, he thought. He realised her own journey home would have taken her in the opposite direction across the square. He was glad she had decided to walk with him.

'Here,' he said, taking off his jacket and handing it to her.

'No, it's all right.'

'Please.'

Reluctantly, it seemed, she took it and put it on. They continued in silence. When they reached the corner of Jiménez, Felisa stopped.

'I should go,' she said.

'Won't you come back and have something to eat?'

They'd arrived in front of the *El Tiempo* offices. She looked at him and then up at the building.

'I said I'd wait for Camilo.'

'I see,' Luke said. 'What we're doing with the redevelopment, it's going to improve things, Felisa, for the people.'

'Perhaps it will,' she said. 'I was thinking about that during the speech.'

'So was I.'

'I don't know if Deputy Martin, or those in power against Gaitán, see it like that.'

'But I do. Why shouldn't that money be used for this?'

Felisa looked at him and came close. 'You really believe that, don't you?'

'I do, actually,' he said. 'I have such ideas, Felisa.'

She looked up at the building again. 'I don't know how long Camilo will be. Perhaps there is time to eat first?'

When they reached his apartment, they were hardly inside the door before they were kissing again. It was urgent and restless, as though something had been building since the square, since the silence that had been forced upon them. Both of them, he thought, knowing that this might be their only chance, that today, they were under some sort of spell that wouldn't last into tomorrow.

And now here Felisa was, sleeping soundly in his bed beneath his arm, her dark hair spread across the pillow. They were naked, and he was content to stay that way. He looked down at her. Her breasts were small and beautiful and her figure light yet firm beside his. Beneath his. She had cried out early, or maybe it was him. They'd held onto each other a long time afterwards. He couldn't remember a moment like it. Only if he stretched back far enough would he find something that came close, that felt as sacred. He didn't want to do that. Not now.

'Luke,' she said, looking up at him. 'I dreamed I'd left.'

'And should you?'

He wasn't ready to let her go and so kissed her again.

'Camilo might come looking for me.'

'He won't come here. I don't think I want to talk about him,' Luke said, laying his head down on her chest.

'Are you mine, Luke?'

'I think I have been for some time.'

Felisa sighed. 'It feels hopeless though, doesn't it?'

'What does?' he said, sitting up and kissing her again, not wanting an answer. He couldn't help himself. He wanted, needed to show her how much she meant to him.

'Please, Luke. You must let me speak.' He drew back. 'You must hear this. Everything I am, I owe to him.'

'To him?'

'Yes, to Camilo.'

'But not like this, surely.'

'He's given me so much.'

'He doesn't deserve your pity.'

'It isn't pity. I am grateful.'

'And now, here, is this gratitude too?'

'Why would you say that?'

'I don't know,' he said. 'Because of what he has, of what you're saying now. He's become a friend to me, but I think I hate him.'

'What have I done?'

'Nothing, you've done nothing,' he said, taking a deep breath. 'It's me.'

She waited for him to speak again.

'Jealousy,' he whispered. 'It's that.' He smiled but it felt weak and sickly. He felt weak and sickly and he was sure she saw it. Saw that she had made a mistake.

'Oh,' she said, rising. 'I should go.'

'No, don't.'

'I think I should.' She kept dressing.

'The article Camilo wrote, it wasn't wholly true,' he said, letting it rush out before he could stop himself.

'Enough, Luke. If you're suggesting he'd make something up, that he'd lie…'

'No, Felisa, I'm not suggesting that.'

'Then what is it?'

'There were things I left out.'

'Well that doesn't matter, does it? You don't have to tell the world your business, if it's private.' She sat down again. 'You don't have to tell me.'

'I do,' he mumbled. 'I can see that. The thing is, Felisa, what I didn't say wasn't private. It was actually quite public.' He folded the sheet over himself. 'This is very white,' he said. 'I hadn't noticed before.'

'The sheet, Luke?'

'Where I come from, if you were presented with a white feather, during the conflict, it meant you were a coward. It meant you thought your life was worth more than those who went to fight.'

'White feathers, Luke? I'm confused. What does this have to do with the article? You were an architect, then you went to work for the ministry, that's fighting of a sort, isn't it?'

'Yes, I went to work in government and for a time, a very short time, I did fight as you call it. But then I stopped believing in it. You see, the type of fighting I was doing meant I had to use what I knew, what I had learned as an architect. What I wrote up in my reports informed where the bombs would drop. I had to look at detailed maps of those cities and say – here, and here, and this place, these are the best targets.'

'Oh, Luke, not really?'

'It's true. It was guesswork, to some extent. I had no way of knowing whether those locations had been turned over to residential use. I hadn't been to some of those places since the early thirties. Christ, some I'd never been to.'

'Luke, your hands are shaking.'

'Are they? I need a drink. Do you need a drink?'

She nodded. 'I'll go.'

Felisa rose and pulled on a shirt from a pile. She left the room. He couldn't breathe. He'd told her. It had been pressing down on him and still was, although he'd managed to let some of it out. Some of it was free. He rose to open the window.

'No, Luke, you're naked,' she said, smiling at him shyly as she came back into the room. He got back into bed. Felisa handed him one of the glasses and placed the other on the table beside him. She went over to the window and opened it.

'Thank you,' he said as she got back into the bed.

He handed her the other glass. They clinked them together. To celebrate the truth, he supposed.

'I don't think there's any shame in not wanting to be a part of that,' Felisa said. 'Using something beautiful, a gift, for something ugly, like war.'

'If only that were it,' he said. 'I can't believe I'm going to tell you this. I took something, you see, and that something hurt more people.' He drank. 'You can't just leave a position like that. You sign up. You have to stay, by law. So, I took the coward's way out. I stole reports and maps for upcoming bombardments – things I had written which I knew they'd never forgive me taking. They still trusted me then, so it was easy to simply walk out the front door with whatever I wanted.'

'You stole from the government, for what you believed in?'

He nodded. 'It held up the effort for months afterwards. They arrested me, questioned me, really questioned me, quite a few of them were involved in that. Then there was the trial. The evidence said that thousands more had died because of what I'd done. Good British soldiers and civilians, because I had allowed Hitler to advance his munitions factories.' Felisa nodded. 'At the time I'm not sure I cared. The whole thing was rotten. I took whatever they threw at me, but it was when they called my work into question, when they wanted to wipe out all of that – any knowledge of it... My name was mud. Luke Vosey, Public Enemy, I— I remember the headlines, the beatings, all of it.'

'What evidence did they have?'

'None to start with. I wouldn't tell them what I did with the papers; I mean, I burned them, obviously, in the pit of a firebombed house at the end of my street. I thought that was quite clever at the time, but it was a bit stupid, really. Someone saw the fire. You see, you had to report everything then, as a matter of public duty. They had this as proof, I mean the woman who'd seen me was a local drunk, but they didn't care. I didn't care. That truth didn't feel as bad as when I was a part of it. It was the photographs that haunted me, that finally convinced me to turn. We'd get these aerial shots sent back from each mission, those weren't so terrible as everything looks manageable from above – a blackened hole here, untouched areas there. No, it was the photographs taken on the ground. In those, you'd come face to face with someone's arm, someone's husband, or a baby... I mean, what was a baby doing in a munitions factory?'

'Stop, Luke, that's enough.'

Felisa put both glasses down and took hold of him. He let himself implode. Disintegrate. He was right back there, to the moment after the trial when he realised what had been lost and what would never be brought back.

Felisa kissed the top of his head and it brought him back into the room. He turned his face to hers and kissed her back, wanting her to know how much it had taken to get this far. He felt she understood – the urgency, the need – everything he did. It coursed through him. He'd been so lost for so long. So without hope of coming back to this moment of belonging. This moment. This. Her face was wet. Was she crying, even now?

No. He was.

'Luke,' she cried out. 'It's you.'

Late that same night he went out with her to find a car to take her back to Tres Esquinas. She had insisted on returning. Luke drew his jacket around her for the second time. When he closed the door of his apartment and was alone again, it was well after midnight. He collapsed onto the bed, wondering whether any of it had been real. In the sheets he could still smell the perfume in her hair, like she had bathed inside the cup of some sacred flower, but even this was more an idea of the smell than the thing itself. Nothing about the evening had seemed real. On Monday, he thought, they'd meet again, and everything would be different.

19

The light was so bright that it became heat – the sky embraced it – falling masonry, bricks, glass shards blocking out the sun. It was gone – all of it – all of them. Luke sat upright in the bed. He couldn't breathe. Another night lost. He rose and stumbled from the bed towards the kitchen. He found the water jug and lifted it to his lips, finding repose at last, resting back against the cool sink. The nightmares had returned. Yesterday's encounter with Felisa had left its mark. Had he agreed to Osorio's project for her and the people, or was it another selfish act, like those he'd been accused of in the past? He was no Gaitán. Last night he'd been followed by a thousand pairs of eyes, and the bodies they belonged to were piled one against another in the scattered basements of the cities he had loved, Hamburg, Dresden...

Dresden. He saw it again now, as fresh as this morning. He'd been there in the late twenties as a student, staying in the Altstadt in a small rented room overlooking the Elbe. There had been a cocktail party in an apartment on the Schloßstraße. He'd snuck in with a friend. A local boy named Robert. They'd met at college, were studying together. The party was Luke's first taste of something grander than himself. They'd pinched cigarettes and flirted with the women. One day, Robert took him to where he lived on the Striesener Straße to meet his mother, father and younger sister. The small apartment looked onto one of the city's central arteries. He remembered the address again later, in '45, when it was marked as a point of focus for the incendiaries. That's how he saw them, civilians and soldiers both, strewn across urban battlefields.

He went back into the bedroom and opened the window, closing the curtains again so he might undress. A gust of fresh air blew through the drapes – it was a welcome breeze just passing through the neighbourhood. It was sobering to feel alive. He grabbed a clean towel and went to wash.

When Luke arrived at La Merced for their last day on site, Felisa was already there. She was sitting cross-legged on the floor, her sketchbook open and the tin of watercolours at her feet. The desks and chairs she had shared with the foreman and her one-time rival Alfonso Blanco were gone, as was Blanco, now that the work had been completed.

'Come and sit upstairs,' he said at last. He hadn't wanted to disturb her.

Felisa looked up and smiled.

'There'll be three of us, though,' he said, wondering how she could look at him after what he had revealed. 'Telma will be here soon.'

'She already is,' Felisa said.

'Are they almost finished?'

'Yes,' she said. 'But if you'd prefer, I can get started on the new project.'

'What I would prefer...' he began.

Felisa smiled sweetly. 'Yes?'

'Should I come and sit down there too?' Telma called from the top of the stairs.

'You're fine where you are,' Luke replied.

They laughed.

'Señor Vosey,' Felisa said. 'I'll be up shortly.'

There wasn't much furniture left in his office and he wondered if he might choose a new space or relocate to his apartment sooner. Inside the room, Telma had already formed a new working space for herself, taking a corner of his desk since her own had gone.

'I'm paid until today,' she said, shrugging, when she caught him staring.

'As you wish, Telma.'

'And the girl in here, too?' Telma rose when Felisa entered. 'I'll make coffee,' she said, squeezing past her and out into the hall.

'Take this spot, there's more light,' Luke said, clearing a side table and positioning it in front of the window.

Felisa followed and placed her tools on top. 'Thank you.' She pulled a spare chair over to the desk and sat down but didn't pick her brush up right away.

'Is everything all right?' he asked.

'Yes,' she smiled, laying a hand on his. 'Did you know there's been more violence outside of the city this week?'

'Where?'

'To the north. Twelve men killed in a skirmish with the landowners.' She sighed. 'If only Gaitán were president now. If only we didn't have to wait another three years.'

He nodded. 'And he'll be able to bring the two sides together?'

'Of course – as long as they do as he says.'

'Without compromise.'

'Don't underestimate him,' she said, throwing a pencil at him. 'Or me.'

'I suppose he wouldn't change the city either?' Luke picked it up and handed it back to her.

'He would... probably find another way,' she said.

Telma came into the room with a tray and they broke apart. She put it on his desk. 'This will be one of the last times I do this.'

Luke looked at Felisa and they both tried not to laugh.

Inside the red folder that Martin had given him were instructions for the areas of the city designated for redevelopment. It was as the deputy, and Osorio before him, had said. The historic centre would be modernised. The redevelopment would run across at least three blocks, sandwiching Plaza de Bolívar between them. The entire document had been translated into English for his benefit. Luke took paper and pencils of his own and, seated at his desk, began the rough outline of a new city centre that would fill the space left behind by the clearance. He had to get it right. It wasn't like before the war, when he'd ridden a tide of praise, slipping easily from one project to the next. If this failed, that would be it. No more chances. They were relying on him. He worked carefully, to give the minister what he wanted, dressing it in something Felisa would be proud of too.

The three of them worked on into the afternoon without disturbances. By late afternoon, Luke had achieved a rough skyline, close to what he wanted. It had to be both residential and commercial, but it needed a third thing too, something that was almost impossible to maintain – a sense of the new. He looked at the sketch again, tidied up the corners and held it up to the light. Stark skyscrapers and low-level commercial buildings ran linear through a new centre. The buildings opened up the skyline and the streets below were wider than they were now. Creativity in space, he thought, his mind turning just then to one of his earliest projects – Madrid's Centro Inglés. There, he'd come up with the idea of introducing thousands of panes of glass inside cantilevered steel frames that as good as gave the building back to the clouds. At the time, it was a huge success. And the skyline here is so beautiful, he thought.

20

To finish the drafts, Luke moved Felisa and Telma into his apartment. They went on like this for weeks, Señora Rojas fuelling the proceedings with a constant supply of fresh-bought bread and fried empanadas. Luke was getting fat. Well, not fat exactly but 'healthier looking', Señora Rojas told him. He didn't care. He felt stronger and his clothing held his shape better. The question of his 'wholeness', as Luke considered it, was a personal one because only he knew how incomplete he'd felt before Felisa came into his life. He enjoyed her company daily and saw Camilo just as much. The journalist made sure of that. Felisa had told him of the project as Luke said she should, but on the proviso that he wouldn't write about it. At the apartment, Luke had sworn him to secrecy too. There'd be an exclusive interview in it for him once it was all signed off and construction begun. When Camilo wasn't off reporting some new rural horror, he'd taken to working there too, turning the apartment into a newsroom of sorts. He took a keen interest in what they were doing. He shared his working life with theirs. Luke would listen as Camilo read the latest news stories to the three women before packing up the transcripts to be couriered away to the editor. He read without sympathy and sometimes, despite his fondness for him, Luke wished he wouldn't. Señora Rojas was quiet and withdrawn on more than one occasion and when Camilo noticed this, he exaggerated the brutality of the stories. 'Enough!' Felisa would shriek until a single look from Camilo returned her to silence. What power his young friend held then. At night, Felisa was always the last to leave when Camilo wasn't there. Otherwise they hid their feelings around him. She asked Luke to do that, saying it wasn't right to change how things were for Telma or Camilo. That it was theirs alone. He'd gone along with it. It wouldn't be for much longer, he thought. He'd signed the contract for the new office. They were due to move in the new year, close to the mayor's office on a street that wouldn't be touched by the development. Close, as he had been with La Merced.

For now, they'd developed a system for working, Felisa choosing to sit cross-legged on the floor, while Luke took the table, picking over plans as she handed the finished drafts up to him. Today, Camilo's notebooks lay sprawled at the far end of the table where he'd left them. Telma was absent too. She'd taken the day off for a communion.

'The last one,' Felisa said.

She rose and handed the draft to him. His housekeeper was out of the room and so she stayed close, running a hand through his hair. She had passed him an artist's impression of a street scene with a curved building at its centre. Felisa called it the Frigate, saying it resembled the bird in flight. She was right: raised off the ground on concrete pillars, it would look airborne from the right angle when it was built.

'It's very clever,' he said.

Felisa left his side. He tried to return to what he had been working on before, the tree-lined avenue that would run the full length of the development. He could still feel the ghost of her fingertips. She was in the kitchen now. He ran his fingers through his hair. Felisa was discussing lunch with Señora Rojas to celebrate Camilo's promotion to senior reporter. Camilo had gone out to track down a bottle of champagne. For now, Luke was alone with the two women. For now, there was enough space for all of them. There was a knock at the door.

'Camilo,' Felisa said, running to answer it.

He'd been very quick.

'Is this the right place?'

It was Karl. Felisa moved to one side so he could enter.

'This is Señorita Mejía,' Luke said.

Karl had been drinking. Felisa nodded but didn't hang around for introductions.

'New housekeeper?' Karl's face was flushed and excited.

'Our draughtswoman for the project.'

'If you say so,' Karl said, poking Luke in the ribs. He found his way across the room and dropped down into a chair.

'We're about to have lunch.'

'Not for me, thanks. Can't stop,' Karl said, drawing out a cigar and struggling to light it. 'Come for these plans you've been promising.'

'They're not due yet,' Luke said. He went over and helped Karl with the lighter. 'I'll deliver them to the mayor's office myself.'

'I insist,' Karl said. 'Told Osorio I'd come personally. Speeds things up. Also,' he added, puffing away, 'he wants me to invite you to some New Year's soirée he's got going at his place.'

With his free hand, Karl felt about in his pockets. He brought out the invitation and handed it to Luke.

'At the hacienda?'

'Yup.'

There was a second knock at the door and Luke went over to open it. It was Camilo this time, grinning from ear to ear.

He held up two bottles. 'Champagne,' he said, breathlessly. 'I went across town to my uncle's in the end. He wasn't there but he won't notice.'

'He's very particular, I'd say,' said Karl.

'Señor Draper. I didn't see you there.' Camilo handed the bottles to Luke and came forward to greet Karl formally. He sat down on the edge of the sofa and crossed his arms. 'You could always join us.'

'You're too late.' Karl leaned forward and stubbed his cigar out in the ashtray. 'Luke here already invited me.'

'You two know each other?' Luke asked.

'We've met. At your uncle's, right, boy?'

'That's right,' Camilo said.

'What's the celebration, then?' Karl asked.

'Camilo's promotion, actually,' Felisa said, coming back into the room.

'Congratulations! Promotion to what?'

'It was the article on Señor Vosey that did it.' She placed her arms around Camilo's shoulders. 'Now he's a senior reporter.'

'Enough,' Camilo said, freeing himself.

'Got a copy for me?' Karl asked.

'I do, actually.' Luke put the bottles down and took a newspaper off the top of a tall pile.

'Jesus, Vosey, did you buy every copy in town?'

'Camilo did,' Felisa said.

Camilo picked up one of the bottles. 'Let's open this, shall we?'

He called into the kitchen for glasses and Felisa returned with five of varying shapes and sizes. Señora Rojas came too. Luke took the bottle from Camilo and popped the cork.

'To our dear senior reporter!' Felisa said.

They raised their glasses and drank.

'Tastes like it belongs to Osorio,' Karl said.

Luke put his down and went over to the plans on the table. He worked them together into a pile and rolled up the stack, Felisa's Frigate on top. He secured the bundle with a couple of loops of string.

'Here,' he said, handing it to Karl.

'Good work, Vosey.' Karl stood, finishing his drink in one.

'Shall I call you a car, Karl?'

'Got one, haven't I. Waiting outside.' Karl took the roll and headed for the door. 'I'll tell Osorio you're thrilled about the invitation.'

After he had left, Felisa went over to the door to check it was closed.

'What's this?' Camilo asked. He picked up the invitation that Luke had left on the chair. 'What fortune! Please say you're going, Luke.'

'I thought you didn't get on?'

'I'm family, aren't I? I don't have a choice. And if you're there, it'll make it completely bearable.'

Luke took the card from him. 'I don't think I can refuse.'

'Is it a celebration for your birthday?' said Señora Rojas, winking at Luke.

'You know perfectly well that it isn't,' Luke said. He hadn't wanted it mentioned. He would be forty in two days.

'Ah!' Felisa cried. 'Your birthday! Why didn't you say?'

'To avoid this. It makes me feel old.'

'He's ancient, Felisa, you heard. Best not to mention it.' Camilo grinned at him.

'He doesn't look old,' she said. 'We should take Señor Vosey away, Milo, out of the city.' Her eyes were big and Camilo's too, although they'd only had a glass apiece.

He sighed. 'And where would we go?'

'Guatavita, of course,' Camilo provided.

'Yes, Guatavita,' Felisa said. 'It's the week before Christmas. We can leave offerings.'

'I'm not sure.' Luke looked at them. They were waiting, expectant as children, for him to answer. 'Señora Rojas, is Guatavita a nice place to visit?'

'Beautiful,' she said, poking her head back into the room. 'And the girl is right, it's a spiritual place.'

'There, it's decided,' Felisa said, gaining in confidence. 'We've finished the drafts and Camilo is a senior journalist, and it's your birthday.' She touched Luke's sleeve.

'Perhaps he would rather we went without him,' Camilo said, 'and left him here, in peace.'

Luke looked at him. Something unspoken passed between the two men.

'All right,' he said, emptying his glass and turning to Felisa. 'I'll come, if that's what you want.'

21

Estación de la Sabana, the city's main train station, was a forty-minute walk from his apartment. Luke didn't mind it. He planned on travelling light, taking a beat-up leather bag containing only a change of shirt and trousers to last the week. He also had the straw hat he'd purchased for ten centavos, far more than he should have, determined to put it to use on this, his first trip outside of the city. Without questioning it, he'd also packed the photo of *Catherine on the Rocks* – the one of her taken all those years ago on that beach. He'd started thinking of it by that name, because in some small way it offered distance, as though she were nothing but a pretty face locked in a painting of sorts. Thoughts of Felisa swam closer to shore now. He was taking the photograph with him to get rid of it. Felisa had mentioned a sacrifice of sorts and in a moment lacking total clarity, he'd decided to bring it with him for the purpose of exorcising himself of her.

Over yesterday's lunch, the three of them had made a rough plan. They'd agreed to take the eight-thirty train out of the city the next day – 'There's no time like now,' Felisa had insisted, as though her urgency to leave was greater than theirs. Camilo,

Luke noticed, went along with practically anything she said. And so it was set, their adventure would begin on the last Saturday before Christmas. Felisa had explained the journey. They would take the north-eastern line, stopping at Puente Aranda, Chapinero and Usaquén on the outskirts of the city, then on to Ramel Samper, San Antonio, La Caro, Briceño and Tocancipá before reaching their destination, Gachancipá. She counted the stations out on her fingers. From there, they'd take a bus, Felisa had shown, weaving her hand along the tablecloth to show how the road cut alongside the mountains to Sesquilé, and then between the peaks, keeping to the low road that would lead them to Guatavita. Six and a half hours, if they were lucky.

'Everyone is leaving,' Camilo had added. The city would be empty by Sunday. Luke didn't know whether he'd meant everyone was leaving for elsewhere or with them. What kind of a place was this Guatavita? It had all come about so fast and in the fresh morning light seemed rash now. How might it look to Karl, to Osorio? Karl had taken the plans for the city centre. There wasn't time now to call at the mayor's office to check whether he'd delivered them. He'd have to trust him, and he did trust him, didn't he? I need to get away, Luke thought. There had been no let-up between La Merced and the new project. Until now, the furthest he'd managed was Osorio's hacienda. These things; these things stopped him thinking about Felisa. A whole week away with her – away from the project and her politics. They'd be alone, almost. Did Camilo suspect them? Camilo was a journalist and journalists were good at detail. I will have to learn to mind myself, Luke thought.

La Sabana station was big and imposing and looked a lot like Europe, Luke thought, taking in the tall columns that ran the length of its main concourse. He was early but there was already a crowd gathered at the ticket desk and luggage stacking up beside porters, official or otherwise. He spotted Camilo almost immediately, leaning against one of the pillars. Luke went over.

'What time did you get here?'

'I can't say.' Camilo laughed, nervously. 'Last night, perhaps?'

'And Felisa – is she here, too?' Luke looked around as casually as he could.

Camilo shook his head.

'There's time,' Luke checked his watch. It was ten past now. There was an awkward silence in which he struggled for something to say. 'I never said thank you, properly, for the article.'

'You didn't need to,' Camilo said plainly. 'They promoted me because of it.'

'Congratulations again, then.'

'Thanks. I've booked us seats already.' Camilo's face broke into a grin. He lifted his arm, waving their tickets above his head. 'She's here!'

Luke turned to see Felisa coming towards them.

'Have you seen the line of people?' she asked, coming up beside him. She snatched the tickets from Camilo. 'Tickets already? This is very out of character, Milo.'

'Queue if you like, Felisa; Luke and I are leaving.' He picked up Luke's bag as well as his own. 'It's Platform 1 when you're ready. Come on, Luke.' Camilo walked off in the direction of the trains.

'Very out of character,' she said, when they were alone.

'Shall I take your bag?' Luke asked her, noticing she'd packed as lightly as he had.

'Thank you, no,' Felisa said. 'We should hurry.'

They found Camilo on the train. He had secured them a

private compartment and Luke wondered how much it was down to his uncle's connections, as opposed to his increase in salary. The carriage was old-fashioned and ornate. Luke, in his weekend clothes, felt underdressed.

'Don't expect the same treatment on the way back,' Camilo said. 'I could only afford one way.'

'Leave that to me,' Luke said.

'Already I feel less... absorbed,' Felisa said, stretching out along one side of the car.

Camilo smiled at Luke.

'You've no idea what awaits you, Luke. Camilo,' she said, turning to him, 'you haven't been to Guatavita either.'

'Why would I go to Guatavita?' Camilo asked. 'I've had no need to.'

He had that look again. Luke hoped he wouldn't sulk the entire week.

'Luke,' she said, making the K sound softer than it was. 'Guatavita was special to the Muisca people.'

'El Dorado,' Camilo cut in.

'In Chibcha it means high peak, or end of the fertile fields,' she continued. 'Their king, the Zipa, would be painted in gold and then rowed out to the centre of the lake by his subjects. He would jump in to wash it from his body and then, before returning to shore, he threw offerings of solid gold to the goddess, Chia.' Felisa looked at him. 'As he had offered himself.'

'You realise it's long gone,' Camilo said.

Felisa reached across and hit him. 'They sacrificed sacred items, Milo. Gifts from the people to their deity.'

'It sounds wonderful,' Luke said as a whistle blew, drowning him out. The last of the passengers caught on the platform boarded. They hadn't left yet but already Luke was imagining a lake of solid gold and Felisa at its centre. He closed his eyes and sat back. Beneath them the train came to life. He became aware of it edging slowly away from the station as a boat might, pushed away from the shore.

Once the train pulled away from the platform at Usaquén on the outskirts of the city, he left all thoughts of Bogotá behind. The landscape unfolded before them, flat, wide and unending. The train travelled faster when it was outside of the city. Its tracks gripped the savannah like a bird in shackles, sometimes frenzied, sometimes rested. They never broke free of the Andes, whose peaks kept watch to their right as the train skated its way northwards across the flat. Felisa kept up his education. She told him of the crops that grew further north than Guatavita; onion, potato, wheat and barley, stretching far into the distance and blanketing the ranges. She had distant cousins who lived there and she had once seen whole fields ripe with them, pressing her face to the glass as though that time were now. What she imagined, the big wide world of it, seemed to awaken something in her, Luke thought. At these moments, she seemed at her most beautiful and free. Luke tried to listen politely but it was hard to not get carried away by her enthusiasm. Camilo, seated beside him, was trying his best to ignore her, or at least look like he was. He had tasked himself with copying something long and indecipherable from one notebook into another.

It was three in the afternoon when they reached Gachancipá. Camilo sprang into life after they'd exited the train, finding them the bus that would take them the distance to Guatavita via Sesquilé. Everyone else who'd got off the train wanted to board the bus too and so Luke found himself giving up his seat and pushed to the back. Camilo was with him at the rear while Felisa was at the front chatting to the woman in the seat beside hers.

'She makes friends with everybody,' Camilo said.

'Some people have that gift.'

Camilo eyed the back of her head as though fixated on some dark thought. The bus hit a pothole and they were thrown sideways. Luke tightened his grip on the rail above his head.

'I knew a woman who was much the same as her,' he said.

'The one who died?'

'I'd forgotten I'd told you that.'

'I hadn't. Part of the job.' Camilo tapped the side of his head and the bus rocked again. Luke reached out an arm to stop him falling. 'Thanks,' Camilo said. 'Can I ask, how did she die?'

Luke swallowed hard. In that small space, there was nowhere to hide. 'She was a nurse; field work.'

'On what you call the front?'

'Yes.'

'And you didn't follow her? To protect her, I mean?'

'It doesn't work like that.'

Camilo nodded. 'How *did* it work, for you two?'

Luke thought back. He tried to remember. 'You get a commission and are placed in the department best suited to your experience. For me, I suppose that meant Whitehall. It must have been my knowledge of buildings, my experience in those cities, it all counted for something. It could be used. I could.'

'And so she was placed far from you and you from her.'

'It wasn't as romantic as that.'

'No?'

'She could have stayed. Catherine chose to go.'

They stopped at Sesquilé and there was a chance to get down and buy refreshments or smoke. Luke stepped off and stretched. His muscles ached. He was too long and the bus too short but he felt constricted by more than just that. He looked around him. They'd stopped on the town's main square. For a small place, the cathedral was huge, rendered in a sandy-coloured stone that stood out from the other whitewashed dwellings. It was about as foreign as he was.

'Luke, Luke!' Felisa called to him from the steps of the bus. The engine was running and it looked as if it was about to leave. He ran back over to join her.

The bus had emptied at Sesquilé and for the final run of the journey they had two seats apiece. It was late afternoon and they'd been travelling for hours. Luke stretched out luxuriously and felt sleep overtake him. It was cold, numbing and deep.

He was woken by Camilo.

'Guatavita?' he asked.

'Yes, Luke, we're here.'

Some friends of Felisa's were there to collect them. The three of them, along with the woman Felisa had been talking to on the bus, piled into a truck. The woman was related to the driver, he discovered. Her name was Sofía. The journey to their destination was waited out in laughter and conversation. These were old friends of Felisa's that she hadn't seen for a while. Eventually, the truck pulled up outside a farmhouse at the end of a secluded track. Luke got out. The air was fresh, smelling of wet leaves and dried bark. The quiet that surrounded the farm was something else. It was everywhere and inside of everything. He'd grown too used to the city. Much about this place reminded him of the past, actually. He'd spent a lot of time in similar, quiet circumstances. Luke listened for the silence to break. For one accustomed to the city, it was alarming when it didn't.

22

———

Luke sat upright in the bed. He didn't know what time it was or where he was. He'd slept the entire night. Felisa was leaning on the door frame. She was already dressed. It must have been early because it was still dark inside the room, although behind her in the hall, there was daylight. He'd woken to her telling him the story of their arrival – that on the road to Guatavita, they'd passed under the nose of the sacred lake. He had no idea how long she'd been standing there.

'Did you sense the lake as we went by?'

'Should I have?' Luke heard himself croak.

The room was dark because of a pair of heavy shutters drawn across the window on the far wall. It could be the middle of the day, he realised, and he wouldn't know it.

'You wouldn't have seen it anyway,' she whispered, looking past him to the second bed beside his. 'We'll need to trek upwards for that.'

Luke looked over at Camilo, still sleeping. Last night, the pair had shared a room and it reminded him of those days later in the war, after the trial, when he'd been posted to the farm close to RAF Hemswell for field work. There were six of them in that room.

'Will you have coffee?' Felisa asked.

'Yes, thanks,' he said.

When she had gone, Luke slipped out of bed and went across the room to the window. He put his face close to the wall and pulled open a corner of shutter. He squinted as a stick of light cut a path across his cheek and hit the wall behind him. He looked back at the bed but Camilo slept like granite. Luke peered out again and made out a rough dirt square. A pair of chickens were pecking and clawing at the loose earth in search of food. Behind them was a low building that looked like a stable block.

He heard laughter coming from somewhere inside of the house. It's Felisa, he thought, smiling at the newness of the tone, as though here, her voice had wrestled free from some powerful grip and was enjoying a newfound freedom of its own. Sofía sounded happy too. Somewhere in another room, somewhere he hadn't been, they were happy together. Luke closed the shutter so as not to wake Camilo and went to see.

The bedroom led out onto a sunlit corridor, along the width of which were closed oak doors, much like the one that opened up into the room he shared with Camilo. The laughter got louder the further he got. He still felt half asleep and didn't hear the person coming in the opposite direction until he turned a corner and collided with Felisa. She was pushed backwards and both of the coffee cups she was holding fell to the floor. The liquid ended up on the wooden boards and his trousers.

'Step back,' she said, already down at his feet gathering up the shards from the hot puddle. Luke bent down to help too and as he did so felt something slice his heel. He lifted his foot in time to see the wound open.

'Ay Dios!' Felisa said.

'It's fine,' he said, although the pain was sharp.

Sofía appeared. 'With me,' she ordered.

Luke limped after her, trying not to leave a trail of blood behind him. Felisa followed, carrying fragments of broken clay. Sofía led him down a short stairway into a vaulted kitchen.

'Put your foot up,' she said, bringing over a low stool and telling him to sit.

'I'm so sorry,' he said.

She took a cloth and plunged it into a bucket of clean water.

'I'll do it,' Felisa said, taking the cloth from her.

'I'll make some more coffee then,' Sofía grinned at him.

How much did she know?

Felisa knelt at his damaged heel. She started to peel back the leg of his pyjama trouser.

'I can do it,' he said.

From the corner of the room, someone coughed. It was the man who had driven the truck last night. Luke hadn't noticed him before. He was seated close to the door. In one hand he held a strip of leather and in the other, a machete.

Camilo appeared after breakfast. 'What happened to you?' he asked, when Luke limped out of the finca into the morning light.

'We patched him up,' Sofía said, so that both she and Felisa laughed.

It was decided that the trip up to the sacred lake could wait; he shouldn't go when the cut was so fresh. It hadn't run as deep as he'd thought, but for a surface wound it throbbed each time he put pressure on it. The man with the machete turned out to be Sofía's brother, José. He agreed to run them into town so they might look around instead. José spoke English with a

German accent he'd picked up from a non-native barley farmer who struggled with Spanish. English had quickly become their common language.

'We might find something to throw into the laguna,' Felisa said.

She was helped up into the truck by Camilo. Luke climbed into the front beside José, who put the vehicle into gear and revved the engine, so that in no time at all they'd left Sofía and the farm far behind.

23

———

They weren't the first tourists to pass through Guatavita. It was a pretty town, similar to Sesquilé. There was a pattern, of course. Here, like there, they thought he was one of the German migrants. These newcomers weren't usually alone with the locals, though. People stared at the three of them. At their familiarity. They didn't trust it.

'They think you're going to carry their women off,' Camilo teased.

'That's funny,' Luke replied.

Camilo had been in a strange mood since they'd arrived. Felisa had disappeared into a store some twenty minutes ago. They were waiting on a low stone wall for her to return. He was waiting.

'It's quaint here,' Luke said. 'But you're right, something about it is unnerving.'

'If you have money here, people will do anything for you. You can get them to do anything. And if you don't have any money, well, you're like clay. Easy to mould.'

A group of young men in rough-hewn ponchos and

cowboy hats passed close by, their faces hard and weathered. Yes, he'd feel better once they were back at the farm.

'And what group do they belong to?' he asked Camilo, once they had passed.

'Not the same one as you.'

'Look,' Felisa said, coming across the square towards them. She was holding something wrapped in brown paper. She pulled the wrapping away to reveal a wide-mouthed figurine carved out of wood that had, at some point in its wretched life, been smeared in yellow paint.

'You realise that's hideous,' Luke said.

'It's for the goddess.'

'She thinks it's solid gold,' Camilo said, laughing.

'Excuse him,' Felisa said. 'He's ignorant. His family are Spanish through and through, aren't they, Camilo?'

'And yours?' Luke asked.

'Felisa is an Indian,' Camilo provided.

'I'm not ashamed,' she said. 'My mother had native blood.'

'And look how proud she is of it.'

Felisa went quiet. If Camilo had caused her pain, he seemed not to notice.

'This town is boring,' Camilo said, yawning. 'Just look at it. Poverty at every turn.' He singled out a man and boy pushing a loaded wagon of refuse across the cobbles. 'Where can they be going with that!'

'Why should you mind?'

Camilo looked at her. 'I don't.' He laughed. 'Thank goodness for your party tomorrow night, Luke.'

'It's meant to be a surprise, Milo!'

'As you keep telling me. He doesn't want a fuss, do you, Luke?'

He didn't, but Camilo didn't have to say as much. Surprises always carried an element of pretence. Everybody knew that.

'I have no idea what you're talking about,' he said, looking at her.

Felisa brightened. They heard a car horn and all looked up to see José driving towards them. They'd spent a friendly couple of hours in Guatavita until now. If Camilo wasn't teasing Felisa, she was goading him. Luke couldn't stand it when they carried on like that. It felt like she'd forgotten the time they'd spent together. He was at their mercy here. There was nothing to do but sit back and watch their childish flirtation, if that's what you could call it, twist and knot itself around the day. José pulled up beside them, and Luke couldn't have been happier to see him. José had been to run a few errands and so they shared the return trip with a couple of large bags of grain and containers of fuel for the truck. Camilo and Felisa were squeezed into the rear with the grain. They were very quiet and, in the front, Luke felt a million miles away from both of them. From her. He forced himself to focus on the road ahead and not check the mirror as he'd started doing when they'd first left the town.

Felisa leaned between the two seats. She was holding the object she'd bought in the market. 'If your injury has healed tomorrow, we can take this up to the sacred lake.'

'All right,' Luke said.

She brushed the side of his arm with her finger. So, she hadn't forgotten him.

Over a late meal back at the finca they discussed the trip. Luke caught some of the conversation thrown across the long table. They spoke fast in a regional accent he didn't understand and Camilo, although a stranger like Luke, was quickly brought into their pack while Luke remained detached and unconsumed by it. He was able to lose the thread if he chose, realising nothing much was expected of him speech-wise. His birthday was mentioned but he lost the rest.

'How do you know each other, Sofía?' he asked, when there was a break in conversation.

His hostess looked at Felisa and smiled.

'Our mothers,' she said. 'Mine and Felisa's were friends back in Armenia.'

'And are they still?'

'They died,' Felisa said. 'Mine giving birth to me and Sofía's not long after.'

'I'm sorry, I didn't know that.'

'Why would you?' Camilo asked.

'We're used to death here,' Sofía said. 'Felisa tells me that tomorrow you'll go up to the laguna?'

'I'd like that.'

'José will have the mules ready early, then.'

'Apparently, they never break down,' Camilo whispered in Luke's ear, 'although I've never been on one.'

'That's why you'll take the one the children practise on,' Felisa told him.

'How kind.'

She turned to face Luke. 'It's uphill the entire way. We'll take the low road from the town but then pick up the old track that'll take us straight there.'

'Less chance the mules will startle,' José said.

They talked on late into the night, José passing a bottle of aguardiente between them. It was thick and sweet, made mostly of aniseed fermented with alcohol. When Luke stood, the pain in his heel had abated. Felisa and Sofía had their heads together and were talking of events in Bogotá, of Gaitán and the rallies.

'The people will have their voice,' Felisa said, passionately.

'It isn't the same here. We can't afford to.'

'Forgive me, but why?' he asked, interrupting them.

The two women looked up at him.

160

'You shouldn't ask questions,' Sofía said.

'It's OK, Sofía. He's been to the rallies. He saw Gaitán.'

'It's true,' Luke said, 'and I'll never forget it.'

Felisa blushed.

José joined them at the table. 'It's better to be cautious,' he said. 'Suspicion is everywhere. Your friends can quickly become your enemies. We're safe here but at any point, if word got around that we were for land reform, well, there are powerful men with deep pockets here too.' He looked at Camilo.

'But you have so much land,' Camilo said. 'Why would you complain?'

Everyone looked at him.

'I mean, surely you'll lose out if change comes?'

'Why?' Sofía said. 'We work all the land we have, which is more than can be said for those who keep hectares clipped short for... for tennis games.'

'You are right,' Camilo said. 'There are some excellent tennis players in this country.'

'Milo,' Felisa said, cautiously. She looked at Sofía. 'He's teasing you.'

'Felisa knows me too well,' he said, smiling at them.

It was the same winning grin he'd thrown Luke all those months back. It had gained him access to his life for the article, to his friendship too. These people were cautious, though. The night wore on. Camilo managed to get José alone and was trying to get him to explain how he kept the farm running, asking questions about the livestock and the land, and all the while casting glances in Felisa's direction. He looked sorry for earlier, Luke thought, as though he might have overplayed his hand and made things difficult for her. It was fine for him to tease Felisa, but not these people who didn't know him. These people could see through his shabby clothing. He held himself too well. Luke was tired and he still hadn't really been alone with Felisa, only when he'd cut his heel. It had not been his finest moment. Perhaps tomorrow on the mountain there'd be time. He said goodnight to her and to all of them but they were too immersed in their conversation to hear him. He left them like that and slipped away, back down the moonlit corridor to bed.

24

'Happy birthday!' Felisa reached up and kissed him lightly on the cheek. 'That one is for today,' she whispered.

'Thanks,' he replied. Something flashed between them and he had a mind to kiss her properly.

'Sit, please, eat,' Sofia said. She placed a plate of eggs and yellow arepa down on the table and moved Camilo along. Luke sat down and ate. The arepa was still hot from the fire. It was fresh and incredibly good. Camilo and Felisa had already eaten theirs, he noticed.

'José's getting the mules ready,' Camilo said. It was obvious that he was treating the whole expedition as a joke. The statue Felisa had purchased in Guatavita was on the table beside her.

'It's a fertility symbol,' she said.

Sofia emptied more eggs onto his plate and looked at Felisa. 'I can't believe you didn't know.'

Luke chewed and looked at it again. The mouth was more a deep slit, really, surrounded by a pair of fleshy lips and below this, exaggerated breasts and a bulbous middle.

'We put our wishes in here,' Felisa said, signifying the space between the lips. 'So that when we cast it into the lake, Chia will hear them.'

'And we can write anything?' Camilo said, with some interest. 'You won't read it?'

'No one can,' Sofía said, 'unless you smash the thing on the floor.' She grinned at Luke.

'We thought,' Felisa said, turning to him, 'that you might like to go first, because it's your birthday.'

'All right,' he said. 'If that's what you want.'

'There might be something you wish to let go of – you can write that down too.'

'What could Luke possibly have to let go of?' Camilo asked. 'What do you know that I don't?'

'My terrible Spanish, my fear of heights, my appalling dancing...' Luke said.

Camilo shrugged. 'God, how average. Do try to wish for something better than that, Luke.'

'I'll try,' he said, catching Felisa's eye. She looked relieved and so was he, in more ways than one. It was clear she hadn't said a word about what he'd revealed to her, not until then.

Felisa ran off to find paper while Luke finished his breakfast in silence. Today, he was forty. Double the age of the friends who'd gone to Europe to fight. Catherine would be forty now, too. They'd all left for the front and never come back. Forty years had brought him here. In his life, there were things he had seen coming and even things he had not, but which had seemed inevitable afterwards, but his life, thus far in Colombia, fell clear of both categories. He smiled, wondering if it might be possible to let go of the past; at least, that which he had revealed, as Felisa said he could. Perhaps, though, it would make more sense to wish for the future.

After breakfast he left them and went to dress. He still hadn't contributed anything to the list of wishes the others were eager to pen and he told them to go ahead without him. He would decide upon what to include later. Something in the way Felisa had presented it to him made him feel responsible for his contribution. From the open shutters he could see José saddling up the mules. Three had been led from the stables to the courtyard. They were a scrawny-looking herd. He lifted his bag onto the bed and found the shirt he'd worn on the journey up. It had been a mistake to bring only two. Luke took the photograph out of his wallet and looked at it – *Catherine on the Rocks*, his one-time goddess. He would wish to be rid of her.

'Luke?' It was Felisa, calling him from the hall.

'Coming,' he replied.

'We're leaving without you!'

He pocketed the photograph and pushed his bag back under the bed.

After the main road, the mules knew what to do, kicking a path along the familiar dirt track that would take them to the summit. On the highway, they'd travelled in single file. José had said this was best before they'd set off, but here they abandoned formation and Luke found himself alongside Felisa while Camilo cut a path in front.

'You're a natural!' Felisa shouted forward at him.

Camilo didn't reply. She looked different out here. The landscape had changed her. She shouted again and the ears of her mule pricked up. Felisa patted its side gently and they carried on side by side at the pace set by the animals. It was the first time they had been alone on the trip so far.

'Last night,' Luke said. 'I heard you talking about Gaitán.'

'Sofía likes to know what's going on in Bogotá,' Felisa said. 'You understand more Spanish than you let on, don't you?'

'Not enough,' he said. 'Is the Pan-American Conference mentioned at the meetings you go to?'

'It is,' she said, fixing him with a stare, 'but not what's planned for the city afterwards.' Felisa kicked her mule so it moved ahead of Luke's. 'Camilo!'

Luke watched her catch up with the other mule. He felt in his back pocket. The photograph was still there. He was completely decided on what his sacrifice would be. Luke smiled a little to think of Catherine ending her days in the gut of a cheap souvenir.

It was a steady two-hour climb to the top of the mountain. At first, he'd been cautious of them heading out alone without a guide or even José's machete for company. You could never be sure who you might meet. Out here they were easy targets. When nothing happened in the first hour, he relaxed. There were times when he was happy to be alone, watching the landscape as one seeing it for the first time. They passed untouched fields with nothing to spoil their greenness but the odd hut for grazing sheep, outbreaks of trees he didn't recognise, and bearing down on this a cap of endless blue, the shade of which forced him to question whether he had ever really seen the sky until then. Felisa came and went from his side, where they carried on safely inside of other subjects.

'This must be very strange for you,' she said, joining him again. 'I mean, the mules, the landscape, us.'

'You're not strange to me.'

Felisa looked away. 'Will you tell me about England? If it's not painful to speak about it?'

'Yes, if you like. Ask me anything.'

'London. Is it as bad as the newspapers said it was? Bomb damaged, and the people too?' She stopped, as if alarmed by something she had said or was about to say. 'I'm sorry, the way

I express things, after what we spoke about that night, it might not be right.'

'No, it's all right to ask questions. Thank you for not telling Camilo what I told you. I thought it might have cheapened things to swear you to secrecy then. I trusted that you hadn't, and this morning, it was clear to me I'd been right to do that.'

'I know. I understood that,' she said. 'Also, can you imagine, ruining his article?'

'He'd be devastated,' Luke said, laughing too.

'Yes, he would. The truth is that I have great respect for what you did. It takes courage to stand up like that.'

'And stupidity.'

'No. You brush off as a joke something which has pained you, I think.'

'You're very wise to say so.'

'Me? Ha! Not really, perhaps I kept quiet because I was flattered. Perhaps I wondered, why is this celebrated man telling me? Why is this Englishman even looking at me? Me, a nobody – a barely-junior draughtsman. A peasant girl.'

'That's not how I see you.'

They both turned forward to look at Camilo.

'He'll want to know what we're talking about,' Felisa said.

'And I haven't answered your question,' Luke said. 'About London. You asked me about the damage there. Let's say places take a long time to heal. A lot of people lost their lives and sometimes buildings can't recover from that, from the absence of warmth – the people too. I was too young to know it at the time, but the Great War was the one that changed everything.'

'Great War, so it was special?'

'That's just an expression they used afterwards to justify the loss.'

She was watching the horizon.

'And Armenia – what is that like?' he asked. 'I'd like to see it.'

'It's a great mess,' she said.

'I'm sure it's beautiful.'

'It is, but sometimes people can make a place ugly, don't you think?'

'The work on the redesign, Felisa, I'm going to make it a success. It'll be something to be proud of. I'd like to think Gaitán will approve.'

She was quiet for a moment. Their mules had strayed close and they were practically touching. Luke waited to see if she would move away. Camilo wasn't very far in front of them now.

'London is very different to Bogotá,' he said when she didn't. 'But the city isn't everything. I grew up somewhere else.'

'Where?'

'In a small village, west of the city. Nothing much happens there.'

'That's what Quimbaya is like, the area I'm from.'

He nodded. 'Mine is called Liddington and from there, if you head south across the Downs, you'll reach the sea. Have you seen it? The sea?'

She shook her head.

'There's a place off the Dorset coast where the waves are as much a part of the landscape as the earth itself.'

'That's where it differs from Quimbaya, then. The Pacific is a long way west. People don't stray far from where they grew up and so everyone looks inwards. They squabble and fight over the most ridiculous things. You're meant to marry and die there.'

Luke smiled. 'Then it's very similar.'

'If you do leave, there's something wrong with you. It's the people you leave behind who suffer. It's unforgiveable.'

'It's normal to want more.'

'They're good people, though,' she said, perhaps feeling that she owed them more. 'For as long as I can remember, my family have been there, working on the plantations.'

'Growing coffee?'

'Yes, of course,' she said, laughing. 'It's the wealthy landowners who benefit. Most of the crop ends up in big city cafés: New York and London, in your skyscrapers.'

'There aren't any skyscrapers in London, not yet. Somebody should draw them first. Somebody good.'

'Don't tease me, Luke.'

He smiled. 'Is that why you fight for those outside of the city?'

'It isn't funny. I don't understand you sometimes. You claim to take our side, and you have been on that side yourself, but now you work for the men who are against change. Not change that benefits only themselves, but social change. I know you would like to but you can't understand. I wish it was different, that we really were on the same side, but we're not, are we?'

'We are,' he said, loud enough so that even Camilo in front turned. 'Only I understand that the change you're talking about has a price.'

When they were close to the summit, they tethered their mules at a drinking spot and trekked the rest of the distance on foot. Luke was upset. He wanted to talk to her again but Felisa had made it clear that she wouldn't; they couldn't whilst Camilo was close by. This wasn't how he'd imagined the trip at all. Ahead of them and around him the route was densely forest-fringed and wound upwards, seeming to curl back on itself.

'Like a coiled snake,' Camilo said, looking at Felisa.

A bird with a wingspan that actually shut out the sun flew overhead. They all stopped and looked up.

'A condor,' Felisa said, 'sacred and very rare.'

They pushed on and the track upwards suddenly dipped and they were walking downhill, through thicker foliage, until the walking became a run and Luke had to bear backwards so he didn't snowball forward as his bad leg gave way.

'Is this right?' he asked.

'Are you afraid?' she called back.

Felisa led the way with Camilo following and him last. Her hair had come down and as she travelled, it seemed to lift and sway of its own accord, adding to his sense of disorientation. In front of him Camilo pursued her recklessly, so that Luke wondered if they were both under her spell. They went on in silence until Felisa broke cover through the trees and they emerged after her onto the sharp bank of the lake itself. It was enormous, an almost perfect circle, its colour jewel-like – a glassy, emerald hue.

'Could be a meteor, or a sinkhole,' Camilo said.

They picked a path sideways, holding on to branches to steady themselves until they came across a small clearing where it was safe to collapse. They all struggled to catch their breath. Felisa opened her bag and brought out the figure.

'You're not going in?' Camilo asked, horrified.

'Don't worry,' she said, 'Luke is tall, he can throw it – he can probably reach the middle from here.'

'How will we get back?' Luke asked. It would be an almost impossible uphill scramble the way they'd come.

She looked disappointed and went back into her bag. This time she produced a cloth which she placed on the ground and unwrapped. It was a picnic from Sofía made up of chorizo and cold arepa. Felisa sat down and broke a piece off from the cornbread and passed it to Luke.

'I thought you'd be braver,' she said.

Luke tore what remained in half and handed the rest to Camilo. The chorizo followed and the three of them ate in silence. It was hard to swallow. They were almost level with the lake and it was easy to see how it might be thought sacred. It was eerily quiet. He heard a bird call somewhere on the opposite bank and the echo of it skimmed the water as though one bird had become many. It was a place for the ghosts of things, he thought, remembering the photograph. She was wrong about him. He could be brave.

'I have something for the goddess,' he said.

He took the photograph out of his pocket and held it up.

'Luke, you shouldn't,' Camilo said.

'I don't understand,' said Felisa. 'Who is she?'

'It doesn't matter.'

'It's the love of his life,' Camilo said.

Felisa just stared at him.

'Oh, give it here, please,' he said, pulling the figure over.

'Don't!' Felisa reached forward. Luke was faster and had already pushed it through the hole.

'Why did you do that?' she asked, on the brink of tears. 'We'll have to break it.'

'It's my offering,' he said, feeling the panic rise up in him. He hadn't intended for her to see the photograph. He hadn't thought what might happen if she did. 'I thought it was meant to be a sacrifice.'

Felisa cradled the figure and nodded.

'Let me,' Camilo said, reaching over and snatching it from her.

He rose, wiping chorizo grease on his trousers, and shuffled carefully towards the edge of the lake. Camilo leaned backwards and sent the object through the air. It was a good throw. They watched as the little fat figure made it halfway towards the centre before disappearing beneath the surface in a single gulp.

Felisa was quiet on the way back. Her head hung low whenever Luke tried to bring his mule alongside hers and so in the end he left her to it. The sun had peaked and gone and with the coming dusk, the journey felt longer, as though the goddess on the mountain was chewing over her precious offering. When they met the main road, they were blinded by the stationary headlights of a car. The animals didn't startle. José left the truck and came towards them.

'Can you drive it back?' he asked Luke. 'I'll take the mules.'

25

Back at the finca, Luke went straight to his room. Sofía, he'd noticed, had washed and pressed his trousers and shirt and left them hanging on the front of the closet. At the lake, the past had been brought face-to-face with the present. The way Felisa had acted when he'd brought out the photograph, she'd looked at him like he'd deliberately tried to hurt her. He hadn't meant it to be like that, but rather a declaration on his part. Camilo had found the whole thing wildly amusing. He wouldn't have, Luke thought, if he knew what was between them.

'Luke,' Camilo said, coming to the door of the bedroom. 'I'm instructed to tell you to hurry up.'

Luke did as he was asked while Camilo waited outside the room. He took some water from the basin on the sideboard and tried to smooth down his hair. He wasn't in the mood for company but would try to look like he was. He joined Camilo in the corridor. 'Can I ask what this is about?'

'You cannot.' Camilo grinned, leading him towards the kitchen. The room was in darkness.

'Go in,' Camilo said, shoving him from behind.

'Cumpleaños feliz! Happy birthday, Luke!'

Inside of the room, Felisa, Sofía, as well as two couples he didn't recognise, had stopped singing and were staring at him. It was unbearable. Sofía came towards him with a cake thinly spread with candles. He blew them out and was grateful to return the room to darkness again. Someone flicked the switch and the single electric bulb that hung over the table was reintroduced and more candles lit to compensate.

Luke took a deep breath. 'Thank you,' he said, smiling at them all.

'These are friends of ours,' Sofía said.

She put the cake to one side and brought a bubbling pot to the table. They all sat down; Luke in the middle with Camilo and Sofía either side of him. Felisa was opposite and the friends further along. José had missed it. He was still outside with the mules.

'Do you like sancocho?' Sofía asked, serving him first.

They were all hungry and had been waiting, it seemed.

'It's a chicken soup from Armenia,' Felisa mumbled.

It was the first thing she'd said to him since the lake. Luke was handed a bowl of broth – chicken, cassava and sweetcorn. It smelled wonderful. He was hungrier than he'd imagined.

'Thank you, this is too much, though, really.'

Camilo slapped his back again. 'We got you, didn't we?'

'I had no idea.'

Luke looked across at Felisa and smiled. She returned it, her face bright and alive again. Whatever had passed between them at the lake and on the climb had been forgiven, he hoped.

After the meal, two of Sofía's friends produced four-string guitars. The table and benches were cleared and the space turned over for dancing. The men of the group had brought a box of beer up to the finca with them. They handed Luke a full bottle each time his current one ran low. It was warm and heavy, but it was the aguardiente he wanted. Back in Bogotá he'd developed a taste for it. He told them this and they laughed. José, back from finishing off with the mules, ran to a cupboard and returned with a jug of the aniseed drink. The way to drink it, they told him, was as a shot after the beer. One of the two men picked up the guitar he'd brought with him and played. This man had a black eye. When he caught Luke staring, his expression hardened. The man's wife came between them with the other guitar and started playing. The tune was simple and Spanish in sound as the strings were plucked to set the rhythm. Luke was pulled to his feet by Sofía and shown how to move through the steps. He was glad for the aguardiente, making clumsy work of what she showed him. Felisa's mood, he saw, had lightened. She was watching him and laughing but he didn't mind. She was asked to dance by Sofía's other friend. Camilo approached the last available woman, so that, except for José, they were all doing it. Although he was a terrible dancer, Luke relaxed into it. After the song finished they threw their hands in the air and glasses were refilled before the music started up again and Luke found himself with a different partner. He saw Camilo now danced with Felisa. Camilo danced with confidence, of course. He'd been born to that. They looked well together. The couple moved as one, like water slipping over a fall, quite differently to how Luke held Sofía's friend, whose name, confusingly, was also Sofía. The evening wore on, partners were changed, and more aguardiente was drunk so that packed together as they were, they seemed to get drunk off each other. Eventually he took his turn with Felisa.

She was quiet when they moved close.

Luke took her hands. 'I'm terrible, as you've seen.'

She laughed. 'Just follow me.'

She showed him what to do and he found her a better

teacher than Sofía. Perhaps, he thought, I'm just paying more attention.

When the song ended they went straight into another one. Luke forgot himself. He forgot all of them but her. He didn't want the dancing to end and he hated it usually, the performance of it. He'd always felt too tall for movement. The music slowed and so did they.

'You arranged all of this, Felisa, didn't you?'

'I had some help.'

'From Camilo?'

'He admires you, Luke.'

'He doesn't know me.'

She looked up at him. 'Do I?'

It was a challenge and she expected a response. They'd stopped moving but Felisa was swaying slightly. He realised she was as drunk as he was. God help him, he wanted to kiss her. She might regret it but he wouldn't. Did she know him, though? Luke opened his mouth to speak but before he could answer, the song was dropped for something faster.

'Oh,' she said, stepping on his foot.

'It's all right.'

'I don't know this one, I'm confused.'

Felisa looked upset. They abandoned the dance but didn't break apart.

'Felisa, come on!' It was Camilo. He grabbed her hands from Luke's and twirled her off and into space. Luke watched them go.

They danced on, all of them, until he was sure the night must have ended and a new day begun. Later, he found himself stuck with one of the Sofías. She'd forgotten he didn't speak Spanish fluently. It was nauseating trying to translate when drunk. He'd lost count of how much he'd had since that last dance with Felisa. It must have been a lot because he was still dancing, but it wasn't fun any more. The words in his head just didn't make sense, not in Spanish or English. He grabbed José as he passed, insisting he take his place. He needed air.

Luke stumbled outside. The night was sobering and cool compared to the heat of the kitchen. He took a deep breath and then another, filling his lungs with the cool, quiet night. No more aguardiente, please, he thought. He tripped across the courtyard to the stable block and leaned over one of the half-opened doors. Luke peered in. He thought he recognised the mule inside as the one he'd ridden to the lake.

'Hello,' he said.

The mule turned its head towards the wall.

'Is the conversation any better out here?' It was Camilo.

'They only speak Spanish,' Luke said, turning to face him. 'I'm drunk.'

'Come with me.'

'And Felisa?'

'Inside. Come on, Luke; let's walk.'

Camilo waited for him before leading the way around to the front of the finca. When they got there, they sat down together on the front steps. From here, the party at the back of the house sounded like a wireless in another apartment. Luke looked up at the stars, but they were a white-hot blur. The drive stretched before them and, surrounding this, a canopy of lifeless trees. Beyond it all was the wide world, he thought, picturing the journey that would take him there in three days' time.

'This place,' he said, throwing his arms in front of him, 'has been slowly creeping up on me whilst my back has been turned.'

'What's that?' Camilo said, looking at him strangely.

Luke couldn't tell if Camilo was drunk too. This place, it brought back memories of another dark time, after the trial, when he'd been shut away from the world and forgotten.

'I've spent a lot of time on farms, that's all,' he said.

'You?'

'My father owned one. I was meant to run it.' Luke laughed at himself.

'Why didn't you?'

'I never went back. Not after the war. I was done with farm work then.'

'I think it's romantic.'

'Liar.'

Camilo shrugged and lit a cigarette.

'Can I have one?'

Camilo lit another and passed it to Luke. 'You belong to the city.'

'I had a brother, younger than me. He would have done it.'

Camilo opened his mouth to speak.

'Before you ask,' Luke said, 'he was killed too. Neither of us went back after the war.'

'You and Felisa have that in common.'

'What?'

'Farms and flight.' Camilo lifted his free hand in the air as though it were soaring away.

'It's different,' Luke said.

'Yes, I bet your mother didn't disappear.'

'Felisa said she died.'

'For her, she did.'

'What happened?'

Camilo ground his cigarette beneath his boot. 'It's in the past now,' he said. 'I had to pay her father to get her away from that life.'

'You bought her freedom?' Luke didn't feel right. 'Does she know?'

'No, and she mustn't. Don't look so shocked, Luke. Do you

think he would have let her go? She was better than all of them and he knew it.'

'She talks as though she left freely.'

'She did.'

'And if she returned?'

'I won't allow it.'

Luke looked at him. He was drunk and he didn't like the way the conversation was going. Things he was only becoming aware of now were finding their way to the surface. Drink did that, he thought, it brought clarity.

'And just what are you getting out of this arrangement?'

Camilo laughed. 'It isn't like that.'

'Then what is it like?'

'Luke, we're friends, you and I, aren't we?'

'If you like.'

'Well, Felisa and I are very good friends.'

'The fucking kind?'

Camilo was on him, his face twisted and close. Too close. Luke was pinned to the porch with Camilo's right knee bearing down on his lower abdomen. The pain was absolute; sobering even. Luke pushed back against him and Camilo was sent with some force down the steps. He landed in the dirt, crying out as his head made contact with the filthy surface. Luke stood up and leapt towards him. He stopped, just in time. On the ground beneath his feet, the boy curled up pitifully into a ball, as though expecting more. He was crying.

'What's wrong with you?' Felisa screamed from behind Luke.

She must have come looking for them. She ran towards Camilo and pulled him up. Luke stumbled backwards.

'It's nothing, Felisa.' Camilo coughed, letting her help him up. He wasn't crying now. 'We're drunk. We've been very foolish, haven't we, Luke?'

Luke tried to hold himself upright, tugging at his crumpled shirt. 'We have,' he said, unable to catch his breath.

'You should know better!' Felisa cried, taking hold of Camilo under one arm.

'You're right,' he said, standing back so they could pass.

'How could you, Luke?' she asked, but he didn't know. It was between them. Him and Camilo. Luke followed them around to the back of the house. When they reached the door beside the stable block he stopped. The sound of the party was louder here. He couldn't face them, any of them.

'I'll say goodnight here,' he said.

'You won't say goodbye to the others?' Felisa asked. She looked so disappointed.

'Will you say it for me?' He held his hand out to Camilo. 'I'm sorry, for what I said. Too much aguardiente.'

Camilo took it. 'Goodnight, Luke.'

He stood there and watched them walk arm-in-arm back to the sound of music and laughter.

26

_____

Luke woke up the next morning wondering how he'd come to end up on top of the sheets, fully clothed and with one shoe on. He lifted his head in search of the other and saw it lying on its side against the far wall. Camilo's bed hadn't been slept in. Luke lowered his head and closed his eyes. The last time he'd felt this awful, he'd been a university man a long, long time ago. This new decade of his life had begun badly. The party and dancing he could remember but the rest of the night had already slipped into the abyss. These Colombians know how to drink, he thought, rising. His clothes were crumpled and sleep-worn. He had a pain in his side which ached as though bruised. He stood beside the bed and stripped down to his underwear, stumbling about in the shadows for what he had worn yesterday to travel up the mountain. Once he was dressed, he went over to the window and pressed his face against the wall. Its coolness was a welcome reprieve. Last night it had been cool outside too. He remembered the scene. It came back to him – the pain in his side caused by Camilo's knee trying to crush him like some unwelcome insect. But what had he said to start this row? Luke couldn't unpick it, whether he had been wrong, or Camilo. The truth seemed lost. One thing was certain, he couldn't stay in the room forever. They were probably all at breakfast. It embarrassed him to think they might suspect he was hiding from them. That Camilo might think he was hiding from him. Luke took a deep breath and peeled himself away from the wall.

When he entered the kitchen they all looked up.

Sofía grinned. 'Do you think you'll want breakfast?'

'Just coffee, thanks.'

Luke sat down across from Felisa and Camilo. The room smelled stale.

'How are your ribs?' Camilo asked.

'Sore.'

Sofía handed him a cup.

'I don't understand it,' Felisa said.

She looked angry but sad, as though something else had happened that he hadn't been able to remember yet.

'Yes, arguing like schoolboys. What was it about?' Sofía asked.

'A test of strength,' Camilo said.

'You men.'

'Felisa stopped us before we really hurt each other, though, didn't you?' Camilo turned and kissed her clean on the mouth. She looked caught, frightened, but didn't try to move away, not immediately. Luke froze.

'It must be this place,' Luke said, addressing Sofía. 'One of your friends had a black eye last night.'

Sofía's face darkened. 'No, Luke. That fighting is real.'

Luke waited for her to continue but she didn't say anything else. No one, it seemed, had an appetite for that conversation.

'We thought we might go back into Guatavita today,'

Camilo said. He slipped his arm around Felisa's shoulder. Luke forced himself to look at them.

'I've nothing clean to wear.'

'I'll ask José,' Sofía said. 'You can borrow something of his.'

It would be out of the question to join them now. 'It's all right, you two go.'

'Sofía, find him something,' Camilo said. 'He's just being polite.'

'It's too hot in here,' Felisa said, shrugging Camilo off and rising.

Camilo met Luke's eye and smiled again. 'You are a terrible drunk, Luke Vosey.'

Luke went back to his room to wash and to hide. Camilo had slept in Felisa's room and in her bed too, no doubt. Overnight, things between the two of them had changed; things which seemed inevitable, really, if he chose to think about them. They're about the same age, he thought. He was so much older. What had he thought would happen? A wave of nausea hit him and he ran to the bathroom. Felisa, then, was gone. He was sick and glad of it. It was a distraction from how he really felt.

While he was away from the room, Sofía had laid out trousers and a shirt that must have belonged to José, on the bed. Luke undressed. He put the new outfit on. The trousers were too short by far and so he swapped them again for the ones he'd worn up the mountain. These were accompanied by an animal smell, something caught between life and death which almost made him vomit a second time. The shirt would do and over this he threw his jacket. He'd have to find a way to return it. He was going back to the city. It was decided. He couldn't stay there. Not with what had happened. He found his bag and put his dirty clothing and few belongings inside. Luke checked the room once more and went along the corridor to tell them. The group was outside, waiting for him beside the truck.

'We're only going into town,' Felisa said, seeing his bag.

'Actually,' he said, addressing only her, 'I'm needed back in Bogotá. I'm going to have to leave you.'

'Impossible,' Camilo said, walking over. 'Who can contact you here?'

'I've known about it for some time.'

'Is it because of the party?' Felisa asked.

'No,' he said, lying for both of them. He turned to Camilo. 'I've left money for train tickets for both of you on the kitchen table. I hope it's enough.'

'And you say you've known the whole time you've been here?'

'As I said—' he looked at him '—it's only fair I pay the return trip. I'll join you as far as Guatavita.'

'Nonsense,' Sofía said. 'José will run you up to Sesquilé now.'

'I'm so sorry to put you out,' he told her, walking over to the truck. 'It's unavoidable.'

José opened the passenger door. 'Jump in.'

Luke turned to his hostess. 'Thank you, Sofía, for everything.'

'Go,' she said, offering her cheek to be kissed. 'You'll miss the midday train otherwise.'

He climbed into the vehicle.

'See you in Bogotá,' he called back to them as it pulled away.

In the wing mirror, he watched the two women lock arms and disappear back inside. It was only Camilo who stood there. Luke watched him in the glass. On the dirt track he didn't budge and Luke could sense he was trying to work things out; to work him out. Let him wonder, Luke thought. He knew that he had to go. That he couldn't stay to hear the night spoken of. That seeing them together, seeing Camilo's happiness, was excruciating. He couldn't stay for that – not having to look at Felisa's face. The truck turned a corner and both Camilo and the finca were lost to him. He squeezed his eyes shut and held on tight. Guatavita might become a place he'd be able to forget, if he tried.

27

The trip to Guatavita seemed another lifetime ago and like it had happened to someone else. The date for Felisa and Camilo's return had come and gone, and he hadn't heard from either of them. He wondered how permanent their absence might be, whether Felisa would be back to work on the project. The events of that final night came back to him at times, like a half-remembered dream. And like a dream he dismissed the more distressing aspects as unreal. As Christmas approached, Luke threw himself into his work, bringing forward the lease on the new office. It was on a street called Calle del Divorcio, which would have been funny any other time. It was also only a block away from the Palacio Liévano where Felisa and he had met with the deputy mayor. Perhaps the new office was too close to what was coming, he thought, when he stood outside of it for the first time. It consisted of a couple of furnished rooms – an office and reception for Telma. It was a reasonable space in which two people could comfortably work. Both rooms were dark and dusty and had been cheap because of it. The electrics were a nightmare and he almost ended his life on more than one occasion trying to mend them. After a couple of days in the place by himself, he contacted Telma and practically begged her to start before Christmas. He hadn't needed to worry about disturbing her. She'd been waiting for him to call, she said. Her sister's son was driving her crazy. He hadn't realised she didn't have a family of her own. She arrived the next day and set about putting the office and him in order. She even bought new plants and the two of them settled in nicely. The only thing missing, he realised, was Felisa.

His phone rang.

'Telma?'

'Señor Draper is here. Shall I show him in?'

The door burst open and Karl stood before him. Out in the hall, Telma still had the receiver to her ear and looked furious.

'It's all right,' Luke called to her.

She rose and closed the door behind their guest.

'She looks familiar,' Karl said, taking a seat. 'I went to your apartment first.'

'I sent the new address.'

'Didn't get it.' He lit a fresh cigar. 'Mrs Draper's taken to opening everything. She thinks I've another woman.'

'You?'

'I know, more like women, hey?' He leaned forward. 'How was your trip with that little draughtswoman, Melissa, wasn't it?'

'Felisa. We were a group actually.'

'Right.' Karl eyed him suspiciously. 'Anyway, come to tell you the board wants to meet you.'

'The Pan-American committee?'

'Yes and no – Osorio's people, those in charge of the city's coffers. They want to shake hands with the man behind the plans for the centre. While you've been away, they've taken a good look and like what they've seen. And that article the young Osorio wrote – I read it and so have they. Osorio's given copies to everyone. Seems you're a bit of a celebrity now.'

'Am I?' Luke asked. He didn't want to think about Camilo or any Osorio right now. 'I don't think I can, sorry, Karl.'

'Wrong answer, Vosey.' Karl puffed on his cigar without drawing breath. 'Make this easy for me, Luke. How's it going to look if I go back without you?'

'What do you mean? When is it?'

'Tonight.'

That evening, Luke found himself outside the Jockey Club across the street from *El Tiempo*. There was no avoiding Camilo, it seemed. Luke had heard about the Jockey Club. It was where the politicians met if they wanted to talk off the record. It was where the rich went if they wanted to talk to politicians, off the record. It was where everyone met, if they wanted to talk about Gaitán. Gaitán had been blackballed, he'd heard. He wasn't a member. 'It's the only place they talk freely,' Camilo had said when Luke had asked about it pre-Guatavita, pre-Felisa too. That evening, Karl had practically escorted him across town and now inside, Luke found himself behind closed doors away from the main club rooms. They were the last to arrive.

'You said eight, Karl,' he said, shaking hands with the men as quickly as Karl was able to introduce them.

'They've been here all day,' Karl whispered back, 'turning over proposal after proposal. Let me get you a drink, Vosey.'

He led Luke away from the group and over to a small bar which had been set up for the purpose.

Karl poured two generous whisky and sodas and handed one

to Luke. 'See that one over there?' He pointed at an elderly man across the room.

'Yes.'

'Judge and philanthropist.'

'And?'

'Makes things happen, or not happen, depending on how charitable he's feeling.'

The judge caught Luke's eye and raised his glass. Luke smiled.

'And the others?'

'Lawyers, politicians, a colonel,' Karl said, singling them out in turn, 'businessmen, like me.' He smiled. 'And I think somewhere we have a pig farmer.'

'Where's Osorio?'

'No, no, Luke. I manage his involvement. Do you think he's got time for this lot?'

Luke was relieved. Karl led him back towards the main group who had sat down at a table set for dinner. He took a seat between Karl and a lawyer called Pino. Steaming bowls of fish soup were brought out. They made polite conversation and ate. After the soup came seasoned lamb and new potatoes.

'You might not know this,' said Pino, addressing Luke. 'But your English houses, I organised the sale of the land from the Jesuits to the oil company.'

'Really?'

Pino reached across and filled Luke's wine glass. 'It's as I said. There's nothing in this city that hasn't been chewed over at this table first.'

'So I have you to thank?'

'How so?'

'If the deal had failed, I wouldn't be here.'

'Oh, that would never have happened.' Pino smiled, popping a thin slice of lamb into his mouth.

'Señor Vosey, you held the rank of Captain, I believe?' It was the man Karl had introduced as Colonel Martínez. He was seated across the table from Luke and so when he spoke, most of the group stopped to listen.

'That's what the article says.' Luke put his knife and fork down.

'Tell us, how did you get the common man to fight?'

'Easy,' Luke said. 'We took away his right to choose.'

'That's one way,' said Pino. 'But it must have its foundations in the law.'

'The war's behind us now,' Luke said, pouring himself more wine. 'And it's my belief that they'd have gone anyway.'

'Why? Surely it's madness to suggest it.' Pino blinked.

'Their homes were at stake.'

'You didn't fight, did you?' It was Martinez again.

'And neither did I,' Karl said, 'too much to take care of on the home front. Wasn't that right, Vosey?'

Luke smiled. 'Yes, Karl, although we were in quite different lines.'

'Señor Draper's talents are well known to us,' Martinez said.

The plates were cleared and glasses refilled. Luke couldn't recall if this was his third or fourth. Was he here to talk business, or wasn't he? Someone must be in charge.

'Karl said you'd looked over the plans I filed?' Luke said, addressing all of them. No one spoke. 'So, which one of you asked me to come here?'

The men sat up straight. That had their attention.

'I did.'

Luke turned to find Gabriel Osorio standing behind him.

'Don't get up, gentlemen,' Osorio said.

A seat was found and everyone edged along to make room. It was placed next to Luke's.

'Tell me, how was your little excursion to the countryside?'

'Enlightening.'

Osorio nodded. 'I hope my nephew wasn't tiresome. I still think of him as a boy.'

Coffee was brought to the table.

'Cream?' Osorio asked, offering to serve Luke himself.

'No, thank you.'

'The Pan-American Conference will be here soon, gentlemen.' Osorio addressed the table. 'The mayor has now agreed to Mr Vosey's excellent plans, which just leaves the citizens themselves. We need them compliant.'

'In agreement, you mean?' Luke asked.

Osorio laughed, although it hadn't been a joke. 'Just the ones who won't listen to reason. A small faction: Los Guaches, dedicated to Gaitán and his preposterous vanity.' He yawned. 'I'm so tired of his simple ways.'

'They're more than a small faction, I'd say.'

'Are they, Karl?' Osorio turned to face him.

'Just something I heard,' Karl said, going red in the face.

'These fanatical lectures…' Osorio continued.

'I've been,' Luke said.

'Then you'll have seen. Nothing but socialism dressed up as liberalism.'

'Your nephew didn't seem to think so.'

'The boy has strange ideas,' Osorio said. 'But still, he should be careful.'

When the party broke up, the judge and a couple of others he'd forgotten the names of asked to speak to Osorio alone. He excused himself and so Luke rose and went over to Karl.

'Glad you came now, aren't you, Luke?'

'What makes you say that?'

Karl frowned. 'Careful, Vosey. Your English sense of humour will only get you so far.'

'I've come to tell you I'm heading home.'

'OK. Have the girl out front call you a car.'

Luke put a hand on Karl's shoulder. 'Get her to call you one too.'

28

It was Christmas Eve and Luke was glad to be alone whilst the city celebrated. Telma he'd had to argue out the door of the office. They'd shut up early; there was no one around to receive phone calls when tables were being laid and whole families squeezed around them. Telma insisted he join her at her sister and nephew's for the meal, but he suspected he'd leave with a new apprentice if he did. He'd enjoyed walking back through the empty city to his apartment knowing there'd be no one there when he arrived. There was the bottle of whisky from Karl, three plates of food from Señora Rojas and the wireless to keep him company. Felisa, he thought, was probably with Camilo. She was definitely with Camilo. He thought of Rocío then. He'd never returned when he said he would. She couldn't have expected much from him, he knew, but it didn't sit right with him, not when he said he'd visit. He stopped in the street. Is that why he was thinking of her? What did it matter now, he thought, changing direction.

It was a fifteen-minute walk to the old house in Las Cruces. From the outside it looked pretty shut up but he knew better than to believe that. Luke crossed the street and opened the outer door. He stepped inside. The interior was gloomy and still. Perhaps even the inhabitants of this household were able to return to their families, he thought, suddenly dreading the idea of being alone now he'd opened himself up to other possibilities.

'Who's there?' Rocío asked.

'It's me, Luke.'

She came forward, out of the darkness. Yes, it was her.

'Luke!' Her face broke into a wide smile. 'What are you doing here?'

'I was just walking by and…' He trailed off. It was a pathetic sentence. 'Are you alone?'

'I am,' she said, coming towards him. 'The other girls have taken the little ones and the mistress is sleeping. She won't wake now, not after what she's had.'

'Can you leave?'

'Are we going out?'

She looked excited.

'My housekeeper has left me a feast and I can't very well eat it alone.'

She crept closer. 'And you want to share it with Rocío, Papi?'

'Are you coming or not?' he asked. Perhaps this hadn't been a good idea after all.

'All right, all right,' she said. 'Wait here.'

He went back outside to wait for her on the street. It was a foolish thing to do in a rough part of town where he didn't look local. Rather than feeling absolved for his earlier abandonment of her, Luke felt more alone than ever. He'd have been better off approaching Christmas solo. Now he'd have to entertain all of Rocío's expectations too. At least she didn't keep him waiting long. When she appeared, she was modestly dressed in a plain skirt and wool jumper. She wasn't wearing any make-up, he noticed, and looked better for it.

'My night off,' she said, registering his surprise.

'Shall we?' he said, offering his arm.

She slipped hers into his and the two crossed the street together. Luke paid for a taxi to take them the distance to his apartment.

Once inside, Rocío set about laying the table and preparing the food left out by Señora Rojas. Luke offered to help but she shooed him away. She seemed to understand where everything was.

'I forgive you, of course,' she called out to him from the kitchen, 'for not coming that time. It was your birthday, wasn't it?'

'How did you know that?'

She came into the room with plates. 'You told me.'

He couldn't remember doing that.

'Some friends had a mad idea to take me away.'

He poured whisky into two tumblers and handed her one.

'Happy Christmas,' he said, raising his.

She went up on her toes and kissed him on the mouth.

'Happy Christmas, Luke.'

They had everything they needed, Señora Rojas had seen to that. Luke pulled out a chair for Rocío. With her knees she pushed out the one beside hers, but Luke rounded the table and sat down in the seat opposite.

'Let me,' he said, taking her plate and serving from the first of the dishes. It contained rice, and the other two, boiled pork and then a mixed salad of papaya and leaves.

'Thank you,' Rocío said, taking her plate.

She waited for him to fill his own before raising her wine glass.

'What shall we drink to?' Luke asked.

'Loved ones.'

'To those we love.'

They drank deep.

'I was surprised to find you alone tonight,' Luke said.

'Why?' Rocío picked up her fork. 'My parents died years ago and I have no aunts and uncles worth speaking of.'

'Me neither,' he said. 'I'm alone now too.'

'Oh, I'm not that. I've a brother,' she said. 'But he hasn't been seen in years.'

Luke filled her wine glass. 'Where is he now?'

'South of Bogotá, last time I heard. Even if he knew where I was, he wouldn't come looking for me.'

'It's his loss.'

Rocío laughed and raised a hand to her mouth. 'Do you think he's ashamed of me?'

'No, I...'

'Luke, that's not it. His business is much worse than mine.'

'Worse, how?'

Rocío's eyes narrowed. 'Men pay him to do things they'd rather not do themselves.'

Luke nodded. 'We need more wine.'

'My goodness, have we almost finished the bottle?'

'I've another,' he said, rising.

Luke stayed away longer than he needed to. Rocío and her brother both worked in the shadows, she'd said so herself. How many like him were there, willing to spill blood in exchange for a few notes? Luke uncorked the new bottle. He returned from the kitchen and filled Rocío's glass before topping up his own.

'This one tastes expensive,' she said.

'It's the same as the last.'

'I know.' She looked unsure, he thought, watching her eyes flit about the room. 'You have interesting tastes.' She gestured to the pile of magazines on the table end.

'*Jornada*? A friend lent them to me.'

'He has no real power, not outside of the city.'

'Gaitán?'

Rocío nodded. 'But he wants to help all women. Even me.'

'I'm pleased to hear it.'

'That's what they say. All the girls talk about him. What he'd be like. I'd know how to stop his tongue!'

Her foot found Luke's leg beneath the table.

'Who do you hear talking about him, other than the girls?'

'The politicians all talk,' she said impatiently, giving up on his thigh. 'I do read the papers, Luke – Spanish as well as English – anything that gets left behind.' A blotch of red crept into her cheek. 'It's how I learned.'

After they'd eaten, they moved to the sitting room. Luke took the armchair and Rocío the sofa. It had been a long and pleasant meal. He was glad she had joined him in the end. He was glad he'd gone looking for her. Rocío rose and went to the bathroom. He looked over at the plates, still piled high with the food they couldn't manage. He would go into town and buy Señora Rojas something nice to say thank you, he thought, leaning back and closing his eyes.

'I'm so full,' Rocío said, returning.

There was a party going on in one of the apartments below. He could hear it, rising up through the floorboards.

'Luke, did you hear me?'

He opened his eyes. Rocío was standing over him. She smiled and dropped to her knees.

'I don't think you listen at all,' she said, finding the buttons on his trousers.

He took hold of her wrists gently. 'I don't want you to do that,' he said.

'Is it broken? I can fix it.'

She was drunk.

'No, Rocío. Just friends tonight.'

She shrugged but didn't rise. Rocío sprawled out at his feet and closed her eyes. Why hadn't he, Luke thought. The music in the flat below grew louder. It was just a moment, but he closed his eyes too. Then Rocío screamed. He opened his eyes to see Felisa standing in the room. She was looking at the table. At them.

'I didn't know it was unlocked,' she whispered.

'What are you doing here?' Luke asked.

'Otherwise I wouldn't have…'

Rocío laughed. She was still sitting on the floor at his feet. Why wouldn't she get up?

'I'll call you a taxi,' he said, looking down at her.

'For me, or her?'

He looked up, but Felisa had already gone.

'Wait here,' he said, running over to the door and pulling it closed behind him.

'Felisa?' he called, afraid of not finding, or finding her. She hadn't gone far. Out in the corridor, he found her slumped low on the top step. He approached slowly and sat down.

'Why did you come here?'

'I didn't want you to be alone,' she said.

'She's only a friend,' he said, because it was partly true.

Felisa was quiet.

'And you're alone tonight?' he asked.

Felisa nodded. He couldn't bring himself to ask her anything else. Luke rose and offered his hand. 'Come on,' he said.

Inside the apartment, Rocío had picked herself up off the floor and was now draped across the sofa. 'Hello,' she said, addressing Felisa.

'Hello.'

'Have you eaten?' Luke asked her. 'Can I take your coat?'

Felisa looked again at the table and shook her head. 'I

shouldn't have come. I'm sorry. I want to go home. Will you call me a taxi? I've missed the last streetcar.'

'No, don't go,' he said. If she left like this, he was sure he'd never see her again. 'Please, have something. You have to stay.' He picked up a clean glass and filled it with wine. 'Here.'

'I don't want it, Luke.'

'I'll take it,' Rocío said, rising. She took the glass and swallowed. 'Should I stay too?' she asked, looking at Felisa. 'She's pretty.'

The two women looked at him.

'Perhaps it's best if you went, both of you. We can talk tomorrow,' he said, addressing Felisa.

He ordered two taxis and sent them off in opposite directions. Rocío looked furious when he'd bundled her into hers, as though robbed of something she couldn't yet measure. Felisa went willingly. He didn't blame her. She had found him with another woman. In Guatavita she'd been with Camilo, though. He'd wanted to mention the new office, to say she could come whenever she chose, there was a desk there waiting for her, but couldn't bear the thought of mixing this night with the days he hoped would follow. He led her to her car silently and handed the driver an extra note, as if this might alleviate some of his guilt.

He rose early the next day, dressed and left the apartment. He made his way down a deserted Seventh Avenue and onto Plaza de Bolívar where he boarded one of the few trams that stuck to the timetable over Christmas. He was going to see Felisa at any cost. He was going to put things straight. He hadn't slept at all and was grossly hungover. Perhaps he should have shaved, presenting a better version of himself than the one she'd seen last night. It was too late for all that now. He stifled a yawn picked up from a man seated across from him. The tram reached Tres Esquinas. He jumped off and walked the couple of blocks to her building, trusting his instincts to get him there. He hadn't been back to the neighbourhood since the raid. He could smell it though, the remnants of violence from that day. It was a lazy form of malice. On these streets you'd be killed for no reason other than the turn in someone else's mood.

He reached Felisa's apartment block. It was as he'd imagined it would look by day, crumbling and, by some miracle, still standing. He went up to the door and knocked hard. No one came. He tried the handle. It was locked. He looked up at the window she'd said was hers and understood she wasn't there. There was no way of knowing for sure – her room was on the second floor – but he knew. He hadn't expected her not to be there because it's where he'd asked the taxi to take her.

29

Christmas came and went without Felisa. On the eve of Osorio's party Luke pulled himself out of his malaise and went to a barber. He returned to the apartment riding high on the pretence that he'd changed. To add to this, he'd also had his tuxedo pressed and it felt new again against his skin. Señora Rojas' attempts to ply him with larger portions at dinnertime had paid off and the suit fit better than it ever had. He stood in front of the bathroom mirror and adjusted the necktie. Camilo would be there tonight. Would Felisa have mentioned her visit? Luke worked his cufflinks into place. Something told him she wouldn't have.

He hired a car to take him to Osorio's. As it pulled away from his apartment block he relaxed. It felt good to leave the city behind, as it had before. On the streets, the New Year's Eve festivities had begun. From the window, he watched a young couple chase each other down the street followed by the pop of cheap, homemade fireworks. When the car slowed, he saw two old men embrace. I'm fine in here, he thought, not sure if he meant the car, the starched tux or some other border. It didn't pay to get too involved. Look what had happened with Felisa when he had. In Osorio's world, wrongs were settled in currency, not conversation. He could guess at where the money for Osorio's project had come from and he'd probably be right. By signing up for the work on the centre, he'd already aligned himself with their way of thinking.

The car rolled into the grounds of the hacienda and stopped some distance from the house. There was no trouble getting past the guard on the gate tonight, although that was as far as they did get. The drive was jammed.

'It's all right, I'll walk,' Luke said, opening the door.

The air was fresh and he inhaled it like medicine. The hacienda glistened, more so than before, illuminated by thousands of tiny low-level lights that made the entire building look as if it was levitating. Perhaps it was, Luke thought, Osorio was capable of many tricks. As he got closer, he could see the entrance to the inner courtyard too, glowing, like the open jaw of a golden snake. The serpent's mouth pulsed with people and it made him afraid to approach it after his recent weeks spent in near solitude. Somewhere on the grounds he heard a dog howl. Luke looked about for Osorio, remembering the mutt from last time. The cry came again, but it was more a whimper this time. It was coming from behind the house. Luke changed course and headed towards it. The rear of the hacienda was unlit. It took his eyes a while to adjust to the darkness and when they did it was a forest of tall trees he saw, running off into the night. On the edge of the forest was a low hut that could have been a pen or a workman's shed. Luke heard the dog whimpering again. It was inside.

'I think you must be lost?'

A man he'd missed stepped out from among the trees. He recognised him from last time.

'Is that your animal in there?'

'It might be.' The man smiled.

'I used to have a dog,' Luke said, 'a pet.'

'Neron!' the man shouted, running forward. As if on cue the dog appeared from the hut and launched itself towards Luke. A thick chain, wrapped like a noose around his neck, stopped him from making contact. He snarled and bit wildly at the space between them. Luke, backed up against the hacienda, had nowhere else to go. The man took a pole that had been lying against the side of the hut and beat the dog until he backed down. Luke didn't hang around. He needed to find a drink. The man's laughter followed him back around the house and up the front steps of the hacienda.

'Luke.'

It was Osorio and he looked genuinely pleased to see him.

'I thought I saw you arrive but then you vanished again.'

'I'm afraid I got lost,' Luke said, extending his hand.

'We need more lights, perhaps.' Osorio smiled. 'Come, there are many friends here you should meet.'

He led Luke inside. Even for the host it was hard to get through the crowd of people, packed together against the papered walls and fine furniture. It was like the time at the opera, Luke thought, recognising some of them from that night. He passed Pino, the lawyer, and recalled a few others from the Jockey Club, picking them out with slim smiles. He thought again of the dog called Neron. Was he here to protect the likes of Pino, to keep them safe? The way the crowd pressed and squeezed Osorio, it might have been the other way around.

'Here.' Osorio handed Luke a glass of champagne. 'Most of the city has come, you see.'

He led him down the lit passageway and into the courtyard. The fountain had been turned off and covered by a platform. It was being used as the base for an eight-tiered cake. Around its sides the year, 1948, had been iced in cursive script.

'Quite the party,' Luke said, sipping the cool liquid. 'Thank you for inviting me.'

'Luke,' Osorio said, taking him by both shoulders. 'You're one of us now. No more pleasantries.'

'If you say so.'

'Will you make yourself at home?'

The grip on Luke's shoulders was firm. 'Yes,' he said, hoping this might free him.

Osorio smiled and let go. Those in the passageway recognised their host and went forward to claim him. Osorio turned just once and caught Luke's eye. He shrugged, as if to say, what can I do? Luke watched until he disappeared, swallowed whole by his guests.

The courtyard was more naturally lit than the rest of the house. Luke looked at the people gathered there. He didn't recognise any of them. A passing waiter filled his empty glass and Luke sat down on the bench he'd shared with Karl on his last visit. Where was Karl tonight? He hadn't seen him.

'Hello, Luke.'

'Camilo.'

Camilo sat down beside him. He looked tired, like a schoolboy who had stayed up late studying. Despite the events in Guatavita, Luke had missed him. It seemed perverse, but he couldn't hate Camilo for what he felt. For loving Felisa. If they stuck to politics, maybe they'd be OK. 'You've been working late again, I can tell.'

'Always,' Camilo said, being handed a glass. 'Happy Christmas, New Year, and anything else we can consolidate,' he said, raising it to Luke's.

'Salud.'

They both looked up. A woman standing perilously close to the cake was saved by her friend and now they were shrieking over what might have been.

'Has there been any progress in government?' Luke asked. 'Even in Guatavita, you could sense it.' He took a deep breath. 'The tension, I mean.'

'There's been nothing. They can't control it. Not even Gaitán can reach outside of the city to stem the flow of violence.' Camilo lit a cigarette. 'A few days after you left, one of Sofía's friends from the party was murdered. Showed up face down one morning in the centre of town.'

'The guitar player with the black eye?'

Camilo shrugged. 'Probably.'

'How did you know he'd been murdered?'

'Hard to stab yourself in the back. All his fingers were broken too, the local paper said. God, the women! They were very shaken up. Luckily, I was there.' Camilo grinned. 'I suppose it could have been the guitar player, on account of the fingers.'

Luke swallowed. 'And the president – Ospina?'

'He doesn't care. He's preoccupied by the coming conference. Did I tell you how much money he's given to Gómez's department to paint the city?' He looked again at the two women who had spotted them too.

'How much?'

'Four million pesos.'

'I bet the people don't like that.'

'Why should they? They're pinched harder than ever.'

'So why do it?'

'To show the Americans what their investment looks like. It'll be worth it, you'll see.'

Camilo gestured for a waiter and helped himself to a second glass of champagne. He yawned. 'I'm down to cover most of the bigger openings when the conference comes. I have to arrange accreditation for some of the senior figures flying in from overseas, so yes, there's a lot keeping me up. It's Felisa too. Has she spoken to you?'

'Felisa? No.'

Camilo leaned in close. 'You should know, in Guatavita, we got close.'

'Like you always wanted.'

'Yes, it was always going to happen.'

'It must be nice to think so.'

'What's that?'

'Nothing.'

'That night, Luke.' Camilo grinned. 'You can't imagine. She's wild.' He leaned in closer. 'It's better when you don't have to pay, hey?'

Camilo didn't know when to shut up.

'I'm joking, Luke! Your face. Anyway, when we got back to the city, she changed. No, it happened before that, after you left us there.' He laughed. 'As though the two of us can't be happy unless we're a three. Does that sound crazy to you?'

Luke shrugged. 'You knew each other before I came along.'

'She's fond of you. It's nothing but a schoolgirl infatuation, you understand.'

'Of course.'

'In the meantime,' Camilo said, 'it seems you're necessary to our happiness.'

The two women by the fountain shrieked again and Camilo, Luke noticed, was grinning at them.

'She's very pretty, isn't she?'

'Beautiful, when she's not telling me how to do my job.'

'Not Felisa.' Camilo turned to him. 'The blonde over there.'

It was the woman who'd lost her balance minutes before.

'She gets these dark moods, you see,' he said, still staring at the blonde. 'Came to see me just after Christmas in one.'

'What did she say?'

'What?' Camilo sat up as the woman and her friend came across the courtyard towards them. 'She said she was looking forward to work – to getting everything back to normal.' Camilo extended his hand and the blonde took it. 'I mean, what's wrong with her?'

As the New Year struck, Luke found himself alone again, craning upwards along with the other guests who'd crowded out onto the front lawn to watch the sky blister and explode. He'd bored of the blonde and her friend, both American it turned out. The blonde, who called herself Ruby, was over from the States visiting her diplomat father. To the girls, everything was either wild or cool; his British accent was cool, Colombia was wild, as was Camilo for being so handsome and it was also wild (and cool) that they were all hanging out together, the friend had told him repeatedly. The wildest thing of all, though, he learned, would be when they told the girls back home. Luke soon tired of them. He was tired of Camilo too, leaving him in both their company and wandering off alone. That was at least two hours ago and he hadn't seen the three of them since.

After the fireworks had finished, the guests returned to the main house. Luke watched them go, passing through incendiary fog. He felt bitter about the whole evening. Karl had failed to show. Lucky him, Luke thought, looking for Osorio in the crowd gathered on the front porch. He wanted to say he was leaving. Across the lawn, Luke spotted his driver and waved.

'Luke!' It was Camilo, coming across the grass towards him. He looked as if he'd fallen over and taken some time to get up again. 'I thought you'd left?'

'What happened to your friends?'

'Who?' Camilo asked, looking behind him. 'The thing is,

Luke, I'm quite stuck here. If you're leaving, can I get a ride back into town?'

'If you like,' Luke said. 'Let's tell your uncle.'

'Leave him,' Camilo said, putting a hand on Luke's shoulder. 'I'm not sure I can face that mob again.'

Luke forced a smile and the two turned and headed towards the car.

'Do you mind if the windows come down?' Camilo asked, as they pulled out of the estate. Luke turned the handle of the one on his side. He was glad for it. Camilo smelt like cheap perfume. Luke leaned his head against the window. The first hours of the New Year were cold and sobering. When he turned back, Camilo had his eyes closed.

'There were two girls, Luke. You could have enjoyed yourself more.'

'That sounds like a reproach.'

Camilo turned towards him. 'Got to let go sometimes.'

'I thought—' he paused '—I thought you might have spent tonight with Felisa.'

'I told you before, Luke. I couldn't invite her here. Anyway, she's no fun.'

'I'm sorry,' Luke said. 'It's none of my business.'

'Oh, but it is,' Camilo said. 'At least, it feels like your business. She won't stop mentioning you. Luke thinks this, Luke said that…' He prodded Luke hard in the arm. 'Any other man would be jealous.'

'I'm not sure she'll listen to me, not now.'

'Now?' Camilo sat up. 'That's it. I should go there now. Wish her happy new year. Good idea, Luke.' He leaned forward and passed instructions to the driver. Camilo turned back to face him. 'We'll drop you off first, though.'

30

Luke went out early the next morning to buy a copy of *El Tiempo* which he took to a nearby café because back at the apartment, Señora Rojas had arrived early. He found the only empty table in a room packed with people, all keen to breakfast on 1948. The penultimate year before they were all tipped towards the fifties and then what? A whole new decade he already felt unfit for. He sipped his coffee and, above the bubble of noise, tried to concentrate on what he was reading. There had been a protest at the oil refinery in Barrancabermeja. The workers there were in dispute with their bosses over pay. It looked like the economic situation was worsening all round – and poverty spreads faster than wildfire, he thought. More minor riots had been reported closer to Bogotá because of hikes in the price of food, along with steep taxes placed on general goods. The harvest, it said, was going to fail again – more violence and murder, this time in the district of Caldas, west of Bogotá. In large cities like Manizales and Pereira life was being lived increasingly lawlessly. And it's only January, he thought.

When he arrived back at the apartment, Señora Rojas already had lunch underway although it wasn't yet midday. Luke went into the bedroom, opened the closet and reached back into the furthest corner of the top shelf, pulling out an envelope. He counted out Señora Rojas' salary for the month and then an extra hundred centavos before replacing it. He liked to keep some money at the apartment. The banks, with their public siestas that stretched wide-armed across the middle of the day, were less reliable. In the kitchen, Señora Rojas had her head over the pot.

'This is for last month,' he said, handing her the money.

'But it's too much,' she said, blinking at him.

'How can you tell?'

'It's heavy.'

Luke smiled. 'You would say if there was anything you needed?'

'Yes, señor... I... thank you.'

'It's all right,' Luke said, leaving her there before either of them said anything that might embarrass them both.

The doorbell rang.

'Oh, Señor Draper,' Señora Rojas said, answering it. 'Look at your eye!'

'Don't fuss, woman.' Karl came in and closed the door behind him.

'I'll get something,' she said, going back to the kitchen.

'What happened, Karl?'

'Can I have a drink?'

Luke found the bottle and a glass.

'Got robbed,' Karl said, collapsing onto the sofa.

'Robbed?'

'Not far from here.'

Señora Rojas appeared with a wet cloth and tried to place it over the cut lid.

'I said don't fuss!' Karl said, snatching it from her.

'I'll be in the kitchen,' she said.

'It's not her fault, is it?'

'Damn it, Vosey! Little buggers took my wallet and my coat. Why would they take my coat?'

'How did they get it off you?'

'I was holding it, wasn't I?' He lowered his voice. 'Just finished up with a nice little secretary I've been seeing. It's a fine day so I decided to walk back. They must have seen me carrying it and recognised it for a piece of work. Some of these lowlifes aren't without taste.'

'I should call the police.'

'Don't even think about it, Vosey, they'll be long gone by now.'

'Come on, Karl, you should report it.'

'For Christ's sake, Luke, sit down. I just need to think, that's all.'

Karl looked agitated, as if he'd been knocked off balance and was trying to remember how to walk.

Once his former boss had drunk another whisky, he let Señora Rojas tend to the cut above his eye. It looked like something hard, other than a fist, had made contact with the skin there. It grew puffier by the minute. Karl eventually calmed down enough to decide he would leave. Luke called him a taxi and walked him down to the lobby.

'Best you don't come outside with me, Vosey.'

'Why not?'

'You might be seen, and, the thing is, well, the thing is... I don't know if this girl's boyfriend or brother aren't behind this. I don't want to make trouble for you. They might think you're in on it too.'

'If you like.'

'No need to tell anyone about this little incident, hey?'

'In case it gets back to Mrs Draper?'

'Yes,' he said, 'in case of that. You're a good friend to me, Luke, and I hope I've been a good boss.'

'So far, yes,' Luke said. Karl was acting strange, even for him. 'Are you sure I shouldn't come with you?'

'No thanks, it's as I said.'

He patted Luke on the arm and left.

'Karl?'

'Yes?'

'I didn't see you at Osorio's.'

'I was there,' Karl said, smiling painfully. 'See you.'

He disappeared through the door. Luke waited in the lobby for the car to travel past the glass and out of sight.

31

The first week back in the office brought Felisa. Luke tried to hide how glad he felt on seeing her. He knew better than to ask after Camilo and what had happened the night of Osorio's party. She was here and that was enough. She seemed happy, arriving on her first day in a suit of dark blue wool. It was a brilliant colour for her. It didn't look cheap and he felt Camilo's hand in it. Telma welcomed her cautiously, as he expected she would. They'd make a good team, the three of them, until he'd be forced to bring others in on the plan. Karl he hadn't heard from. Luke wondered how he'd explained away the eye to Mrs Draper. If anyone could extricate himself from a tight spot, it was Karl. He had the address of the new office, though. Soon, Luke knew Karl would find his way back into his life again.

'Would you like refreshments, señor?' Telma asked, coming into the room. It was the end of their first week together. 'I'm going out. And you too?' she said, addressing Felisa.

Felisa turned. 'Yes, thank you, Telma.'

Telma nodded and went for her coat and umbrella. Luke watched her leave and waited for the heavy main door to close below. Felisa, it seemed, had been waiting too. She looked at him and smiled before returning to the work on her desk.

'How are they coming along?' Luke asked.

'Would you like to see?'

Felisa went to rise but he was up before her. She moved the sheet she'd been working on to one side, revealing more pages beneath. In front of him, the redesign jumped into life. Where previous draughtsmen he'd worked with had stuck to inks, Felisa had used watercolour to draw out detail in her design.

'It's quite unusual, the technique,' he said, picking up a street scene and holding it up to the window.

'I hope it isn't wrong.'

'You've captured the feeling of the scene, and that's important.'

He smiled and handed the sketch back to her.

'My mother said I had an unusual talent.'

'Before she left?'

'Excuse me?'

He'd spoken without thinking. 'Before she died.'

'Oh, I see.' Felisa concentrated on reorganising the papers in front of her. 'Did Camilo tell you?'

'I'm sorry.' Luke went back over to his desk. 'You shouldn't feel the need to explain, not to me.'

'He must have told you.' Felisa turned her chair to face his and sat down. 'She did leave. Do you really want to know?'

'I do,' he said.

'All right then. I was eight years old. She knew she was beautiful, my father told me that. Now I think of it, he never said she was beautiful himself, just that it was how she saw herself. A friend of the plantation owner used to come and visit us. He was a smart man; an educated man. What does he want with us? my father must have thought. But he was tired. He worked hard for very little and probably didn't have

214

the strength to think about it as someone with more time, with more energy, might have. He didn't see the danger that came finely dressed and scented. My father is a simple man but I never thought him a fool until then. I saw it. At first, this educated man would stop at all the little houses on the plantation, talking with the workers and their families. What a nice man, everybody said of him, what a good Christian. Eventually, it just became our house he stopped at. When the other families realised, we were called names and ignored. The wives were the worst, they hated her. They are jealous, my mother said proudly one night. I watched my father strike her for saying that.' Felisa brushed the hair from her eyes. 'The rich man, I think he was looking at all of the women. He was deciding which one to take. Perhaps the plantation owner, who owned our little house and the land beneath it, told him to do that, thinking that because he'd bought the bricks he'd paid for the people too. That's when we started hiding it from my father. We got into a little routine, my mother and I. When she knew he was coming, she would take me with her, up to the big house and away from the dirt and the bad things that were said about us. But I swear, on all those trips I never went inside the big house. I used to wait outside while they did what they did.' She laughed. 'Do you know, he taught me English. It was in the garden beneath the palms. I risked a lot to discover his real name afterwards.'

'And did you?'

'Never. I used to call him Tío because he was like an uncle to me. He offered her many things, things my father never could have. And she took them. She preferred that life to the one we had. She valued it more. After he took her away, I never told my father what that man taught me. I didn't speak English again for years, not until I met Camilo. It would have killed my father to know he had schooled me.' Felisa looked at him.

'Camilo knows everything. I wish he hadn't told you, though. It's easier to say she died.'

'I can see that you think that but you mustn't feel ashamed.'

Outside the window, the sky cracked and a torrent of rain fell, pockmarking the streets below. Felisa hadn't noticed.

'Telma will be drenched,' he said.

'I have his picture,' she said. 'I drew it soon after they both disappeared.'

The door slammed shut below. Soon after, Telma blew into the space.

'Has it been raining in here too?' she asked, looking between them.

Felisa turned her chair back to the desk.

'No coffee, I take it?' Luke asked.

'I don't mind telling you,' Telma said, shaking out her umbrella. 'I thought only of my hair.'

'I'll go,' he said.

'But the rain,' Telma cried.

Felisa rose. 'Can I come?'

Out on the street they tried to outrun the rain. She was too fast for him. In their rush to get out, to get away from Telma, they'd left their umbrellas upstairs. There was something about what had been revealed that had sent them running. Felisa moved closer to him. Luke took his jacket off and shielded them both from the worst of the rain. They fell into a coffee shop a couple of blocks over. Inside the dark café, Luke ordered tinto and Felisa hot chocolate.

'Should we take something back for Telma?' she asked, wrapping her hands around her cup when they were seated.

'Later.'

Felisa sucked in her lip and then spoke. 'The night of your birthday,' she began.

'It was my fault,' he said, looking at her. 'If I hadn't been so drunk.'

'Yes,' she said. 'You were.'

'Are you happy, now, with Camilo?'

'I'm not with Camilo.'

'But that night?'

'He slept on the floor at my feet.'

'So, you're not together?'

'No, Luke!' She sighed. 'Camilo gets these ideas in his head but it would be very wrong of him to suggest there is more between us than there is.'

'Then I made a mistake leaving you in Guatavita.'

'Is that why you left?'

Luke nodded. 'He seemed so sure.'

'He's mistaken,' she said, taking his hands. 'You can't allow him to draw you into his fantasies. But for all his faults, he is a good man, Luke.'

'He is,' Luke said. 'I believe you.'

'Can I ask you something?'

'Yes.'

'The beautiful woman in the photograph at the lake, do you miss her very much?'

'Catherine?'

'Catherine. That was her name?'

'It was.'

Her eyes narrowed. 'Is she dead like my mother is dead?'

'She's dead to me in every sense.'

'Then I'm very sorry, Luke, for acting as I did.'

'Catherine and I didn't end on good terms. The last time I saw her we fought.'

'What did you fight about?'

'It's insignificant. I've tried hard not to think about her. I carried her around for a long time, both in my head and that

217

stupid photograph. That's why I took it to Guatavita. I wanted her so much to love me too. Like a child might, I suppose. Like Camilo, perhaps. I suppose I can understand some of his actions.' Felisa was quiet. It was the most he'd said to anyone about Catherine. 'But you make me reveal too much.'

'Do I? How?' she asked.

'I don't know. Perhaps the gods are on your side.'

'Then you should be careful, Señor Vosey.'

His knees brushed hers beneath the table. He felt it, the air shift and everything explode into wonder once more.

They arrived back at the office with hot chocolate and cake for Telma.

'Did they have to bake some more?' Telma asked.

Luke handed her the parcel and flask. 'Drink it while it's hot,' he said.

In the afternoon the sky cleared and the office was lit by an extraordinary sunset. If only all days were like this one, he thought.

32

The next morning, Luke went out early for a copy of Camilo's paper. He reached the newspaper seller and paid over ten centavos for the daily edition before turning for home again. He'd needed to get out. Camilo had been on his mind all morning. He couldn't get it straight in his head. Had Camilo actually said he'd slept with Felisa? Luke could have sworn he had at Osorio's party. No, it went further back than that. Right back to Guatavita. The way Camilo had looked at him over Sofía's table at breakfast. Yes, something had definitely been implied. Luke arrived back at his apartment building. Camilo was waiting for him in the lobby.

'You already bought one?' Camilo said, holding up a copy of *El Tiempo*.

'Afraid so. Are they making you deliver now too?'

Camilo smiled and as good as flung his copy at the porter without looking to see where it might land.

'Not working today?' Luke asked, leading him away and up the stairs to his apartment.

'No.'

They arrived at his door.

'Actually, I am working on something. Something new, about Gaitán.'

'Oh?' Luke unlocked the door and stood aside so Camilo could enter.

Camilo went in, crossed the room and threw himself down onto the sofa.

'Make yourself at home.'

Camilo stretched out. 'Gaitán's speech in the square – some months back – do you remember it?'

'Of course I do. I don't think I've ever seen anything like it.'

'Really? What did you think of him?'

Luke shrugged and went into the kitchen to see what food, if any, Señora Rojas had left him. 'Formidable,' he called back. He found a cool package and unwrapped it to find soft, white cheese. 'I can offer you coffee, and cheese,' he said, poking his head back into the room.

Camilo raised a hand.

'Formidable,' Camilo said, chewing on the word instead. 'It's true, he spoke well. Not a man listening farted.'

Luke laughed and put the coffee on to boil. He came back into the room and picked up the paper.

'Is that what you're going to write in your piece?'

'He wants a war,' Camilo said with all seriousness.

'I don't think that's what he asked.'

'Ask? Gaitán doesn't ask. He commands and the people follow. Ospina knows that. Gaitán wants him out of government and an end to the old ways.'

'Yes, it's Gaitán against them.'

'Gaitán and the pueblo against them. You never told me what happened to you during the war in Europe, not properly, not for the article.'

'You didn't ask the right questions.'

Camilo nodded. 'And if I ask them now?'

In the kitchen, Luke heard the coffee boil over and the liquid fizz against the flames. He rose and went to see to it. In the living room, Camilo was silent, as though he was waiting for an answer to his question. Luke took two cups down from the shelf and burned himself on the pan handle pouring the hot black liquid into each. If Camilo thought he was going to tell him everything now, he was mistaken. Luke took his time wiping up the mess he had made before taking the cups through into the other room.

'I'm struggling to remember what I told you already.'

He handed one of the cups to Camilo and sat down opposite him.

'Well, let me think. Something about Whitehall and not seeing any action.'

'No direct action.'

'Of course. Everyone had their role, etcetera, etcetera.'

Luke took a sip of coffee. 'My role, yes. When I became an architect before the war, the reason I did so well was because there weren't a lot of men like me around.'

'You were the best.'

'I wanted to be, Camilo, but actually, so many men fought and died in the first war that it was easy. I was very young when I received my first commission.'

'You can't blame yourself for that.'

'It's what came next that I blame myself for.'

'Which was?'

'It isn't important now. You got what you needed then, didn't you?'

'OK then. What if I asked you about Catherine, as a friend?'

'I would ask you why?'

Camilo sighed. 'In Guatavita, you called her name in your sleep.'

'Catherine's?'

'Who else? We need to find you a woman. A live one. Someone your own age.'

'Age isn't everything.'

Camilo put his cup down. 'I want you to leave her alone, Luke.'

'So that's why you're here, is it? To talk about Felisa.'

'You're old enough to be her father.'

'She doesn't think so.'

Camilo's face hardened. 'Do you think she loves you?'

He didn't have an answer for that. He didn't think so. Did Camilo think she did?

'No, Luke. She'll grow tired of you. That, I can guarantee.' Camilo took a cigarette out of a pack in his jacket pocket and lit it. 'There was someone else before, did she tell you that?'

'I wouldn't have expected her to,' Luke said, letting his heart absorb the blow.

'She was going to leave me, to be with him. Can you believe it?'

'Leave you?' Luke looked at him and smiled. 'That's good, Camilo.'

'Anyway, it was all very tragic,' Camilo said, dismissing him. 'He fled town and as soon as news reached her, she came straight to me to mend her broken heart. With my help, my connections, we tried to find him, but he had simply disappeared.'

'I see. People have a habit of disappearing around here, don't they?'

Camilo stubbed out his cigarette in the ashtray beside him and rose. 'I would hate for her heart to break again.'

A few days after Camilo's visit, Luke was back in the office. He hadn't mentioned what had taken place in his apartment to anyone, least of all Felisa. Camilo, who had come bearing threats. He had shown that he'd do anything not to lose her. He never had her in the first place, Luke thought.

They were all of them speeding towards the Pan-American Conference in a couple of days' time and after that, the public announcement for the redevelopment. Both were welcome distractions from thoughts of Camilo. Until the plans were made public, they had to keep quiet, Karl said. Only a few in government, including the president, knew about the project. Nobody wanted a riot, which is what would happen if Gaitán got wind of it.

I have other things to keep quiet about too, Luke thought. He had wanted to talk to Felisa – but how would it sound to her to suggest that Camilo had made her lover vanish? He knew what it was to drag up the past. He wouldn't do that to her. One thing was certain: any friendship between the younger Osorio and himself was over.

'This came for you.' It was Telma with a telegram.

'Thanks,' he said.

Across the room, Felisa worked on in silence. Luke opened the envelope. It was from Karl.

Big news. Big bucks too. Can you trust the journalist?

Meet at Casa de la Risa nr. Plaza.

6 sharp tonight. Karl.

La Casa de la Risa; he knew it, and the journalist – Karl meant Camilo. Yes, he could trust him, except where Felisa was concerned. Luke put the telegram into his jacket pocket. Felisa was watching him.

'Is it important?' she asked.

'I don't think so,' he said. 'Are you hungry?'

She smiled.

'Telma, we're going out for lunch,' he said.

'Again?'

When they were clear of the building, he took her hand.

'Luke, you can't,' Felisa said, looking around.

'Who do you suppose will be watching?' he snapped, immediately regretting it. She didn't reply. 'If this is too public, come to mine for supper soon. No one will notice us there.'

'Please let go of my hand, Luke,' she said, trying gently to free herself.

'Say you'll come and I will.'

She nodded and laughed. Felisa looked up and down the street and when she was happy they weren't being watched, leaned upwards and kissed him.

'I thought you minded?' he asked, stealing a kiss back.

They forgot the time over lunch and sat for more than an hour. After they'd eaten they walked around for a bit. Felisa didn't want to go back yet. There was something she wanted to show him, that she'd mentioned while they were eating. They crisscrossed La Candelaria and ended up eventually far from the office at the foothills of Monserrate. They'd stopped in front of a bronze statue of a woman seated on a plinth.

'This is Policarpa.'

'Hello,' Luke said. The statue was larger than life – too large. It appeared clumsy because of it.

'She was beautiful,' Felisa said.

'You admire her for that – for her beauty?'

'No,' she said. 'Not that. She was more determined than any man to fight for what she believed in.'

Luke looked up again. The figure did look defiant, with her arms stretched behind her back. He could see why Felisa might like her.

'During the fight for independence, she was a spy for the revolutionary forces. She was captured but steadfast to the end.

The Spanish shot her because of it.' Felisa looked like she was about to cry. 'Why do you think they did that?'

'Because beautiful women frighten ugly men.'

Felisa smiled.

'We should head back,' he said. 'Telma will be worried.'

'Yes.' She put her arm around him and the two of them made their way back like that.

Policarpa is an unusual name, he thought, turning to catch sight of the statue one last time. From the back, he saw that the bronze-cast hands were in fact tied.

When they got back to the office, Telma wasn't in her usual spot. Perhaps she'd gone out for lunch. It meant another brilliant hour alone together.

'What's wrong with you two?'

They'd almost missed Camilo, waiting for them in the shadows. He was seated on top of Felisa's desk.

'Move, or you'll ruin it,' she said, going across the room and pushing him aside.

'All right, all right,' he said rising. 'I brought this.'

He produced a thick white card and handed it to Luke.

'What is it?'

'Invitation. The National Museum opening in a couple days' time.'

'Oh,' Luke said, looking across at Felisa. It would mean a whole night with Camilo.

'It's inside of the old prison, the Panóptico,' Camilo said, looking between them. 'You do know my uncle insists you be there.'

'Your uncle? I thought you didn't get on?'

'Oh, don't let's go into it, Luke. We'll go together, then?' Camilo smiled slowly. 'It'll be like New Year's again.'

He took his time kissing Felisa on the cheek and then left. Luke went over to the door and closed it.

'He'll hate to be there if his uncle is,' Felisa said.

'Perhaps.'

'You know they don't speak.'

'I'll have to go. If Osorio's involved I have little choice.'

'Why should you mind? Isn't it what you wanted?'

He crossed the room and slipped his hands around her waist.

'I'm sorry. I'd rather spend the time with you, that's all.'

'You're like a boy,' she said, kissing him.

La Casa de la Risa was as he remembered it – the old man behind the grill in the kitchen and his sometime daughter waiting tables. He looked up when Luke entered and grinned. In the gloom he spotted Karl seated towards the back and went over.

'You know they say the socialists come here?' Luke said, sitting down opposite him.

Karl brushed the accusation away.

'All the better for it. Means we won't be seen.'

'By whom?'

Luke looked back towards the door. True, there were men huddled in groups around the tables, but none looked threatening. Karl had a beer in his hand. Luke ordered another two from the girl.

'Your eye has healed, then?'

'What? Oh, that. Yes, I suppose it has.'

'Your wife wasn't too upset?'

'More upset about that coat.'

The girl brought the beers.

'It was a gift.'

Luke took a sip. He counted three empty bottles on the table already. 'What did you want to tell me?'

'Christ, Luke, I don't know if I should.'

'You must have thought so earlier.'

Karl just sat there.

'I've got a lot on my mind, Karl.' He wasn't sure where this was going. Felisa had said she would spend the night at hers, but he couldn't shake the feeling that Camilo would be there waiting for her when she arrived home.

'All right, Luke, but it's big. I mean huge, really.' He knocked back the remains of his bottle and picked up the new one. 'It's Gaitán.'

'You're the second person to mention him to me this week.'

'And why not? He wields a lot of power.'

'What about him, then?'

'Not a friend of Osorio's.'

'Osorio is a powerful man. I'm sure he has as many enemies as friends.'

'Don't be poetic, Luke.' Karl leaned forward. 'Osorio and his pals have got it in for this Gaitán. Like, really got it in for him. It comes up in conversation a lot.'

'But there's more?' There was definitely more.

'His nephew, that young journalist. You think he can be trusted?'

'Camilo? Yes,' Luke sighed, 'he can. Hasn't breathed a word about the project.'

'Can you arrange for us to meet?'

'I'm not sure that's a good idea, Karl. They don't get on.'

'I know they don't, but that's precisely why it has to be him.'

'I'll need a bit more to go on.'

Karl took a long swig of beer. 'Your planning permission. Someone in Gaitán's administration got word. Didn't like what he heard Osorio and his bully-elite were planning to do. He told Gaitán and Gaitán didn't like it either.'

'We've already been over this,' Luke said, a little too loudly. 'It's all been pushed through.'

'Yes and no,' Karl whispered. 'It'll cook up a shitstorm if word got out Osorio was filling his own pockets without a thought for the people he's evicting.'

'But I've built in housing,' Luke said. 'You've seen the plans. You all agreed to them. New model homes for the poor.'

Karl grimaced. 'You remember Blanco, the draughtsman? One-time employee of yours. Osorio wasn't quite sure about some of your designs. Got his own man to adapt them before they were put to the committee.'

Luke felt the blood rush from his face. 'And you knew? For Christ's sake, Karl!'

'I'm sorry, Luke. We all stood to gain. You too, of course. We still do, but there's a threat now from Osorio to Gaitán that could wreck everything. Also, I'm broke. Osorio's had me paying city officials left, right and centre since this thing began, but not coughed up a penny in return. Mrs Draper can't live on thin air, you know.'

'What threat to Gaitán? Karl, what's Osorio planning?'

Karl drew his hand across his throat. Luke had never seen someone do that before and mean it.

'You've got to get me a meeting with the boy.' He produced a cigar and lit it. 'He must have something on his uncle I can convince him to leak. Some woman or family tucked away that Señora Osorio doesn't know about. It might be enough to make Osorio back down.'

Luke nodded. 'It might, but why do you care what happens to Gaitán?'

'I might be a glutton, Luke, but I'm not a murderer. Christ, the man's got a daughter.'

'It just seems crazy. Osorio is ruthless, but this?'

'As I've said. I had no idea, Luke. I thought it was about making a quick buck out of bricks and mortar but not at this price. I mean, Jesus, we just fought a war to be free of dictators.'

Karl pulled a crumpled old cloth from his pocket and wiped his brow. 'Arrange the meeting, please, Luke. I'm tired of this. Mrs Draper wants to go back to Michigan. Her mother's sick. To be honest, I couldn't care if the old crone died before we got off the plane, but the sight of her face, compared to what I've seen here, is a fair thing to aim for now.'

'Does Osorio suspect you, Karl?'

'Of course not. I've been very discreet.'

'If I help you, will the work continue as it did before? My way instead of Blanco's?'

'If we can get to Osorio, shake him up a bit, then we might be able to reverse what's been done. The alternative is much worse, believe me, Luke.'

'All right, Karl, but I'll tell Camilo. You stay away from him.'

'There's one more thing, Luke. The money – please, it's embarrassing to ask.'

'Of course, Karl. How much do you need?'

They parted on the corner of Seventh Avenue. Luke walked the rest of the distance to his apartment trying to make sense of it all. Osorio had lied to him since the beginning. He was nothing but another hand to be turned, manipulated at will. Luke thought of the brilliant plans Felisa and he had worked over, of what had gone into them. He wondered which bits that worm Blanco had erased. It was like ripping the heart from a body and saying it would live. All of it must be true. Karl was afraid; Luke had seen it in his eyes when they'd parted. He knew it would take something beyond words to divorce Karl from making a pile of cash. Why not leave quietly, though, and abandon Gaitán to his fate? Karl, it seemed, had a conscience after all. And so did he. He had to see Camilo, regardless of how he felt about him now, otherwise they'd all have blood on their hands. Felisa would never get over the loss of her beloved leader. She would never forgive him if she found out he'd stood by and done nothing. This time, Luke thought, I will do the right thing.

33

The following day the Pan-American Conference blew into the city with all the fanfare of a travelling circus, bringing with it the outside world. Luke was in his apartment getting ready to leave for the office on Divorce Street, as he now thought of it. He urgently needed to see Camilo but couldn't find him. It was as though the newspaperman had completely disappeared. Or he was hiding. After he'd left Karl last night, Luke had phoned the number Camilo had given him for his office and then again this morning, only to be told each time by the operator that they couldn't find him. Was he out covering the conference, Luke wondered? At all hours? No, Camilo had to know he'd been calling. He was avoiding him. Luke had no way of knowing if Osorio's plan was already in motion. A telegram from Karl had arrived at the apartment that morning, demanding an update. If Osorio was as bad as Karl said he was, he'd have people in every part of the city. Karl was becoming careless. Luke had to get hold of Camilo, and soon.

God damn it, he thought, pricking his finger on his tie pin, I'll have to go there in person. He crossed the room. He'd make Camilo listen. Whatever he thought of him, he suspected his sympathies would lie with the paper and politically with Gaitán. He was relying on Camilo's vanity to blind him to any sense of loyalty he might feel towards his uncle. Luke grabbed his jacket and pulled the door of his apartment shut.

He reached the corner of Jiménez and looked up at the news board. Not even two days in and it was already singing the praises of the delegation. Jesus, it was boring and predictable. It wasn't real news. Nobody knows what's coming, Luke thought – if it's true. The Americans had taken over the Hotel Granada a week ago. It was almost impossible to get a drink there uninvited now. Most of the senior delegates would be at the museum opening tomorrow. He had to get to Camilo before that. Before facing down Osorio – he knew he had to get the project back on track. He wasn't going to lose the housing for the people – it was what connected him to Felisa.

Inside the lobby of the news building, Luke asked the woman on the reception desk if he could see the reporter, Camilo Osorio. He had a big story, he said, giving over a fake name. He wasn't sure if Camilo wanted to see Luke Vosey. She told him to wait while she contacted the switchboard. At the far side of the lobby was an elevator. Some of the men passing through it looked like Camilo but none of them were him. He smiled at the receptionist. He didn't want to go too far in case she had Camilo on the line. He wasn't going to leave without telling him what Karl had said.

'I'm sorry, they can't find him,' she said, taking the receiver from her ear.

'I keep being told that,' he said. 'Can you try again?'

She sighed. She didn't want to. There were other people waiting in line.

'Just once more?'

'Once more,' she said, putting the phone to her ear and dialling again. She said Camilo's name down the receiver.

Then she said it again but slower, then she spelled it. 'You're sure it's Osorio?' she asked, muffling the mouthpiece with her hand.

'I saw it in print myself,' he said. 'O.S.O.R.I.O. Osorio.'

She repeated what she had already said to the operator, but this time she looked annoyed because she had already spelled it correctly and wasn't going to do it again.

'There must be some mistake,' Luke said to the man waiting behind him.

'No mistake,' the receptionist said. 'Are you sure you didn't mean *El Espectador*? Have you got the right paper?'

'No,' Luke said. 'I didn't mean *El Espectador*, or *Jornada*, or *El Siglo* or anywhere else because I won't find Camilo Osorio there, and the reason I know that is because he works here, at *El Tiempo*.'

'And do you know,' she said, matching his tone, 'why I know you won't find Camilo Osorio here at *El Tiempo*?'

'No,' Luke said. 'I really don't.'

'You won't find him here, because there's clearly no one by that name that works here.'

'Got your answer, my friend.' It was the man in the queue, but Luke hadn't heard, he hadn't understood.

'Look,' he said, dropping his voice to a whisper. 'My name's actually Luke Vosey and I have something very important to tell Camilo Osorio, so you better find him.'

She stared at him in disbelief.

'Listen pal, I'm Camilo, OK?' It was the man from the queue. 'You tell me what you've come to say and leave this lady alone.'

'I'm not mad,' Luke said. 'He wrote a piece on me!'

'Uh huh,' she said.

'He brought copies to my apartment.'

'I'm sure he did,' she said.

233

'Stop bothering the miss now, will you?' The man from the queue had been joined by building security.

'Thank you,' Luke said to the receptionist. 'I can find my way.'

The men followed him until he was clear of the doors.

Luke walked blindly into the street and was almost run over. He made it to the pavement across from the office block and looked back at the *El Tiempo* building, just in case it wasn't real, and he'd turn and find a bank or shop front. Why had she said Camilo didn't work there? Of course he did. Luke stood in the street for some time, confused about what to do next. He wondered if, if he waited long enough, Camilo might come out, as he had seen him do before. Then he could explain about the switchboard error. Then he could tell Camilo what Karl had told him about Gaitán. He thought about going across the street, about trying again but with his real name, perhaps that had been it? Or perhaps he needed to pay them? Yes, that must be it: there wasn't a Camilo Osorio because he hadn't asked in the right way. He'd try again. He stepped into the road but caught sight of the security guard still standing in the window of the building. The man was watching him, and had been for some time, apparently – long enough to have called some friends in. Luke stepped back up onto the pavement and walked away.

He made it across town to his office. As soon as he arrived, he phoned Karl. No answer. He tried him again an hour later at his office, but his secretary said he'd taken some time off. Perhaps he'd already fled with Mrs Draper. Luke didn't know what to do about Gaitán and spent the rest of the afternoon trying not to think about Camilo. It didn't make sense. He'd checked the afternoon editions of all of the papers but the story hadn't broken. Gaitán was fine. Things weren't fine, though. There were too many unanswered questions for him to feel everything had just worked itself out. And the one person he wanted to talk to, the one person he wanted to ask, who he usually couldn't get rid of, had vanished.

'Have you seen Camilo?'

Felisa looked up. 'You asked me that ten minutes ago.'

'Did I?'

'Yes. What's going on, Luke?'

'Nothing,' he said. He couldn't tell her. Tell her what? That Karl suspected Osorio was going to murder her hero? That Camilo didn't work at *El Tiempo*? 'It's nothing.'

Telma came into the room. 'Any plans for this evening, señor?'

'Not yet,' he said.

'And will you be seeing your sweetheart tonight?' She meant Felisa, and she meant Camilo.

'Why not head off now, Telma?' he asked her.

'But I've not finished filing.'

'Do it tomorrow,' he said. 'Friday is a good day to finish things.'

She stood there for an irritatingly long time.

'Just go,' he said.

'In truth, señor, my nephew has a young lady coming to tea. I'd rather like to be there before she is.' She stood staring at them both long after she'd finished talking.

'Goodnight then,' he said.

'Goodnight, Telma,' Felisa said.

Luke waited until he was sure she had gone.

'And will you see Camilo tonight?' he asked.

'What is the matter with you, Luke?'

'I'm sorry.' He sighed and sunk lower in his chair. 'He's been on my mind lately. You did a good job today, on the designs. Thank you.'

'Luke,' she said, coming across the room towards him. 'I

need to tell you that I've broken ties with him.' She took a deep breath. 'He hasn't been a good friend to me. I see that now.'

'Really? Do you think that's why he won't see me?'

'He won't?'

'It would make sense,' Luke said. 'He's crazy about you. My god, that must be it.'

'He's not in love with me, Luke.'

'Of course he is. Did you tell him about us?'

'I did.'

'Come back with me tonight.'

'Don't you want to know what he said?'

'I don't know if I do.'

'He said he didn't believe me. That I was infatuated with you. That it would pass and he would wait for me when it did.'

'He's infatuated with you.'

'Then I'm glad it's over.' Felisa leaned down and put her arms around him.

'Are you really?' he asked.

'Yes,' she breathed. 'Yes, I am.'

On the way across town, they picked up a meal from a cantina. They passed the *El Tiempo* building and Luke could tell she was thinking about Camilo then. He was thinking about him too. Although he could still see lights on the building's upper floors, it seemed empty somehow, as though something had been taken from it and couldn't be put back. He put it from his mind. He put Camilo from his mind. Felisa had chosen him. He wouldn't let Karl, or even Gaitán, a man he didn't know but had briefly set out to defend, come between them. They stopped on the corner of Santander Park where Luke dipped into the Hotel Regina and paid an extortionate price for a bottle of champagne. By the time they'd reached the apartment, they were ravenous. Luke tore off the paper wrappings from the bundles of food and Felisa went into the kitchen for plates and glasses. Luke remembered the wireless and wound through the stations until he found one playing jazz and tango. They sat side by side and made their way through the rice and beans that Felisa said was the food of the workers. It was delicious. She laughed, sipping at her champagne, saying they went together surprisingly well.

After they'd finished, Luke rose and went in search of a copy of Camilo's article. He found it where he'd left it on top of a pile of old magazines. He brought it over to the light and held it up.

'Does this look real to you?'

'What?' she asked.

'It is real, I told them it was.'

'It's as real as me, or that table there,' she said, laughing.

The wireless crackled and then a beautiful violin filled the room.

'Luke, it's Volver,' she said.

'You like Carlos Gardel?'

'You know it?'

Luke put the paper down. It was probably the champagne that made him put out his hand. Felisa took it, rising from the table. He led her towards the space in the living room and turned up the wireless before taking her other hand in his. They moved along with the slow tango, self-consciously at first but then relaxing into it. The song hadn't finished before the power cut. Not just the wireless, but the lights too, so that they were pitched into darkness. Outside on the street, he could tell that others had come out of their apartments to investigate. He could hear them cursing – the husbands and wives – and thought Felisa could too. That everyday world belonged to a parallel night.

'Do you know what it means – volver?' she said, her breath hot against his sleeve.

'To return,' Luke replied. He lifted her off her feet and carried her into the bedroom.

He woke up to the sound of someone screaming. Felisa was there, shaking him – trying to bring him back. She looked terrified.

'Luke, what is it?'

There was no one else there – no one at all. Felisa rose and left the room. She returned with a glass of water and handed it to him.

'What did you dream?' she asked, climbing back into bed.

'It's always the same,' he said, swallowing.

'But it will be the first time I hear it.'

Luke turned to her.

'Cities burning,' he said, 'the ones I told you about in the photographs, and the people, I can't save them. I don't even try.'

'It's not your fault, remember?'

'Yes, but I wasn't there. So many of my friends were brave enough to fight; my own brother, even her.'

'Catherine, again?'

'Yes, I'm sorry. I just can't…'

'You still love her.'

'No. And she never loved me, Felisa. There was someone else.'

'Someone for her?'

'She told me that. The last time I saw her, before she left for the last time. I've seen him too. At least part of his arm in a photograph. I'm sure it's him.'

'They're ghosts, Luke,' Felisa said. 'We're real. We're here.'

'We are,' he said. 'I know that. I want you to know that this is different.'

'Shall I tell you something?'

'Yes.'

'Do you remember I didn't want you to put the photograph into the figure at the lake?'

'You got very upset.'

'It was because of what I wrote down. What I asked the goddess for.'

'Which was?'

'You.'

34

Last night, he'd talked and Felisa had listened. They stayed up into the early hours. He told her everything he could about himself, wanting to give her the best chance of loving him. He'd woken late and alone. Felisa had left a note to say she would meet him at the office, that there was no need to give Telma the best gossip of her life, not yet. The first thing Luke did when he rose was to call the offices of *El Tiempo*. This time he didn't bother with a phony name. They still claimed they hadn't heard of Camilo. He remembered afterwards that he still had the museum opening to go to. Camilo had given him the ticket. He would see him then. Even if he was still upset about Felisa, Luke would say what he had to say about Gaitán and leave. He'd promised Karl that much.

Luke dropped into the Café Windsor on Seventh as he often did on his way into the office. He found a table and lit a cigarette.

'That will kill you.'

He recognised the voice but couldn't place the man. He turned.

'Señor Osorio?'

'May I join you?'

'Of course,' Luke said, offering the chair opposite. He needed to act normal. Luke scanned the rest of the room. It could be that it was a chance encounter, Osorio finding him here, but perhaps not.

'You come here?'

Osorio shrugged. 'Sometimes I like to sit at the bar. To watch the world go by alongside the next man.'

'I've never seen you.'

'No, well, it's fortunate perhaps.' Osorio coughed. 'The smoke, but please, continue.'

Luke took a deep draw and then stubbed it out. 'Fortunate for me, actually.' He cleared his throat. 'Have you seen Karl?'

'Karl?'

'He came to see me a couple of days ago.'

'Did he?' Osorio's eyes gave nothing away. 'And may I ask what about?'

'Nothing important,' Luke said.

'Yet you are worried about him?'

'Should I be?'

Osorio sighed. 'I probably shouldn't be telling you this, but perhaps you already know. Yes, I think you do know. Karl is bankrupt.'

'Bankrupt?'

'He's put his name to enough debt to chase him out of town. He's left his wife, you know.'

'He can't blame her?'

'His wife?' Osorio laughed. 'Oh no, Luke. Liquor and women, the former coming at a greater cost than the latter, you understand. He's run up huge bills he can't pay back with all the clubs in town.'

'I don't believe it. That's not what he told me.'

'Oh? Why not question him yourself?'

'I can't find him. His secretary said he'd left.' Luke felt hot and uncomfortable. 'He seemed so genuine. Afraid, actually.'

'As would you if you knew the men he owed. He'll do anything to help himself. It's better if you forget Karl Draper, we've too much to do here.' Osorio finished his coffee and rose. 'One last thing, and I ask this as a friend: you didn't give him any money, did you?'

Luke took the side streets back to his office. It felt like those first few months, when he hadn't known which way the streetcars ran – feeling out of sorts with the city and his place in it. Had Karl been lying? He had given him all that cash. And he'd almost told Camilo. He had been going to tell him tonight, in fact. He didn't know what to think. It was easier to believe Karl's excess. He'd experienced that first-hand.

When he arrived, Telma and Felisa were hard at work and barely registered his presence.

'New instructions from the mayor's office,' Felisa said, not looking up.

'New? That's good,' Luke said. So, things were fine. The designs were safe and corrections were rolling in as they should.

The three of them worked on all morning and he wondered how Felisa could do it, being in the same room as him. He couldn't focus at all with her sitting there. As lunch approached Luke rose and went to her side. He'd tried to forget the events of the last two days. He was going to murder Karl before anyone else did if they ever met again. Felisa worked on. The sketch in front of her was new. She wasn't working on the city plans at all.

'What's that?' he asked.

'The new work,' she said, looking up. 'I told you when you came in.'

She sat back so that Luke could lift the page free.

'I know this place,' he said.

'Yes, it's Señor Osorio's hacienda. You know, Camilo's uncle.'

He looked again at the sheet. It was the hacienda, but the building had been extended by Felisa's hand so that it had grown a new wing. It was now double the size. He handed it back to her.

'No doubt the money from the work for the city stretched further than anyone imagined,' she said.

'And it came via the mayor's office?'

'That's what Telma said.'

'I see.'

Luke went back to his desk. So now he was Osorio's man in every respect? Part of him wished he'd had the guts to leave like Karl. After this, they couldn't keep him here. He wasn't designing houses for all of them.

Some time around one, Telma went out to collect lunch for the three of them. It felt as though she'd never leave. When she did, Felisa was the first one to rise. She wiped the ink from her hands and came across the room.

'I still haven't decided what we're to do after this,' he said, pulling her onto his lap.

'After this?'

'It's just this business with Osorio's hacienda. He has me where he wants me.'

'There's more, isn't there? Tell me, Luke.'

'I can't.'

'Even if I make you?' she asked, pinching him gently.

'It's better if you don't know.'

She nodded. They stayed like that for some time, enjoying the quiet that bound them.

'How do you feel about Europe?' he asked.

'London?' Her eyes widened, as if every fantastic thing had been invited to pass before them.

'Perhaps.'

'I don't have any papers.'

'If you're my wife you won't need them.'

Felisa looked at him. He'd just said it and felt stunned too. They kissed, and it was as if they were back in the apartment, with Gardel on the wireless. They didn't hear when the front door opened below, nor the person on the stairs, nor moments later when Telma burst into the room.

'Gaitán is dead,' she said.

Felisa tried to rise and Luke too. She hadn't heard, but he had.

'How?' he asked.

'He's been shot,' Telma said, breathless. 'Save us all – Gaitán has been shot!'

'What?' Felisa rose. 'I don't believe you. What are you saying? What's she saying, Luke?'

'She says he's dead.'

'No, he isn't.' Felisa backed away from them, towards the door. 'She's lying!'

He stepped towards her. 'It isn't safe, Felisa. We need to stay here.'

'I can't,' she said. 'Why are you so calm?'

'Please, Felisa.' He edged closer.

'I'm sorry, Luke, I can't!'

She ran from the room. He heard her on the stairs, and then silence. Telma began to cry and then to wail. He guided her to a chair and then sat down himself. He had to think. Karl was right – Karl knew, and he had told him. Luke had known and had done nothing.

'It's true,' Felisa said, coming back into the room. 'I heard it from a man below. They've got him.'

'Who?' he asked.

'Gaitán, didn't you hear?' She let out a cry so raw it pinned him to the spot. She cried out again and he went over to comfort her. He held her tight in the hope of containing anything else that might pour out and drown them both.

35

There wasn't a wireless in the office and so Luke told them to stay where they were. He fetched whisky and made the two women sit with a drink apiece, saying he'd be back shortly. He went down the stairs and out into the afternoon light. He ran towards the main square. It was how Karl had said it would be. Gaitán was dead.

Luke wasn't alone. Everyone was running in the direction of the old town or towards Seventh Avenue, he couldn't be sure. That's when he saw them. A small group of men with weapons – wooden batons and machetes – moving slowly before the cathedral. They were dragging something – Luke couldn't see what from where he stood. He crossed the street and reached the centre of the square, pausing beside the statue of Bolívar. From there he had a better view. The number in the group was growing – men and women together – heading in the direction of the presidential palace behind the Capitolio. The delegation must still be running inside, he thought, looking up at the flags of the nations dotting the skyline. Something told him to stay back, to not let himself be seen, and so from behind the stone plinth he tried to see what it was they were dragging.

At first sight it could have been rags or a large dog, but then he recognised a leg, and then another, followed by two arms. The body of a man, almost naked, was being dragged by the feet across the hard stone. A boy of about fifteen ran past Luke and right up to the body. Luke watched him lift his boot and, without fear, bring it down on the head. The group cried out. Luke turned and headed back towards his office.

'It's probably best if you go home,' he said. 'It's not safe here.'

The two women hadn't moved since he'd left them. Telma was up before he had finished speaking, but Felisa just sat there.

'I can't believe it,' she said again.

'Telma, shall I arrange a car for you?'

She seemed unsettled by this and fumbled with the buttons of her coat. 'I'll be fine, señor.' She put her arm on his and looked down at Felisa. 'Will you make sure she is?'

Luke nodded. She took up her handbag, looked between them and left.

'He's dead,' Felisa cried, burying her head in her hands after Telma had gone.

'He might not be,' Luke said, thinking again of the faceless figure in the street. 'We'll go back to mine,' he said, taking hold of her. 'We shouldn't stay here.'

Felisa rose and seemed to snap out of her misery long enough to find her coat.

'Did you see where Camilo went?' he asked her. She shook her head and he wished he hadn't said anything because she started crying again. 'Let's go.'

When they reached the square together, Felisa stopped.

'Look,' she said.

Across from them the mob had grown and was screaming for the president now, demanding his resignation. They were trying to break through the official army barricade that protected the Capitolio and the presidential buildings beyond the square.

'They're calling "Fuera Ospina!"' Felisa shouted.

'Ospina out?'

Felisa stepped forward. 'Has the president killed Gaitán?'

'Come away,' he said, guiding her towards Eighth Avenue instead.

They walked fast, passing people heading in the opposite direction. Some of them were too preoccupied by what was going on around them to make it to the square and had turned their attention to the storefronts full of expensive goods. He shielded Felisa as a window was punched through. The store's cash register exploded onto the pavement at their feet. They were almost caught up by the hands and feet that stamped most of the contents to shreds before it could be claimed. Luke made them walk in the street, preferring this to the pavement, as it became obvious that each of the storefronts had met the same fate. Suits, cashmere and silver were thrown from the windows. Some of it was salvageable, some was not. It didn't matter; it was all piled up for the taking. Felisa let go of his hand and went towards something shiny that had sailed before them moments before. She picked it up from the gutter and handed it to him. It was a silver shoehorn. Luke threw it to one side and led her onwards.

It was amazing how quickly it took hold. Further down the street they stopped again. The American Embassy was the first building they saw burning. Felisa had left his side to ask a passer-by what had happened to Gaitán. The man had an armful of silk shirts and didn't linger long but she got what information she needed and almost fell into Luke's arms when she came back over.

'They say he really is dead,' she said. 'And it was just a boy who shot him.'

The body from the square, Luke thought. Over her shoulder, he looked up at the building and watched as the embassy staff fled. Where were the fire trucks, or the police to stop the mob? Someone struck out violently at a small official, who'd counted himself lucky in getting free of the building. The fool had stayed to watch. The first punch was followed by another as a second man joined in. Luke ran over and managed to get the first one off so that the official could escape. The second man turned and hit Luke square in the jaw so that he staggered backwards. He heard Felisa scream. He grabbed her hand and they ran.

'Your face!' she cried, when they stopped for breath in a doorway.

'Where are we?' Luke asked.

He'd lost all sense of direction. His jaw throbbed and his lip was bleeding.

Felisa peered out onto the street.

'It isn't safe,' he said, pulling her back.

'We're on Fourteenth,' she said. 'I'm sure we are. It's close to Seventh.'

'It's not far from the apartment.' It wasn't, was it? But he was struggling to control his breathing. There was blood all over his hands and his shirt. The mob were looking for people like him, people who stood out a mile. 'We'll have to run,' he told her.

Luke peered out at the street again. It was filling with smoke and he rubbed his eyes. They both did. It was hard to know which way the fire was turning. It was hard to know which way to run. As they hesitated, more buildings were being torched, to their left and to their right. And the noise, that was the most disorientating thing of all – the rawness of the people's rage played out in smashed glass and falling masonry. Soon, they'd be trapped.

'We need to move,' he said, pulling her back onto the street.

They ran up to Seventh Avenue, taking cover when they needed to – Luke pulling her one way, then Felisa pulling him another, working hard to keep each other alive. When they reached Seventh, they didn't have time to feel relieved. The entire street was on fire. He looked towards the old town – Plaza de Bolívar and La Candelaria. There, the flames engulfed the skyline, blocking out any views of the mountains above. He heard the familiar ding of the streetcar bell and instinctively jumped up onto the pavement. Luke turned to see a stationary tram consumed by fire, its interior a pit of smoke. There was another tram further up the street loaded with people, rocking it dangerously back and forth. He tightened his grip on Felisa's hand and pulled her away from the centre. If they could just get back to his apartment, he was sure they'd be safe.

'I can't!' she cried.

'It's not far, come on.'

'Luke, stop.' Felisa wrestled free. 'I have to go back.'

'What do you mean?'

'These are my people, Luke.'

'What? You'll be killed!' He grabbed her again.

'Luke, please.' Felisa broke free of him and ran.

'No!' He went after her but was almost run over by a mob pushing a looted sedan into the street. When he'd picked his way past it, she had gone.

He stood in the street for some time, as though waiting for her to return. He had never felt more lost. Machine-gun fire rang out from the direction of the square and he hit the ground along with the other people in the street. A man crouching at his side stared at him in disbelief, as though he were unwelcome to share in his misery. Luke rose as another round of bullets came to meet them. He didn't care. He ran towards it, towards the square and what he hoped would be Felisa.

As he got closer, he tripped over something lifeless, landing in agony on his damaged leg. He knew what it was he'd fallen over but didn't stop to look; Felisa was out there somewhere and he had to find her. The smoke from the building fires sunk lower and it got harder for him to see where he was going. He ran until he was forced to stop and admit he was lost. Aside from the pain in his jaw and leg, he was unscathed. Thinking he'd reached the square, he'd ended up down a side street walking over broken glass that crunched underfoot. Luke turned and tried to retrace his steps. Everywhere, people were carrying things from the newly breached shop fronts and those who weren't were running for their lives. He should be doing that too, he thought. Luke emerged onto what he hoped was the main road again. Instead, he'd come closer to the foothills of the mountain. He rubbed his stinging eyes. How had he arrived there? He must be in La Candelaria. His jaw wasn't broken. He'd forgotten to check before. He turned around. Each direction seemed familiar, carrying with it shocked cries, gunfire, or both.

The first blow came from behind, so that he felt as if he'd stumbled. The second one spun him around to meet his assailants, before the last sent his head against the wall behind him with such force he thought he heard the brickwork crack. He lost consciousness like that, upright, as though anything was possible.

Luke opened his eyes. It was raining. He could feel it on his face and the parts of his body that had become exposed in the struggle. His shirt was torn and his jacket gone. He'd been robbed. He was alive, though. His head felt light and unhindered. He tried to rise and almost blacked out with the pain of it, remembering the boy's boot on the head in the square as though the weight of it had found him here. Luke closed his eyes, unsure how long he'd been on the ground. The day was turning to night. No one came and he wondered if he looked dead. In his unconscious mind he'd heard footsteps passing and people shouting but he wasn't sure what was real or imagined. He tried to open his eyes again and found this time it was possible to keep them open. He sat upright, forcing himself to do it whatever the cost. Waves of nausea came and went, and then came again. He checked his limbs. They weren't broken. He raised a hand to his head, afraid to touch the spots that were numb, even now. He brought his fingers away and looked at them. The blood was dark and like jelly, as though it had tried to clot. Good, he thought. Luke pulled the remains of his shirt around himself and tried to stand. He moved slowly, using the wall for support. He felt the nausea come again and vomited. It was better after that. His wallet and papers were in his jacket and gone now. Christ, he thought, taking one step and then another, finding it got easier once he'd remembered how it went. The numbness in his head was quickly replaced by pain as his body remembered it was alive, punishing him for it. He used the buildings to stumble onwards, trying not to draw attention to himself. He turned down one street and then another, confused and without direction. They all looked the same; it was disorientating. He vomited again. It helped. Faces hurried past him in the half-light. Soon it would be night and here he was, wandering the streets where the ack-ack echo of gunfire could still be heard. That was coming from the square. He knew this at least. A gunfight was going on there. Where was she, he thought, looking around himself, hoping she wasn't one of those stretched across the flagstones with nothing but the sky for cover.

That's how they all ended. That's what the photographs showed that he'd seen in the British press, and his name beside them, as though he'd singlehandedly murdered them all. Bodies piled one on top of the other indiscriminately, as though death came without order. Which it did. People who were strangers in life twisted and split apart so that it was hard to tell whose limbs belonged where. And Catherine hadn't returned. That's when he had the idea that she could have been one of them. That's when, from his cell, he'd started searching each photograph for her – especially the ones the military police forced him to look at during those long, painful questionings. What seemed impossible at first became an obsession. If he only looked hard enough, close enough, he'd find her, or at least part of her. Catherine, Catherine and Catherine again.

Luke's head throbbed. A young woman, startled by his appearance, flew past and disappeared into a side street.

'Catherine!' he shouted after her, and again at someone new who'd crossed the street to avoid him.

Maybe she was here, in Bogotá. It was possible. Wasn't he looking for her anyway? That's why he'd come out tonight. Yes, she was here and he needed to find her.

'Catherine!' he shouted again, walking into the road to pass a burning building. It'd be easy to find her now he knew how to look. Dark-haired and eyes the colour of sea spray, like no colour at all. He approached an elderly couple and grabbed the man, asking him if he'd seen a woman who met this description. The man swore at him and struggled free. Someone was sure to know. He couldn't breathe, couldn't see, squinting to check each figure who passed, going towards those who wouldn't. Eventually he stopped. The pain in his head was getting worse. She had eluded him here as she had in London. He sunk down to the pavement edge and buried his head in his hands.

'Luke!'

Someone was calling his name.

'Luke, oh Luke, it is you.'

He looked up and there she was, at his side. She was here. He hadn't been wrong. She had found him.

'Catherine.'

'Let's get you up.'

Rocío put an arm under his and the two of them rose.

'You're here.'

'I am,' she said.

36

___

In Rocío's room in the boarding house in Las Cruces, he thought he was back on the farm again. The one on the Dorset coast. The war was raging and he was on holiday. No, that wasn't right. It wasn't a holiday. He was confusing the trip with Catherine and this later journey. He kept returning to that farm, remembering how it felt like the ends of the earth after the verdict. There hadn't been enough evidence to convict him of treason in the end. Cowardice, however, he was guilty of that. It was written all over his face. He stank of it, they said. A banishment – that's what he got. The farm with the others, stuck there turning the land. He'd been cast out. You're not an architect any more, they'd said at the trial, you're a labourer. He'd laboured all right – he'd made that word his own – head pressed deep to the earth, sinews stretched, raking up the soil, sweat-rashed. The farmer had not been kind. He had a son gone off to fight – a son who'd stepped on a mine in a field in France; been sown by other soldiers' boots into the ground like his limbs might grow again. 'But you're the rotten crop,' the farmer had spat when he'd first arrived, fresh and untouched by any of it. After that day in the field early on, when Luke had fallen from the fence and broken his leg, it was the great barn he'd been dragged to, half-conscious and in pain. It hadn't been a room. A room implied walls, a window, and a door, not a vast chasm, ancient and forgotten. It was a week before he realised they'd just left him there. Less than basic rations, a bucket to piss in and plenty of time to pray. The doctor didn't come for a full fortnight. Too busy, he'd said. Hadn't been told for a week, he said. He reset the bone without ceremony – the only hymn Luke's screams which set the skylarks free from their nests in the rafters. 'I've done it, but you're not worth saving,' he'd come in close to whisper. A broken leg and on your back in the dry? What sacrifice was it, really?

Luke was aware of Rocío leaning over him, washing his body and binding his head. He heard the shooing of children and then the madam standing in the doorway, saying he couldn't stay here. He opened his mouth to speak but nothing came out, just an inward cry, a sadness locked so tight inside himself it frightened him to hear it. He was restless and kicked off the covers, which Rocío replaced again and again. His leg throbbed. The old break returned. As much as sleep tried to overtake him in the darkened room, he kept waking, looking about for some lost thing. It didn't make sense; he was here and so was she.

'You called me Catherine again,' Rocío said.

'Did I?'

'She has quite a hold over you.'

He watched her cross the room and dip a bloody cloth into a bowl of water on the nightstand. Outside the window, a torrent of rain fell. He could hear it.

'How do you feel, Luke?'

'By the look on your face, terrible.'

'I was so worried.'

She returned and sat down, running the cloth gently across his forehead. He flinched.

'The city is on its knees and you were just sitting there, Luke, as though you had gone for a stroll.'

'Gaitán is dead. There was a boy, on the square.'

'Yes, I know it. Such a good man. The communists took hold of the radio stations. They say Gómez is dead too. You know him?'

'No,' he said.

'A minister. I know some of his friends. The wireless called it a rebellion.'

'By the communists?'

'Yes.'

'No, it was the people.' And she had run to join them. 'Felisa,' he said, trying to rise.

'No, Luke, you have to rest.' Rocío gently pushed him back down.

Felisa. He had gone to find her and had failed.

'Sleep now,' she said, watching him, waiting until he closed his eyes.

Luke did as she asked and in the darkness was a worse nightmare than any he'd imagined possible, Felisa running towards that gunfire.

Luke waited until he could hear Rocío leave the room and move downstairs with the other girls before pulling back the covers, rising and finding his clothes. He quickly dressed, picking up a rough woollen poncho from the back of a chair. He went along the corridor and down the stairs. He didn't want them to come running. He still felt nauseous, although the worst of the pain had passed. He reached up and touched his face. It was badly swollen and it took most of his energy not to cry out. At the foot of the stairs he could hear a wireless turned up loudly. The women were there, in the back somewhere. At the front of the house the inner door was locked; he slid the bolt across as quietly as he could. Thankfully, the outer door was open.

Outside, it was dark. The boarding house had felt safe and now he was exposed again. A foreigner and an easy target. He pulled the poncho tight and took a moment to remember the route. He planned to avoid the most obvious path to the main square and stick to the roads closest the mountain. At some point he would have to bear downwards and hit Seventh; he didn't know another way and didn't want to risk being seen. Many of the roads in the centre had been used as blockades to stem the mob's progress and so he found himself turning first one way and then another to reach it. After what felt like hours, he ended up close to the main square. This was where everyone had been. Bodies, piled one on top of the other, meant many hadn't left. Lone rebels were still fighting from the rooftops, picking off those stupid enough to break cover. Most of the mob, he noticed, had grown tired and were running away from the square. In front of him a boy of about twelve dragged a rusted machete along the roadside. Keeping close to the buildings, Luke edged closer to the square. That was where Felisa had run.

A metallic wail split the air close to his head, the shock of which made him stumble backwards. The bullet had come close to his right ear and taken a bite out of the plaster behind him. He kept low, covering his head, forcing himself to move forward. The buildings either side of him fell away and he was back out in the open again. He looked across the square. A whole corner was on fire. The Palacio Liévano and the government buildings, where Gaitán had made his speech months before, were missing. On the side closest to him, the palace still stood, as did the Capitolio. There was a wide, ugly gash in the police barricade in front. People were still running towards it, trying to make for the steps. The police were nowhere to be seen. He recognised the army, firing at anything, regardless of which direction it ran. A small group of men and women flew past him and he followed, managing to get as far as one of the smaller fountains in the centre of the square before three of the group were cut down ahead of him. A woman fell to the ground beside him. He reached down to help her, his hands pressed to her stomach, so that she died staring up at him. He covered his ears. Couldn't catch his breath. If Felisa was here, there was a chance she was inside these buildings. That's where he'd have gone.

The firing stopped. He looked out from behind the fountain. The army weren't looking at the government buildings. They were focussing in on a small group of rebels with guns of their own. No one was watching the steps of the Capitolio. Luke left his hiding place and ran. He jumped the barbed wire lacing the barricade and fell up the steps, ignoring the searing pain in his leg. He ran through the columns and across the inner courtyard, slamming the heavy door behind him.

Inside it was quiet, in stark contrast to everything that had come before it. But he could hear his breath, all right. He put his hands on his knees and threw up. It was the stench that did it. Piss and faeces. The lowest offering for the highest office. The destruction here was worse than the square. Amputated tables, chairs, curtains torn from hooks and windows smashed through so that moonlight poured in. A man ran past him carrying a pair of gilt candlesticks. He pulled open the main door and ran out. Moments later, the sound of gunfire.

'Felisa!' Luke cried, taking the stairs two at a time. He reached the landing, a wide corridor, and pushed open the first door, nothing, just an office, paper strewn everywhere. He tried another, empty again. Everyone had fled already. A hand on his shoulder spun him around. His assailant raised a finger to his lips.

'In here,' the man said, leading Luke inside a darkened room. As soon as the door was closed the man flicked a switch and the room lit up. It was a washroom. The man straightened out the soap and then busied himself tidying cloths that had fallen to the floor.

'Nobody's been in here,' he said, his accent American. 'Seems they'd rather defecate on the carpets.'

'Why haven't you escaped?'

'It's safe here.'

'Safe?'

'Forgive me,' he said, wiping his palms on his trousers. 'I'm Peter K. James, from Boston.'

Luke held out his hand. 'And why are you hiding in the bathroom?'

'I told you, it's safe. I'm only a secretary and a badly paid one at that,' he laughed. 'Not important enough to shoot.' He went over to the door, opened it and peered out. 'At least that's what I'd tell them if they'd stop.'

'Why didn't you leave with the other Americans?'

'Because I was in here!' He closed the door and then slid down to the floor. 'When they all ran.'

'They torched the embassy.'

'Oh my!' The secretary rose. 'We'll be next! They'll come for us.'

Something like a mortar, fired from a tank, made the whole building shake. The secretary ducked and Luke joined him.

'Just breathe,' Luke said.

'We're trapped. I heard them running, but then I heard the gunshots.'

'There has to be a back way out of here,' Luke said. 'One that doesn't lead onto the square.'

'There's a garden. I saw it through the windows but I don't know how to get there.'

'We'll try.' Luke rose. 'Come on, I promise you'll be safe.'

It was easier than he'd thought. Keeping low, they found a set of old service stairs which snaked down to the ground floor. The back of the building was much quieter than the front. The destruction hadn't reached here. He realised too late that it was because the area had been cordoned off. No member of the public had been able to breach this section because of the huge army presence. Luke stepped outside with the secretary cowering behind him. The garden was dark and as far removed from what was going on at the front of the palace as was possible to get.

'We're alone,' the secretary said.

Luke's heart lifted. Perhaps they were, with only the swaying trees and shrubs for company. Joy was short-lived as what he'd taken for part of the landscaping was a heavy-set soldier walking towards them.

'Hello,' Luke said, extending his hand as the soldier had.

'What are you doing!' the secretary spat, grabbing hold of Luke's arm and forcing it down.

As the man got closer, Luke saw he wasn't aiming for a handshake. He had a rifle pointed right at him.

'American?' he said.

'That's right,' Luke lied.

By this time more men had arrived, more guns were aimed.

'Oh God, oh God,' the secretary mumbled.

Firing squad, Luke thought. If it was to come to this, if he was to be shot alongside a man he had just met in a washroom, if he was never to see Felisa or anyone who could identify him again, let it be here, in the garden of the presidential palace. Somewhere inside of his delirium, he smiled and then he laughed. The secretary started to cry. Before Luke knew what was happening, a real hand was placed in his, a face up close – a man with a big grin to match his own leading him away, explaining that he was Commander Hernández. The secretary was no longer with him, Luke realised. When he looked back, he was gone.

Luke was led to a quiet corner of the presidential gardens. He was sure Peter K. James would be fine. The secretary was American, after all. Luke wasn't, though. Because of his face it looked like he'd been fighting, fighting back against the government. The spot they took him to was landscaped and beautiful. He wondered if he was going to be shot by this Commander Hernández. It happened like that. Something mundane, like snapping a twig beneath your shoe and then crack. Instead, he was questioned for at least an hour. What had he been doing in the building, they'd asked. He'd become trapped, he said. He was part of the delegation and his papers had become lost, somewhere up there, in all that destruction. He needed them to believe him. Commander Hernández left him alone for a short time. Luke thought about running but he knew how that might look. He might end up with a bullet in his back after all. He was losing valuable time. Felisa could be anywhere.

It was late when they let him go. He took a wide, circulatory route back towards La Merced. Exhausted, he tried to pick up the search for Felisa. He didn't know where to start – he could be wandering all night. After a time, he realised he was walking home. She could have gone there. He was so stupid not to have thought of that. There was a chance, at least. Luke picked his way past smouldering buildings, rubble, and trams that had been stopped mid-route and torched. They were hissing now, crackling because it had started to rain. It looked like a twelve-pound bomb had fallen on Bogotá. Things were worse at the junction with Jiménez Avenue and Luke wondered if it had all started here. He'd almost forgotten about Gaitán. The Granada, where most of the delegates were staying, was intact, although it looked somehow depleted. Opposite, the Hotel Regina was burning strong – flames had engulfed the roof and by the morning, he knew there'd be nothing left. He passed the churches, de la Veracruz and San Francisco; these had also been spared. He had to keep moving. Felisa might be waiting for him at the apartment. She might think he was dead.

When he eventually reached his building, it was pouring. The streets were empty on the way back; had it really only taken rainwater to drown the pueblo's spirit? The lobby of the apartment block was deserted. Luke reached behind the desk where he knew the spare keys were kept. He found his and left the rest behind the counter. He needn't have bothered; when he reached his apartment, the door was open and the frame split. He stepped inside and flicked the light. Someone was moving about in the back. Someone was in the bedroom. Moments later, Camilo walked into the room.

'Christ, Camilo! Where have you been?'

'Hiding from the curfew,' Camilo said.

'Curfew?'

'The government's will. Anyone found on the streets will be shot on sight, weapon or not. By order of Ospina.'

'Even an Osorio?'

'Even an Osorio.' Camilo went over to the drinks cabinet. 'May I?'

'You already forced the door.'

'Sorry about that.' Camilo poured a large glass of whisky and handed it to Luke. 'Here, you look terrible.'

'I was detained. Questioned.' Camilo didn't look so bad. 'Where were you?'

'Reporting, Luke.' He raised his glass and drank.

'But where were you yesterday, and the day before that?'

Camilo shrugged. 'I don't know, Luke. Really? You want to ask how my week's been, after this?'

'I knew this was going to happen.'

'What?'

'Karl told me.'

'Draper?' Camilo looked surprised.

'He asked me to tell you, about Gaitán. He knew. I said I'd find you. I tried, but you weren't at *El Tiempo*.'

'I was out, covering the conference, you know this.'

'No, Camilo, they'd never heard of you.'

Camilo's eyebrows raised. 'My editor said that?'

Luke's head was starting to hurt again. 'Well, no, it was the girl on reception.'

'Reception? A piece of agency skirt?'

'I guess. I don't know.' He put the whisky down. It wasn't helping get things straight.

'And who did Karl say was going to kill Gaitán?'

'He didn't say.'

Camilo nodded. 'That's good.' He picked up Luke's glass and handed it back to him. 'Did you know it was the police who supplied the people with weapons?'

'The police?'

'And the National Guard cut them to shreds.'

Felisa. Sitting there he'd forgotten the most important thing. There was a good chance she was dead. The two men were silent and he wondered if Camilo was thinking it too. Luke finished his drink and reached for the bottle. He needed it now. If she was dead, he didn't want to feel. He craved numbness. 'And Karl saw it all coming. If I'd listened to him she'd be fine.'

Camilo looked at him. 'No, Luke. This was something else. They say the communists are to blame for Gaitán's death, for the craziness out there.'

'That's a load of shit.'

264

'Really? Why do you say that, Luke?'

He rubbed his eyes, including the one that throbbed. The pain felt good. What was Camilo saying? Yes, there had been communist supporters in the mob but he remembered them from the rally in Tres Esquinas. They weren't organised enough for this. There weren't enough of them. He felt sick.

'I don't know any more, Camilo. As you can see, a small group of your countrymen beat me up tonight.'

'Christ, Luke. I didn't even know where you were until you turned up here.'

'Yes, and here you are.'

'You and I don't matter. This destruction has spread beyond the city. The other papers, we've been pooling the news all night. The nationals too.' Camilo poured himself another drink and downed it in one. 'The Liberals took control of Cali, they've torched the port in Buenaventura and the oil refinery is under siege, and that's still going on. There are pockets of rebellion everywhere; the radio stations have had their part to play. Nacional was taken over by some students and some journalists took control of Nueva Granada, working with Guzmán. There's a police station to the west that's holding up pretty well too.' He took a pack of cigarettes from his pocket and lit one. 'The army's mainly interested in the buildings surrounding the palace, everything else has been left for the rebels. It's been a land grab, political or otherwise.'

'How do you know all this?'

Camilo's eyes narrowed. 'I'm a journalist, aren't I?'

Luke took the cigarette Camilo offered him. 'I saw the bodies.'

'Mainly peasants,' Camilo said dismissively. 'There was a rumour about Gómez being killed but it wasn't him. Bastards got his manor in Fontibón and his newspaper too. *El Siglo* is no more.'

'And *El Tiempo*?'

'Still standing, along with *El Espectador*. That's where *Jornada* is printed, so.'

Luke's head spun. Camilo was trying to make him forget. Forget about Felisa. 'Why are you here, Camilo, really? You're press. You don't need to hide.'

'I was wondering when you were going to ask me that.' Camilo rose. 'I've found her, Luke.'

'Where is she?'

'She's safe.'

'You have to tell me where she is.'

Camilo poured himself another drink.

'For Christ's sake, Camilo!'

'OK, Luke, I'll tell you, but don't overreact.'

'Where's Felisa? Where is she!'

'All right, she's at my uncle's hacienda.'

'What? How?'

'She was found in police custody. She was already pretty beat up.'

Luke buried his head in his hands.

'It's OK, Luke. She asked for me. The Osorio name holds weight, even now. Actually, especially now. A car was leaving the city with my uncle's staff from the town house. She was picked up and taken with them.'

'OK, that's good.' He rose. How would he get there? No cars, no buses. He could walk. He'd just leave, and they wouldn't stop him. They couldn't. 'I need to go to her, I need to see for myself.'

'She's OK. Please, calm down. It's the safest place for her.'

'Camilo, please. I need to see her.'

'You can't. The curfew. There aren't any cars. You can't move unless you're diplomatic.'

'There has to be one, someone still working.'

'No, Luke: listen.'

Camilo was right. He couldn't hear a single engine. From the street there was nothing. They'd be shot if they went outside.

'But how did you get here?'

'I'm a journalist. They let me through.'

'You mean, you're an Osorio.'

Camilo shrugged. 'Stay here, Luke. Recover. Recuperate and then in a few days' time you can see her again. If she wants to see you then.'

'You know I'll try to go there, with or without your help.'

'It's out of my hands, Luke.' Camilo moved towards the door. 'Rest. This isn't your fight.'

After Camilo left, Luke went into the bathroom to assess the full extent of his injuries. He wanted to see what Camilo had seen. Looking in the mirror he saw his eyelid was red and sore and the skin around the socket blotchy. The throbbing to the back of his head had never left. He removed his soaked shirt and found his ribs had turned black. It didn't matter, though, none of it. Felisa was alive. He went into the bedroom and found dry clothes. He needed a plan, a plan to get past the army checkpoint out of town. He noticed the dresser. The top drawer had been pulled out and replaced, but not fully. He went across and opened it, shifting the contents, searching for anything which should have been there but wasn't now. It all looked fine, didn't it? Perhaps it was his head that wasn't, the concussion, lingering. Felisa, Felisa; how would he make it to the hacienda? It was miles away. Back in the living room he tried the wireless again. The same order to stay off the streets was repeated across each of the stations. Out of the window the road was completely deserted. The message had been delivered to most of the city, then. People were hiding. He heard a woman weeping and looked out of the window again. Nothing. He sat back down and tried to think. The door to the apartment was pushed gently open and Mrs Draper, Karl's wife, walked in.

'Mr Vosey?' she sniffed. 'Thank God, you're still here. I knew there'd be one friend.'

'Mrs Draper, I thought you'd left. Where's Karl?'

'Don't you know?'

'Take a seat, please.' Luke guided her forward. 'How on earth did you get here?'

'My Karl is very well connected,' she sniffed. 'That car out there.'

'But the curfew.'

She shrugged. 'I don't know much about that. The driver had no problems, besides, rules are for natives. If you don't mind me asking, Mr Vosey, are you OK? Your face, I mean, it looks painful. Do you want an aspirin?' She went into her bag.

'No, it's all right,' he lied. 'Where is Karl, Mrs Draper?'

'I haven't seen him for a couple of days now. He has his girls, you know, and so I thought he was off with one of them, but then this happened and... and it was so frightening!' She started crying.

'Please, Mrs Draper. Did he tell you anything, anything at all?'

'He said something big was coming. That I should be ready to go. I don't suppose you have anything to drink?'

Luke went to the kitchen and found a clean glass. He returned and poured her a drink.

'I haven't seen him. I thought you'd both left.'

'Why would you think that?'

'Something Karl mentioned about going to the US, to see your mother.'

'My mother?' She blew into her handkerchief. 'Do you know, Mr Vosey, you're very kind to say that. That nice Mr

268

Osorio was too when he came around to the apartment. I know Karl's run away with one of his girls.'

'Gabriel Osorio came to see you?'

'Yes, said if I needed anything I should come up to his place. You know, the one he's got just out of town; anytime I want.'

'To the hacienda?'

'Yes, worth a fortune it is, too. Came with his nephew – the one who wrote that piece on you.'

'Camilo?'

'That's his name, yes. Looks just like Osorio.'

'I was under the impression they didn't speak?'

'Nonsense, everyone knows he adores the boy, and the boy him.'

'What?'

'You've gone very pale, Mr Vosey.'

Luke had to think. The day in Guatavita, when Camilo had watched him leave. There had been something in it… no, it went further back than that, the article, the invitations to join them… Camilo had always been there – hanging around. He'd thought it was for Felisa.

'I think I know where Karl is,' Luke said. 'Is your driver still outside?'

'You don't imagine I sent him away, do you?'

When they had left the city behind, Luke told the driver to go faster. Felisa. He knew where she was. He knew where to find her. If Camilo hadn't lied about that too. In the car he'd thought of something else. He knew what he hadn't found in the drawer earlier after Camilo's visit – the envelope containing a handful of old letters and, most importantly, his passport. It was missing.

37

Luke told the driver to pull up some distance from the hacienda. He'd seen the armed men posted on the gate.

'Mrs Draper, I'd like you to go now. Don't wait for us to come out.'

'Shouldn't we drive in?' She had started crying again.

'Let me speak to Karl alone. I'll find him. We'll stay here with Osorio until the morning, then we'll have one of his men take us back into town.'

'But why can't I come?'

'See those gates?'

She nodded.

'We don't know for sure what's on the other side.'

'But you said Karl was!'

The men were getting suspicious. A couple of them had left their post and were walking over.

'You need to trust me now, Mrs Draper. Go to the next village, the next town. Don't go back to the city centre.' He turned to the driver. 'Is there somewhere safe you can take her?'

'We'll go to Usaquén. The violence hasn't touched it,' he said.

'I'll send word to you tomorrow.'

'Thank you,' she said, squeezing his hand.

'Now go.'

Luke got out of the car as the men reached it. The driver turned the vehicle and sped off. Luke watched until the rear lights were eventually extinguished by the night. He turned to the two men, meeting two faces that said they'd been here before. Perhaps not with him, but with others. Something they enjoyed was about to happen again.

'Come with us,' one of them said.

He went willingly, thinking only of Felisa.

'Something funny?' he said to a third man leaning against the gate. He was chewing on the end of a piece of tobacco and spat into the earth at Luke's feet.

'I don't think so,' he said, standing back as the gate was opened.

Luke walked into the grounds of Osorio's villa. The man didn't follow; none of them did. The gate was closed, he heard the bolt slice back across its middle, more shrill laughter and then just silence. He was alone again.

The house sat in darkness. As though nobody's home, Luke thought. He set out slowly down the gravel drive, cutting inwards onto the clipped grass where he might continue undetected. If what Camilo said was true, he was getting closer to Felisa now. He remembered the fireworks at the party when the jewel-studded night had held them all captive. He looked up at a sky as tawny and unwelcoming as Osorio's hacienda beneath it. He was close to the house now. He planned to knock; if no one came out, he'd go in uninvited. Then he heard a dog whimper. He remembered the woodshed behind the house. It was the last place he wanted to go. Luke heard voices inside the house. He wasn't sure what to do now and hadn't thought of what to say yet. The men on the gate knew he was here and it would only be a matter of time before Osorio, if he hadn't fled already, would too. The dog whimpered again and the voices got louder. Luke crept around the side of the house, away from the men and towards the sound. The back of the building seemed darker, as though it were a different sky overhead. Luke blinked, seeing first the low hut and thankfully the dog too, connected to it by the chain.

'Neron,' he whispered, remembering its name.

The dog looked up and growled, low and deep. Luke walked wide of him, as before; the chain could only reach so far. Neron ignored him, turning his attention back to the thing he held between his paws. What was it? There was no one on this side of the house, just him and the dog. Luke found a long stick, as the man had done last time, and approached. When he got closer, Neron looked up and released a growl that seemed to mock the first, as if to say: I remember you, I remember how you fled last time. Luke held the stick out in front, between him and the dog. He approached the animal.

'What have you got there?'

Luke looked down. The dog was nursing something like an empty sack. Neron did nothing. He was afraid of the stick and had learned to obey it. He caught the material up in his paws, turning it over, and Luke saw then what he hadn't before. It was finer than rough hessian. There were buttons, pockets and a collar. It was a man's coat. The dog picked it up in his jaws, stretched and padded off. He cast one final look at Luke before retreating to the shadows of the hut. Luke's attention was drawn from the low building to the trees beyond, caught now in a fierce wind. There was something suspended there, turning like a half-felled branch. He dropped the stick and went forward.

It was a man's body. Karl.

'Neron is such a beast.'

Luke turned to find Osorio, his face milky white, coming out of the darkness towards him.

Luke swallowed. He felt sick. 'I'm not sure dogs climb trees.'

'No,' Osorio conceded, looking up. 'Come, Luke, let me explain.'

At the front of the house, Luke recognised the three men from the gate.

'You have a habit of getting lost,' Osorio said.

Inside the hacienda, he led Luke through to a formal sitting room. There was a lit fire in the grate.

'Please,' Osorio said, offering him a seat.

Luke took it. He looked out of the window. Christ, Karl. The men kept watch on the porch.

'Getting lost in Bogotá too, I hear.'

'What? Who told you that?' He had to get his breathing under control. 'Was it your nephew?'

Osorio looked at him. 'Actually, it's written all over your face.' He lit a cigar and offered one to Luke.

'No, thank you.'

'You're wondering about Señor Draper?' Osorio sat down. 'I could say the rioting, the mob, came here.'

'But you would be lying.'

'Perhaps. You know he was a greedy man. He tried to blackmail me.'

'It's true then, what Karl told me.'

'That surprises me, Luke, because Camilo says you don't know anything.'

Better to say no more, Luke thought. He needed to get to Felisa. 'Is he here? Your nephew? I'd like to see my friend.'

Osorio sat back and exhaled, setting a wall of tobacco smoke between them. 'You and he are friends, aren't you?'

'Is he here or isn't he?'

'But then this girl, this pretty face, came between you.'

Luke rose.

'Sit down. He's here, arrived a little before you.' He flicked his hand and one of the men appeared at the door.

'You should know,' Osorio said. 'There's still time to put everything right. Once things have calmed down, the project can go ahead.'

'What?'

'Perhaps it's not appropriate to suggest it yet.'

'You're right, it isn't. Please have Karl cut down from that tree.'

Luke rose and followed the man deeper into the house. They crossed the inner courtyard. It was unlit and the fountain ran lazily, its liquid black. Luke looked up at the sky, wondering then if it might be the last time he saw it. He shouldn't have said anything about Karl. Oh God, Karl. He should have kept quiet about the meeting. He was here for Felisa. The man led him through a door in the courtyard's south side. They went into a modest room with a guard stationed outside a second room beyond this one. It was being used as a cell; there was someone inside. The two men spoke to each other. He thought he heard Camilo's name.

Why would he be here? Back at the apartment, Camilo had told him to stay put. What if he'd been trying to warn him? He couldn't get it straight. Was he or wasn't he with his uncle? Luke faced the two guards, unprepared for what was to follow. He wondered which of the two he might overpower if it came to that. He'd have to unlock the door to the cell. How far might Camilo and he get before the other raised his gun and took aim...

The men were grinning at him like the ones outside had. The inner door was unlocked. It was dark inside the second room. He didn't want to go inside. Something about the endless gloom, it was the same as before. It had followed him down the years.

'Camilo?' he called.

The man holding the door sniggered. There was no answer and no way of knowing what was inside. The man who'd led him there gestured for Luke to enter. He froze. The other guard sent the nozzle of his gun hard into Luke's back and he arched forward in pain. The butt of the gun came a second time, cracking him across the backs of the legs. He cried out and stumbled forward into the gloom. Inside there was someone, a figure, hunched over on a low pallet in the corner of the room. He turned. The door was bolted shut behind him.

'Camilo?'

The figure looked up.

'Hello Luke,' Felisa said.

He went to her, crouching down in the darkness.

'Are you hurt?' he asked.

Felisa pulled herself upright and flinched in such a way that he knew. He needed to feel nothing – to see past it. Past what was happening, or what had already happened to her. Otherwise they both might disintegrate. He looked back at the door where he imagined the men were. Opposite, set high into the far wall, was a small broken window. She could never have reached it by herself but he might help her up to it. At his side, Felisa shuffled on the pallet. He could tell, even in the dark, that she was trying to be brave. Luke looked away from her, at anything but her outline that seemed to lack definition now. Maybe part of her had already departed through the cracked glass. For him, the worst thing would be to cry out, because he understood that his stupid pity was indulgent – his vanity rising up in defence of hers. If she saw that, it might be true.

'You've been fighting, Luke.'

'You shouldn't have run away from me.'

'Let's say I won't, again.'

'Is Camilo here? Have you seen him?'

She didn't speak.

'Felisa?'

'Look at me, Luke.'

He was afraid to. 'Was it him?' he asked, meeting her stare.

'No, but he brought me here,' she exhaled, seeming to lose what little structure she'd maintained. Felisa sobbed but there was nothing but the numbness for him – that strange, rare feeling that had been suppressed down the years.

'I will kill him,' he said.

Nobody came for them and in the darkness it felt like hours passed and they were the last two people living. He wished they were. There was release in that thought. He imagined the guards had all fled, taking the knowledge of what they'd done back to their wives and daughters. Felisa was calm now, her head upon his lap.

'I went to the square, to find you,' he said.

She sat up and when she spoke, her voice was no more than a whisper. 'After the firing on the square, a group of us saw a way into the Capitolio and took it. I'd never been inside before and just wanted to look at it, to be away from the bodies hitting the stone outside – they were just women from the market, still dressed in their aprons, the shoeshines and shop boys – they'd only come for answers. The guard didn't see it that way. Not once did anyone official come out of the palace. Not the president, not his deputy, not anyone. It drove us crazy. Those who'd followed me inside the building brought the madness with them. That's what it was – senseless, shameful destruction. They were drunk on grief. You couldn't reason with them. It wasn't about getting to Ospina and his government. With their bare hands the people tore everything apart, stamping on tables, snapping legs from chairs, shitting in corners, on anything – the stench of it – while those inside ran for their lives. That's when I was picked up. Someone official in a suit grabbed me and then added my name to a list. The prison came next – I would have called you but I didn't know where you were. I could only remember Camilo's number – the one he'd given me. It all happened so quickly. I called him. He said it would be all right. The next moment I was freed. He said that, Luke, he said it would be all right.'

'It will be, Felisa.'

'I don't know that. The square was full of boys and women mostly, the ones who couldn't run away. I saw their bodies. I found myself in a car being driven away from them. It was so peculiar. So much destruction and then it was as though nothing had changed, just fields and then here.'

He looked up at the window again. He could put his elbow through it.

'Is he still here?'

'Camilo? I don't know where he is. I don't think he meant for it to happen. He didn't know what they'd do.'

'He came to see me, to the apartment. He took my passport.'

'Then his uncle won't let you leave.'

The door opened and they both looked up.

It was one of the guards. Luke rose and put himself between him and Felisa. The man laughed and told her to get up too. They were led though the courtyard and back into the house.

'I'm here, Luke,' Felisa said.

He squeezed her hand and realised he was doing it to check she really was. They were taken back into the room at the front of the house. Osorio had risen and now stood beside the fireplace. Camilo was with him.

'My dear,' Osorio said, addressing Felisa. 'Take this.' He handed her a shawl. 'It's one of Señora Osorio's but she won't mind, under the circumstances.'

277

Felisa extended her arm and took it. Camilo, he noticed, wouldn't look at her.

'Sit, please.'

Felisa sat down, and Luke beside her.

'A sad state of affairs,' Osorio said. 'This business in town.'

'I would agree with you there,' Luke replied.

'Our beautiful city torn to shreds, our culture up in smoke and our women polluted.'

He looked at Felisa.

'You're forgetting one thing,' she said. 'Gaitán.'

'Who?' Osorio asked, looking at Camilo. 'Oh yes, the Indian doctor. I was as shocked as anyone to hear of his demise, but I have to say, I feel rather grateful to him. The centre has been cleared without the need for bulldozers.' He looked at her. 'Who will take up his cause now? Will you?'

Felisa laughed. 'I would have thought it was obvious. We already have. Soon, people like you will be extinct.'

'Camilo, you were right to bring her here,' Osorio said. 'She is a communist.' He turned to Luke. 'I was surprised to hear you were too.'

'I'm not, and neither is she. Now let us go.'

'Luke, come now,' Osorio said. 'Camilo here saw you both at the rally in Tres Esquinas.'

'I see,' Luke said. 'How long has your bastard nephew been watching me?'

'Since the moment you landed,' Camilo said abruptly, 'and before, actually.'

'You have quite a past,' Osorio said. 'A former detainee from Europe is likely to attract attention.'

Felisa turned to Luke. 'I never told them.'

'You knew?' Camilo asked her, coming forward. 'And you still took his side?'

'Camilo,' Osorio said, smiling.

'Bet he left this out,' Camilo said, taking something from his pocket. It was a letter. 'Found this in your apartment.'

'Stop it,' Luke said, his heartbeat ringing in his ears.

'She has a right to hear it, Luke, doesn't she? After you spun us all that beautiful story. What was it your beloved Catherine wrote before she left you?' Camilo unfolded the sheet and began to read. '*I could never love a man like you*. No, she saw him for the coward he was and left him, as you should have.'

'She isn't dead?' Felisa asked.

'Pathetic, isn't it?'

'Enough, nephew. Get him a drink.'

Camilo went over to the cabinet.

'Luke,' Felisa whispered. 'I don't care.'

He sat back down. He couldn't look at her, couldn't think. That room she'd been kept in, it was so like the darkened space he had known at the farm but before that too, when he'd been arrested. Then, he'd waited an eternity for Catherine to visit. He'd almost lost his mind when the letter arrived saying she was leaving, or rather, had left him long ago and was only getting it down on paper now. That other man had been mentioned. He was an officer in the RAF, some high-level bombing work. She was proud of this man, she'd written. Then the farm, the barn. He'd been left to rot. His leg had never been the same since – a slight limp, that dull ache where it hadn't been set soon enough. During all that solitude, it was the buildings he thought he'd never build again that kept him going. He was saved by the cityscapes he'd been able to see in the dark, using only his fingers to draw through the air. Soon after the war, he'd come across some service medals in a junk shop. What did it matter who he had been?

'The fact is,' Osorio said, taking the glass from Camilo and handing it to Luke himself, 'you are a brilliant architect.'

Luke raised it to his lips. It cut through all of it, through them. 'Is that why you wrote the article? To get my attention?'

'It was nice to see your name in print again, wasn't it?' Osorio said. 'Listen, we'll take care of the past and make sure the truth never comes out here. When the city has calmed, we still want you to rebuild it.'

'And if I refuse?'

Osorio looked at Felisa and smiled. 'Why would you?'

Luke didn't move. He couldn't.

'Let's give him time to think,' Osorio said, signalling for the guard waiting in the hall. 'Take the girl back to her room.'

'Wait,' Luke said. 'Let her go and I'll do it.'

'Do what?'

'Anything you want.'

Osorio nodded. 'See to it that Señorita Mejía is comfortable in one of the bedrooms upstairs.'

Luke stepped forward.

'You can sleep outside the door, if you like.' Osorio sighed. 'And then tomorrow you'll both be taken back to the city. Next week, we'll begin the clean-up.'

'And my passport?'

'What passport?' Camilo said.

The guard stood aside. One of Osorio's maids took Felisa by the arm and led her upstairs. Luke went after them.

'Let her go,' Osorio said, reaching out an arm to stop him. 'In my experience, women don't like desperate men.'

38

Osorio insisted that he have another drink with him. After Felisa had gone upstairs, Camilo had looked furious and stormed out. Luke watched from the window as he paced up and down on the front porch.

'You should settle this with the boy. Make peace. She's only a girl.'

Luke looked at him. Osorio, he thought, believed what he was saying.

'We could settle it in the old way, with pistols at dawn,' Luke said.

'The old ways,' Osorio said, shaking his head. 'Camilo's mother was fourteen when my brother married her. She was a quiet, timid little thing. Her name was Isabel.'

He poured another drink and passed the bottle to Luke.

'My brother was a womaniser of the worst kind. He had no time for her. It took two years of silence, of coaxing her out of hiding, before their first child was born. She gave birth to their son in this house during a storm. One of the worst we'd seen. Trees torn up by the roots and sent like spears for miles, animals raised in barns suddenly finding they could fly, you get the idea. That quiet, timid woman made more noise than anything else that night. How she cried! It went on into the morning too. And inside of that hell, that poor child came.'

'What happened to the mother?'

'She didn't survive. Neither did my brother. Not for long after that; a disease of the blood. I raised the child. I denied him nothing.'

Luke looked outside. Camilo, he saw, had stopped pacing and was leaning against the veranda.

'Go,' Osorio said. 'Go and make peace with my boy.'

Luke stepped outside. The night had turned cool. The guards were far off beside the gate again and Camilo hadn't moved. He looked back up at the house and wondered which bedroom Felisa had been taken to. Behind the glass, Osorio was watching him.

'What do you want?' Camilo asked without turning.

'How could you do it, to her?'

'I didn't take a turn.'

Luke felt the whites of his knuckles tighten.

'If you want to kill me, just do it.' Camilo turned. He had been crying. 'She was mine to give, all right? She never belonged to you. I picked the ugliest and I told him to have fun, is that what you want to hear?'

'So I might attack you?' Luke leaned in close. 'I don't believe you.'

'Well, you should!' Camilo's eyes filled with tears. 'I did it for him! I brought her here because my uncle asked it. So you might come.'

'No, you didn't know what they'd do at all. Felisa said that. Even now she's defending you.'

'What does it matter?' Camilo cried. 'She preferred you and I hated you for it. Why shouldn't you suffer?'

'Help her now.'

'How can I do anything? After this, she'll hate me forever.'

Luke looked inside the room again. Osorio was missing.

'Camilo, listen to me, you know that your uncle is dangerous. He has no intention of letting her leave. I'm sure of that.'

'It might be better if she died. Who will want her now?'

Luke hit out. Camilo fell backwards from the veranda onto the lawn and Luke followed, pinning him to the ground. He sent blow upon blow after the first. 'If you want to die, I'll kill you.' It had come at last, that need to destroy that he thought he lacked. Here it was.

'I want to die!' Camilo cried through winded breaths. He didn't fight back. Luke raised his fist again. No, Camilo wouldn't fight back. Luke forced himself off and sat panting on the grass. In the distance, the men came running over. Camilo put up a hand and they stopped. His lip was split and bleeding.

'I will help you. Please, Luke.' He spat blood onto the grass. 'Please, take her far away from here. Away from me.'

'How can it be done?'

'When the house is asleep there's a way through the trees that breaks into open farmland. No fences. It's about eight miles to the next village from there. They're loyal to Gaitán. There might be a chance. And then you can take a car perhaps, far north to Barranquilla. Flights are still leaving from there.'

The room Luke had been taken to looked out over the back of the house. He went over to the window and forced himself to look at the trees but there was nothing there. The body of Karl had been cut down. Mrs Draper would never know what happened to her husband. He couldn't think of that now. Camilo had chosen three in the morning, when the house was asleep, to show them the way. Even now, Luke could hear the men's hyena-calls coming from below. They might come for her again. He couldn't stop them all. He put his ear to the wall. Felisa, Camilo said, was sleeping in the room next door. As long as the men stayed far below, he could wait, he wouldn't have to act, not yet. Camilo was their only hope. Luke rose and went over to the door again, pressing his ear against it. Nothing. Where was he? It was almost time. Perhaps something had gone wrong? He pulled open the door and crept out into the hall. It was deserted. The courtyard below was quiet too. Luke went along the balcony to the next door. He tried the handle. It was locked. Inside the room, the handle was turned a second time. Felisa. Neither of them spoke. They were too aware of what it might mean and they had survived this night, he thought. She was safe, for now. How would she feel, though, when she knew they depended on Camilo? He heard the maid's footsteps on the stairs and slipped back to his room. He waited another thirty minutes and still Camilo didn't come. Exhaustion sent him back to the bed where he collapsed.

He hadn't meant to fall asleep and he woke in a panic. Outside of the window the moon was high. He checked his watch; it was late, closer to four now. Camilo hadn't come. There was someone else in the room with him, though. He turned over.

'I've killed him,' she whispered in the darkness.

He sat upright. Felisa stepped forward. She had a knife.

'I've slit his throat.'

He went over to her and took the knife. It was light in his grip. He looked down to find a letter opener.

'Camilo?'

'No, his uncle. He came to my room,' she said, breathlessly. 'He unlocked the door. He came… he came for me.'

In the moonlight her eyes were black.

'Were you seen?'

She shook her head.

'I should have been the one to kill him.'

'No, Luke.'

'I didn't act when I should have.'

'This wasn't waiting for you,' she said. 'This has been coming for me for a long time.'

Luke rose. 'Will you show me, Felisa?'

She nodded and led him back out onto the deserted corridor. The door of her room was closed. There was blood on the handle. Luke wiped it off with his sleeve, opened the door and went inside. Felisa followed behind. On the bed, it looked like Osorio was sleeping but as Luke got closer he saw the snarl on his face. An open mouth caught in the gulf between pleasure and pain.

'He's dead, you see.'

Luke nodded. She hadn't slit his throat. There was a single puncture wound which must have opened an artery. Osorio had bled out fast. His face still wore the shock of it.

'Let's go.' Luke took her hand and guided her away from the body and back out onto the landing. He closed the door.

'What's this?' Camilo stood before them.

'There's been an accident,' Luke said, moving towards him.

Camilo registered the stain on Luke's sleeve. 'One of the men?'

'Yes,' Luke whispered. 'Camilo, we have to go. It has to be now.'

He nodded. 'Follow me.'

Felisa didn't move. 'I won't go with him.'

'I had no idea, Felisa,' Camilo pleaded. 'I didn't know what they'd do.'

'There isn't time.' Luke turned to Felisa. 'It's the only way.'

She shook her head but went anyway. Luke took her hand. Camilo led them out of the room and down the stairs, passing away from the main door and across the courtyard to the back room which led to the second. The one she had been kept in before. She didn't want to go in there at first but once they explained, about the window, she followed. Luke guided her upwards and through, realising, once he'd pushed the pallet onto its side, he could climb up and after her with Camilo's help.

'Go, and take her far away from here.'

From inside the room, Camilo reached up and forced something into Luke's hands. It was his passport.

'Thank you,' Luke said.

Inside the room, Camilo must have jumped down from the pallet, because he never replied.

They set off behind the house and into the trees. Past the dog and the place where the body of Karl once hung. They ran and it felt like miles before they were clear of it. He held her hand tight. Glancing over his shoulders, he saw how the forest eventually swallowed up the hacienda. He thought of Osorio, dead in his bed. His plans would come to nothing and everything he'd wished to uphold, his idea of a country governed by the elite, reduced to rubble. He thought of Camilo too, going into the room and discovering his uncle's body. He would set the dog on them then. He was sure of that. Luke pulled Felisa onwards and when she had to stop, he rested too, but neither for long. Other times they slowed to a walk but were always able to keep going. He wondered at her strength then, and at his. Nothing tried to stop them. He thought of the goddess at the lake. The trees were her army. In their stature, Luke saw more structure and stability than in anything he'd ever built.

Acknowledgements

Thank you to every single person who has read, advised, edited, reread, designed, queried, encouraged, whooped and generally celebrated this book with me over the last three years.

It's not your names I want to acknowledge, but your actions. In a publishing culture where individuality is being systematically eroded by the bottom line, your integrity has proved itself limitless.

Helen x

P.S. Unbound rule!

Unbound is the world's first crowdfunding publisher, established in 2011.

We believe that wonderful things can happen when you clear a path for people who share a passion. That's why we've built a platform that brings together readers and authors to crowdfund books they believe in – and give fresh ideas that don't fit the traditional mould the chance they deserve.

This book is in your hands because readers made it possible. Everyone who pledged their support is listed at the front of the book and below. Join them by visiting unbound.com and supporting a book today.

Yulieth Adarbe Hernandez
Omar Al-Khayatt
Chelise Anderson
Frances Ann Young
Matthew Baldwin
Jason Ballinger
Magdalena Baran-Tarakci
David Barker
Nathaniel Barrett
Emily Bedford
Owain Betts
Gayle Blood
Caroline Bloor
Lucy Brown
Jenna Bryan
Tim Cady
Fiona Campbell
Laura Church
Nicci Cloke

Sarah Colson
Monica Connell
Julie-Ann Corrigan
Isabel Costello
Adrian Cross
Cheryl D'Rozario
Emily Denniston
Deepali Deshpande
Lisa Dittmar
Tram-Anh Doan
Clair Draper
Ingrid Eames
Jo Ely
Emily Farley Diamond
Francesca Febbo
Anna Fleming
Elizabeth Fox
Maggie Gallagher
Alejandro Gallego

Cheryl Gardner
Maria Ghibu
May Glen
Pamela Gould
Fiona Green
Petra Green
Helen Greenham
Will Hale
Cleo Harrington
Alex Harris
Lucie Hartley
Sarah Head
Clara Herberg
Jaime Hernandez
Lizzie Hill
Charlotte Holworthy
Jennifer Howell
Camilla Hume-Smith
Laura-Jayne Ireton
Faran Ismailpour
Isaac Jay
Sophie Jennings
Deborah Jensen
Helene Kreysa
Natalia Lopez
Fabia Ma
Anna MacDiarmid
Claire Maloney
Richard Marris
Anna Mazzola
Wyl Menmuir
Felicity Mettam
Veronica Montalbetti
Neil Morris

Carlo Navato
Julian Nicholds
Mikołaj Niedorezo
Katie Nobbs
Claire Norval
Vivienne Pearce
Jolita Pleckaityte
Clare Povey
Vivien Quick
Jessica Rachid
James Rennoldson
Kirsteen Richardson
Victoria Roberts
Ruth Robinson
Emma Salter
Freya Sampson
Josh Somma
Janet Spinlove
joanna Stanbridge
Alessandro Susin
Jessica Tackie
Rob Tebb
Dom Tulett
Tom Ward
Grace Whooley
Ewa Wilcock
Ryan Willmott
Francesca Wilson
Felicia Yap
Chloe Yeoman
Laurence Yeoman
Diane Young
Zoe & Keizy
Nelson Zubieta